A BODY IN THE WOODPILE

An Emma Berry Mystery
Book #3

Irene Sauman

Jakada Books

PERTH, WESTERN AUSTRALIA

A Body in the Woodpile: Format (novel)
Irene Sauman / Jakada Books / Perth Western Australia
Originally published as Book 2, now Book 3 in the Emma Berry Mystery series.

Publisher's Note: This is a work of fiction. Names, characters, places, and incidents are a product of the author's imagination. Locales and public names are sometimes used for atmospheric purposes. Any resemblance to actual people, living or dead, or to businesses, companies, events, institutions, or locales is completely coincidental.

Cover images: depositphotos.com

A Body in the Woodpile / Irene Sauman – 2nd edition
Amazon ISBN: 978-0-6480348-2-7
Ingram Spark ISBN: 978-0-6480348-6-5

CONTENTS

Dedication

This book is dedicated to
the memory of my grandfather
George Bennett
who was a Murray River fisherman
and former riverboat captain

Author's Note

THE EMMA BERRY MYSTERIES are set in Australia on the Murray River, the third longest navigable river in the world, surpassed only by the Amazon and the Nile. Its great navigable length was responsible for the development of the riverboats, the side-wheel paddle steamers that opened the country to settlement and sheep farming during the second half of the 1800s.

In this updated edition of Book 3 Emma Berry (nee Haythorne) is living and working on the PS *Mary B* at the insistence of her brother-in-law Daniel. The trading season on the river is almost at an end as river levels fall during the summer months, but there is still time for murder most foul. And the issues raised over that old promise are not at an end yet.

You will find British/Australian spelling and word usage in this book. For the most part. With the way the English language is distributed around the world these days with books, movies, television, and sport it is getting harder to tell what comes from where and what is local. I hope the story carries you through any regional language quirks. Enjoy!

The Age, May 1875. It is generally believed that a system of petty smuggling has been carried on for some time past, not, indeed, to any great extent, but still sufficient to prove that unless it be checked at once it will soon assume formidable dimensions. It is chiefly indulged in by a class of people who regard the fact of having done the Customs officers in the light of a good joke.

Chapter One

EMMA FINGERED THE SATIN ribbons Dotty Keogh placed on the counter and sighed.

"I must admit to having been quite concerned about him, Miss Keogh," she said. "Bea was worried for her brother as well." Dotty glanced down the counter where her mother was unrolling bolts of fabric for Bea Macdonald to inspect. "Matty was so upset when my husband died. They were such good friends." Emma crossed her fingers behind her back and hoped she wouldn't be struck down by an avenging angel. It was all for a good cause and if it appeased the angel at all it wasn't easy for her to speak of Sam's death, still fresh after six months. "But he was most upset for me, of course. He's always been like a big brother. Very caring."

"Yes?" Dotty said, a little breathlessly.

"And because I was unhappy, he was unhappy and he, well, he simply felt he couldn't come and see you and burden you with that."

"Oh, but I would have understood, had he told me," Dotty assured her earnestly.

"I know, dear," Emma said patting her hand. "We women understand these things, but men, they like to be the strong ones, even when their hearts are breaking."

"He didn't say anything about it when he called on me last month."

"He came to see you?" Emma was certain Matty had and that he had been rebuffed. Bea confided her brother had been like a bear with a sore head lately.

"Yes, but..." Dotty leaned forward and whispered, "...Ma sent him off."

"Oh?"

"She, um, told him not to come back. She said he couldn't be trusted and was just toying with me, filling in time. There was someone else, she told me later, and when that woman crooked her little finger he'd be gone again."

Emma felt as if the breath had been knocked out of her. She glanced down the counter at Mrs. Keogh as if her head were on a string and someone had just tugged it. Mrs. Keogh was looking straight back at her. There was nothing judgmental in the woman's gaze, but Mrs. Keogh knew, or believed she did.

Emma was suddenly reminded that she wasn't the only person who made assumptions about others. Had there been speculation about the young woman at Wirramilla and the young man at neighbouring Nettifield who had been friends for many years? She could imagine the drapery store being a hotbed of gossip between its female clientele and its female owner. There was no way Mrs. Keogh could know about the promise Emma and Matty had made on that lovely spring day ten years ago, but even though the arrangement was now null and void the repercussions, unfortunately, were proving ongoing.

"He did just stop coming round, Mrs. Berry." Tears glistened in Dotty's eyes as Emma forced her attention back to the girl. "He never wrote or anything. I don't think Ma is going to change her mind about him any time soon."

"Would you change your mind?" Emma heard herself ask. "If I told you there was no other woman? That you were first in his mind?"

"I'd give him another chance," Dotty said, touching her eyes with her handkerchief. "But he wouldn't want to do that again."

"No. You are quite right. Once is quite enough." And once too many if she couldn't convince Mrs. Keogh. Dotty might believe her story about Matty's unhappiness, but she was afraid her mother would see it for the flimflam it was.

The bell on the shop door of Keogh's Drapery Store tinkled and several other customers came in, ending any chance Emma had for extending her mission at that moment.

======

"WHY WOULD MRS. KEOGH say there was another woman?" Bea asked, taking a sandwich. "Matty's never even looked at anyone else."

Emma sipped her tea, trying not to catch Catherine's eye across the table as her sister-in-law raised her eyebrows at Bea's comment. Emma had just finished telling them what Dotty had said but she had never told Bea about the promise she and Matty had made. She had, however, told Catherine.

Emma had only met her sister-in-law ten days before, when she and Daniel collected her and Emma's brother Joe at Albury to travel the eight-hundred miles down the Murray River. Joe was to take up his new position as Customs Officer at Wentworth and Catherine was expecting their first child. It was for that last fact Emma had insisted on making the *Mary B* available for them. Coach travel would have been horrendously uncomfortable for Catherine in her current condition, and possibly dangerous.

One night during their journey down river, when the heat and stillness made sleeping difficult, they had sat up late on the upper deck and talked. Emma had told

Catherine about the promise she and Matty had made when she was seventeen and he two years older, that they should marry if they were both still single in ten years. And how Matty's honourable nature prompted him to stop seeing Dotty Keogh in case Emma wanted him to uphold the promise and marry her after Sam died. Emma had managed to convince him that the promise held no sway because she had married even if she was now a widow.

Unfortunately, if Matty didn't marry and bring a wife home to manage the Nettifield homestead his sister Bea, currently filling that role, wouldn't leave her father and brothers untended to marry her own love. Emma felt at least partly responsible for the situation they were stuck in and was attempting to get Matty and Dotty back together before Bea's betrothed, the Nettifield overseer Thomas Quilp tired of waiting for her.

It was too late now to tell Bea about the promise she and Matty had made. She could imagine the hurt Bea would feel at Emma keeping it from her all this time, especially as Nella had known for many years. The only person Matty told as far as she knew was his mother, before her death two years ago.

Esther, Catherine's maid, put a fresh pot of tea on the table and went to unpack some more boxes. The house Catherine and Joe had taken was already looking comfortable. The *Mary B* crew had moved everything in the previous afternoon and Bea and Emma had spent the evening making up beds and setting up the kitchen with Esther's help, while Joe and Daniel hung curtains. Catherine could only sit and direct operations as her ankles were swollen in the heat.

"People make assumptions, Bea," Emma said now. "They see me and Matty, next door neighbours, growing up practically together and next thing they are putting two and two together and thinking they make four."

"You and Matty? Mrs. Keogh thinks you're the other woman?" Bea laughed. "My goodness, she doesn't know either of you very well, does she."

"Not a match made in heaven, then?" Catherine said drily. She hadn't yet met Matty Macdonald.

"Hardly. Much as I love my older brother he and Emma would be at loggerheads in no time if they lived together."

There spoke a wise sister. "It's clear Dotty has feelings for him, but I don't know how we are going to get Mrs. Keogh to trust Matty again," Emma said.

"I still don't understand why he stopped seeing her in the first place," Bea said, her exasperation clear. "What was he thinking?"

"Perhaps he should just propose," Catherine suggested, saving Emma from having to pretend she didn't know the answer to what Matty had been thinking.

Emma imagined Bea was beginning to feel desperate about ever marrying Thomas. His pride wouldn't allow him to marry the boss's daughter, and he wouldn't leave Nettifield and take up land of his own without her. Emma stood and began clearing away their lunch dishes, her mind troubled. She would be leaving today on the *Mary B* as soon as Daniel was ready and unable to do anything more.

"Hello, hello," Joe said coming into the kitchen with Daniel on his heels as if Emma's thoughts had conjured them up. Joe kissed Catherine on the top of her head.

Emma's heart gave an odd lurch at seeing Daniel. Her brother-in-law was tall and dark with a neat beard and enough resemblance to his younger brother to give her cause on occasion.

"You're ready to leave then?" she asked.

"The boys are unloading a wagon of stores and then we'll be done. Half an hour or so."

"Just time for me to have a word with you, Em," Joe told her.

"You haven't had enough time in the last ten days?"

"Hardly got a word in between the two of you," Joe said his hand on Catherine's shoulder.

"Can I get you something to drink, Daniel?" Catherine asked smiling.

"Tea would be welcome, thank you."

"I'll get it," Bea said as Catherine struggled to rise. "We need a fresh pot." She picked up the teapot and emptied it into the slops bucket as Joe ushered Emma into the drawing room.

"What now?" Emma asked taking a seat on the sofa while Joe remained on his feet.

"Ah, it's about your collection of duties on Grandmama's herbals, Em. Or should I say, non-collection?"

Emma felt as if her eyebrows must have disappeared into her hairline. This was the thanks they got for delivering Joe and Catherine and their household down the river? With only Joe's fare paid by the Customs Office.

"Really, Joe? You know what a boon Grandmama's herbal remedies are for people along the river, isolated as they are."

While the herbal remedies originated at the Haythorne property on the Victorian side of the Murray, many were delivered to customers on the New South Wales side, requiring the payment of custom duties for passing across the colonial border. Duties Emma never bothered about. She didn't list the herbals as cargo after all.

"Isolated my foot with steamers passing their door day and night," Joe replied, his grey eyes surveying her. Emma wondered idly, not for the first time, why she was the only one who had inherited their grandmother's green eyes. "Don't give me that, Em. It isn't just the herbals that cross the borders without custom duties being paid is it?"

"What do you mean?" Which transaction was he referring to now?

"Those machine parts you picked up at Lorna Park and delivered across the river to Whitneys for one. But there were others. Did you think I wouldn't notice?"

"That was a favour to a neighbour. Lorna Park's blacksmith had an accident and can't work right now so we took the pieces across to Whitneys to repair at his smithy. No money changed hands."

"No duty changed hands either and it should have. That machinery should have been listed cargo."

Emma wasn't about to tell Joe they would probably deliver the repaired machinery back to Lorna Park on the way up. Instead she had a question of her own.

"How did you know it wasn't on the cargo list?" She stared at her brother. "You checked my books? Joseph Haythorne, of all the underhand things. We give you the run of our boat and you abuse our hospitality by spying on our operation."

Joe had the decency to look embarrassed. "It wasn't like that at all," he muttered. "You left the ledger open on the table in the saloon while you went off to see to something."

"That's no excuse. You didn't have to look at it. And it's a bit much you coming heavy-handed now. You were the first to ignore these things when you lived at home."

"It's the law, Em, and I'm paid to enforce it now. How do you suppose it looks for me in my position allowing my sister and brother-in-law to openly flout the rules?"

"Openly?" Emma said looking at him, eyes innocently wide. "Does that mean we could do it surreptitiously, Mister Customs Officer?"

Joe rolled his eyes. "Just be careful, Sis, will you please? For my sake if not for your own. I've bigger problems here than Grandmama's herbals and a few pieces of machinery."

Emma knew he did. He had been sent to Wentworth for a reason. Quantities of opium were finding their way along the river without duty being paid at the borders. That duty was ten shillings a pound-weight of opium, or any product that contained it. Not that the colonial governments were concerned about any possible health aspect. Opium was freely available and used in a widespread number of medicines, from nerve tonics to cough mixtures to remedies for constipation.

But thousands of Chinese had come into the country to the gold diggings during the past twenty-five years, and the Chinese were associated in the European mind with opium smoking. It was in the hope of deterring Chinese immigration that the colonial governments of South Australia, Victoria, and New South Wales had imposed the hefty tax. Wentworth on the Darling River at its junction with the Murray and the nearest town to the borders of all three colonies, was believed to be at the heart of the problem.

Joe cleared his throat. What now? "I would like your help, Sis," he said, giving her an appealing look.

Emma shook her head in wonder. "First you tell me off and now you want my help?"

Joe raised his eyes to the ceiling. He wasn't as much fun as he used to be. Perhaps the idea of being a father dampened his spirits.

"Just listen. If you could keep your eyes and ears open. The opium is definitely being moved along the river and..."

"You want me to spy on my fellow river folk?"

"Spying is a bit strong. Just..."

"Just nothing. No, absolutely not." Her acceptance in the male dominated world of river trade was tenuous enough.

"All I'm asking is that you keep alert for any hint of what is going on."

"And report back to you? I can't do that. I've never heard any whispers about opium smuggling in any case." Perhaps everyone was particularly careful around her because they all knew her brother was a customs officer. "Besides, how much investigating are you going to be doing with no riverboats working for the next few months?"

It was the height of summer and the end of the trade season until the autumn rains replenished the river levels again. As it was, their journey back to Echuca was going to be hazardous with barely enough water to float in.

"I don't just monitor the boat traffic, Em. I have to look over the Cobb & Co coaches too. And some of the bottom-enders will still be running for a while."

"Mmm, with nowhere for them to go except here in Wentworth. I suppose they could stockpile the opium somewhere," Emma mused.

The bottom-enders were the riverboats that worked between Wentworth and Goolwa in South Australia. From Goolwa, the Murray River fed into Lake Alexandrina and into the sea. The *Mary B* was a top-ender whose port was Echuca in Victoria, six hundred miles upriver and two hundred miles inland from Melbourne.

"I knew you'd find it interesting," Joe smirked.

"I'm sure it must be," Emma said dismissively, "for a customs officer. Seems a pretty thankless job to me."

"Which is why I would like your help."

"If I hear of anything. But I won't be looking or asking questions." He would have to be satisfied with that.

Chapter Two

"I'VE BEEN THINKING," Catherine said, drawing Emma and Bea aside as they were about to leave. "Why don't I see what I can do about talking Mrs. Keogh around. I mean, I've nothing much to do for the next few months and I will be needing to make clothes for Joe junior, so I have a reason for going to the drapery store. What do you think?"

"Well…" Emma hesitated. It was tempting to hand the problem to someone else, but she felt a little guilty about doing so.

"Could you do that?" Bea asked, not in the least hesitant.

"I don't see why not," Catherine said, turning her attention to Bea. "And perhaps your brother and his girl could even meet here."

"Ooh, yes, and I could come as well," Bea said. "I could tell Dotty stories about Matty and Nettifield and talk him up to her."

"I don't think it's Dotty who needs convincing," Emma warned.

"But if she's really keen Mrs. Keogh might not stand in the way. Dotty has to have some say in the matter," Bea argued.

"Perhaps if I could find one or two other ladies in my condition, I could arrange a sewing afternoon and invite Mrs. Keogh to advise us on fabrics and the like. That way I could get to know her better and figure what approach to take and all. What do you think?"

"I know someone," Bea told her eagerly. "Sally Cartwright. She's expecting her second. Her husband works at the livery stable. I'll write and suggest she call on you. Catherine, this is so very kind of you."

"What do you think Emma? Is it a plan?"

"I think you are a devious person," Emma said, her reluctance largely overcome by Catherine's enthusiasm and the hope it ignited in Bea, who was looking happier than Emma had seen in some time.

"It will be fun playing matchmaker," Catherine said.

Emma was sure Catherine could arrange what she had planned. Her sister-in-law was vivacious and outgoing. Emma just hoped she could also be discreet.

======

"WHAT A LOVELY PERSON Catherine is," Bea enthused as they shared Emma's umbrella on the way to the wharf. Dust rose about their feet and the hot dry air seemed to suck all the moisture from their skin despite the shade provided by the umbrella. Daniel walked beside Emma, her free hand tucked under his arm.

"She is indeed."

"Thank you for collecting me on your way by yesterday, Emma. It's been a nice little break and if we can sort Matty out, well…"

"Well, indeed," Emma agreed. She would have crossed her fingers if she'd had a free hand.

"What did Joe want to see you about?" Daniel asked. "Or was it a family matter?"

"It is of sorts. He was ticking me off for not collecting duties on Grandmama's herbals. Among other things."

"I knew there'd be trouble carrying him, but you would insist."

"He's family," Emma pointed out. "We had to offer the *Mary B*, especially for Catherine. She'd have been shaken and jolted to bits on the coach."

"You're probably right about that, I don't doubt. What was the 'among other things' Joe mentioned?"

"The machinery parts we moved to Whitneys."

"I suppose we should be glad he didn't throw the book at us over that."

"He wants me to keep my eyes and ears open among the river folk about the opium smuggling, too," Emma told him, as they reached the edge of the wharf. Her words caused him to pause.

"Struth, Emma, you didn't agree?" He looked at her in alarm. "You wouldn't be so silly, would you? For heaven sake, leave it to Joe. It's his job. We don't need any trouble."

Daniel's response almost made Emma wish she had agreed to help Joe. If he wasn't complaining about something she had done, he was complaining about what she might do even when she had no intention of doing whatever it was. She chose not to respond. They would only end up in a full-scale disagreement and she knew he was concerned about getting the *Mary B* back to Echuca. He wouldn't have made this last trip, but she had begged. What was the point in owning forty-two-and-a-half percent of a riverboat if she couldn't make use of it when she needed?

Daniel went to attend to matters in the wharf office. Ahead of her, Emma could just see the top of the *Mary B*'s funnel above the edge of the wharf. Welshman Shorty Mason, barely five-foot tall and all muscle, was hefting a sack onto his shoulders from a wagon nearby which was almost empty. As Shorty started down the bank to the *Mary B* Blue Higgins' red head appeared from below, popping up like a cork. Emma and Bea followed Shorty down the bank. The *Mary B*'s engine was already tonking quietly as engineer Jake Summers built up the steam pressure, ready to leave when the loading was complete.

There was another boat moored behind the *Mary B*. It must have arrived sometime late last night. It was the *Lisette*. Of all the boats on the river it had to be the McCulloch Company steamer Daniel had captained while the *Mary B* was out of commission. Given the drama of their last trip on the *Lisette* Emma had no desire to meet up again with her engineer, Mr. Shankton. She ducked her head and hurried down the *Mary B*'s boarding plank.

Most of the wagon load of cargo had been stacked against the wall on the rear deck under cover of the flyover. Fred Croaker, their most experienced crew member, smiled at seeing Emma deepening the creases on his weathered middle-aged face.

"All under control, Boss," he said.

Emma took this to mean he didn't need her overseeing the loading. The crew did their best, but having a woman supervise them sometimes resulted in attempts to push back even from Fred who was among the most supportive of the crew. Blue staggered up the plank under a heavy piece of worked iron, some machinery part Emma didn't recognise. He dumped it in an empty spot and stretched the kinks out of his tall frame.

"Shorty's coming down with one more and that's the last of it," he told her.

Emma watched with approval as Fred dragged the heavy item into the centre of the deck next to several barrels of liquor to balance the load. He knew his job, but it was her responsibility as loadmaster to make sure it was correct when all was said and done.

=====

THE *MARY B* STEAMED quietly away from the Wentworth wharf and negotiated the Darling River junction, turning left up the Murray heading east. Emma was already looking forward to the off-season, visiting Catherine and Joe and awaiting the birth of her first niece or nephew. But the future of several of her favourite people depended now on whether Catherine could get Mrs. Keogh to accept Matty as a suitor for her daughter. Bea seemed hopeful. Her friend was still smiling when they dropped her off at Nettifield and Emma watched her walk briskly up to the homestead.

Half an hour later the *Mary B*'s whistle signalled their arrival at Wirramilla. Above them on the small plateau skirted by the river, the sun sent flashes of light off the iron roofed homestead and farm buildings. It was to be a brief stop. They had spent half a day there on the way up to Wentworth for Catherine to meet the family and now they had to hasten.

"You could just stop here, Emma," Daniel said to her as he manoeuvered the boat into the bank. "You'll have to get the coach home if you come with us to Echuca. I don't know why you would bother."

"I promised Hilda. She is nervous about travelling alone with the children."

Hilda Zeller and her husband Zac had a timber concession on the Murray and provided one of the many woodpiles for the riverboats. Hilda was planning on taking the children to Melbourne for the off-season and Emma had promised to accompany her for the river section of her journey and see her off on the train.

"I'm surprised Zac isn't going with her," Daniel commented.

"He's got work at Kulkyne she said, same as last summer. She stayed there with him that time, but she needs a break from the bush this year." Emma did wonder how Hilda could afford the holiday. Woodcutting was not a lucrative occupation but perhaps she had money of her own.

"Well, you've still got time to change your mind."

"Anyone would think you didn't want me on the *Mary B*." She said it lightly, more as a tease. A little reassurance wouldn't hurt. They had been friends before the accident and Sam's death, but he seemed to be always annoyed at her lately. The main reason, she believed, was the half share of the *Mary B* Sam had gifted her after their marriage. The same share Daniel had given his younger brother to engender a sense of responsibility and a secure future. That hadn't worked out so well.

"What are you talking about?" Daniel said now. "I was only thinking of your comfort."

Emma shrugged. "It was just a thought."

"Are you tired of it already?' he asked sharply. "I shouldn't have thought the work was too onerous for you."

"Of course, it isn't." Why had she gotten herself into this conversation?

"Well, once you're back home you can have a nice long rest, with everything done for you, can't you?"

Emma pressed her lips together and refrained from answering. It wouldn't help. She had less to do on the *Mary B* than she had at Wirramilla, but he would never believe it. All he saw were the acres of land, the sheep, the servants.

She felt a bit like an indentured servant herself lately, serving her time to make up for giving boatbuilder George Knowles seven-and-a-half percent ownership of the *Mary B* in return for getting the boat repaired and back on the river quickly. It was a bribe really, almost a payment of blackmail as the boat had been insured but Knowles was in no hurry to do the work. Now Daniel expected her to take the place of a crew member until the mortgage on the *Mary B* was paid and he had bought back Knowles' share. The tension this generated between them flared occasionally.

Emma went down to the lower deck and found housekeeper Lucy Wirra waiting at the landing. She had a handcart laden with fresh vegetables and fruit and a few preserves. Daniel as usual protested at the largesse.

"We can't eat all this ourselves, Capt'n Daniel," Lucy said, waving a brown hand over the cart. "Our gardens and orchards produce so much."

Emma smiled at Lucy's possessive pride. Many of the stations provided fresh supplies to the steamers, sometimes for payment or trade but often as thanks for the service they provided. Emma had told Daniel the supplies from Wirramilla were part of her contribution to the financial success of the *Mary B*, but he seemed to find it particularly mortifying to make use of the family connection. Perhaps Wirramilla's generosity made it harder for him to justify the resentment he felt toward her.

Lucy helped the *Mary B*'s cook, Ah Lo, stash the supplies in the galley store while Emma ran up to see her family. She assured her mother that Catherine was well and their new home perfectly acceptable, collected some last-minute herbals from her grandmother for delivery on the way upriver, and accepted hugs from Nella's brood on her way back to the landing. Nella was expecting again, too. Emma couldn't help the twinge at the reminder of her own loss. It was like a dark shadow in a corner of her mind.

She stashed the herbals in the trunk under her bed. Normally she would have slipped the list of orders between the pages of the cargo register she kept in the saloon, but after her conversation with Joe she put it in a drawer in her cabin underneath her unmentionables. It wouldn't do for a snooping customs officer to find it. She was afraid she was becoming a little paranoid about the matter.

Chapter Three

THE *MARY B* TRAVELLED late into the night and moored at Thandam station. The crew were up and breakfasted by six next morning and unloaded the stores ordered for the station. Thandam, on the New South Wales side of the Murray, was on a ridge making the unloading a tedious job. Emma never envied the crew their manual labour.

Shortly after leaving Thandam she saw the mile marker indicating they were nearing Zeller's woodpile. She hoped Hilda was packed and ready, but they would be taking on wood so some delay on her part would be tolerated.

She and Hilda had gotten to know one another rather well after their first meeting fifteen months ago. The *Mary B* had reached their woodpile one Sunday afternoon and found the family taking their day of rest. Sam had been alive then and Emma had been in her early pregnancy. They had spent several pleasant hours in the company of the German couple.

Emma's expertise as a herbalist had been called into use as well that day. Gertie, Hilda's youngest, had contracted a cough and Emma was able to provide something soothing for the child from her herbal bag. She had replenished the supply of the mixture since, as Gertie seemed susceptible to the problem.

Ten minutes later the *Mary B* pulled into the bank by the woodpile. The crew made fast and put down the single plank gangway. The barge *Owen* floated in a little distance behind and Blue came ashore to help with the wood loading. Emma went quickly down the plank. She couldn't see the Zeller's shack from the water and was surprised when she topped the sloping bank and saw no one about.

The wooden shack, its iron roof dull and rusted in patches, was set back twenty or so yards from the bank nestled prettily beneath the huge eucalypts. A weathered wooden bench, a water barrel, and a tub of red geraniums took up all the space beside the front door. She could hear a hen cackling in the background announcing how clever she had been to produce a new egg.

She knocked on the door. "Hilda, it's Emma. Your transport is here."

She waited, but the shack was quiet. Ominously so. Had she got it wrong? No. She had told Hilda on the way up they would be back this morning. She knocked again. Still nothing.

Emma walked around to the back of the shack where there was a flourishing vegetable garden and the hen house. Four goats were lying at ease in the shade tethered to stakes in the ground. That was odd. And there was the goat cart used to haul the wood to the riverbank. Zac can't have been working today. Well, that would make sense if his wife and children were going away for some time. But where were they all?

Would they have gone to Kulkyne? Perhaps something had happened in the last two days and they had needed help. An injury to Zac or one of the children ill. Zac at least couldn't expect to be away for long as the animals had to be attended to. The goats had water she noted. Emma turned to go back down to the river puzzled and a little concerned when she heard a cough from inside the shack. That was Gertie. She went back to the door and knocked again.

"Hilda?"

Silence greeted her. Something wasn't right. The trouble with living so far from anyone and in these rough conditions was that no one would know if you needed help. Hilda Zeller could be lying on the floor right now. Emma steeled herself for what she might find.

"I'm coming in," she called.

The first thing she saw in the light from the doorway were three pair of blue eyes staring back at her. The eldest boy, Heinrich, called Henry and about eleven years old was kneeling on the floor beside Gertie. She had the immediate feeling he had been trying to keep his sister quiet. His younger brother, Erich was sitting at the table, his head propped up on one hand. He sat up straight when Emma came in. None of them took their gaze off her.

Her first thought was that Hilda had gone somewhere with Zac and left the boys to care for Gertie, but why when she had arranged to travel?

"Are your parents around?" she asked as her eyes took in the dirty plates on the cupboard next to the wash bowl. Hilda had been a meticulous housekeeper. There seemed to be more plates there than needed for one meal.

"Father is in the bush," Henry spoke up at last.

His English was good without a pronounced accent unlike his parents who both had more formal speech with clipped accented tones. She knew they spoke German in the home and had idly wondered where the boys had learned to speak English so well. Gertie began to grizzle. Her face hadn't been washed for some time by the look of the food stains around her mouth.

"Is your mother with him?" Emma asked. She didn't understand how they could be working without the goat cart.

There was silence. Emma had addressed Henry, but it was Erich who answered.

"She's gone away," he said. His lip trembled and he quickly clamped his mouth tight shut.

"Is she visiting one of the stations? Was she unwell?"

She couldn't imagine Hilda going away voluntarily and leaving the children. Certainly not Gertie anyway. She was getting a bad feeling about this.

"We don't know," Henry said, shaking his head and standing up from his position on the floor. Emma saw tiredness and what, wariness, in his eyes?

"When did you see your mother last?"

"In the morning. When we go to work."

"This morning?"

"Yesterday," Henry answered somewhat reluctantly. Emma sucked in a gasp of air.

"She wasn't here when we came back," Erich said his voice wobbly, "and... and..."

"Father went into the bush," Henry finished for him, sending his brother a look.

"Your father went into the bush?" What did that mean? Had Hilda run off and Zac gone looking for her?

"*Ja.* He said he would be back soon." Emma thought Henry was trying to sound confident but not entirely succeeding. "We have to wait."

"That doesn't sound right, Henry," Emma told him. "Did something happen last night? Was there some trouble?"

"*Nein.* Mama wasn't here." Henry emphasised the last words as if Emma didn't understand. He was right about that. She didn't. She was trying to think of what else to ask when a shout from outside drew her to the doorway.

A tableau greeted her gaze as she stepped out of the shack. Blue was on the plank frozen in the action of passing up a cut log to Willy who was leaning forward on the deck. Jake Summers stood behind him. Shorty was on the bank. All the men were staring into the woodpile. Her first thought was that a snake had been disturbed. They often slept in the woodpiles. She might be needed to give aid if one of the crew was unlucky enough to be bitten.

"Capt'n, Capt'n, look here."

Emma picked up her skirt and ran down as Daniel appeared at the stern.

"What is it?" he asked.

Shorty pointed to the woodpile his face ashen. "There's some'un in there."

Daniel vaulted to the bank over the low free board as Emma reached Shorty's side.

"Oh, dear Lord." Staring up at her from among the logs was Hilda Zeller.

No one moved or spoke for several moments. Emma's mind flashed back to the sight of Sam's body on the riverbank. She wavered for a moment, pushing down the feelings of helplessness the image always generated. She knelt and lightly touched Hilda's face. Not that it was necessary. She was clearly dead.

"I thought something smelt off," Shorty muttered.

"Where's Zeller?" Daniel asked his voice low, crouching down beside her.

"He's not here. Only the children. The boys said he went bush last night."

She had lowered her voice to match his. It seemed somehow wrong to speak normally at that moment. She looked back to the shack. Henry and Erich were both standing in the doorway silently watching. They made no move to come and see what was happening, thank goodness.

Emma began to carefully remove the wood from around Hilda's head. One blonde plait was pinned around the way Emma had always seen her, the other loose tangled amongst the wood. Shorty and Daniel were lifting off the wood further down, tossing it to one side. Revealing more of her showed there was blood on her clothes.

"It looks as if she's been shot," Daniel said.

A chill went through Emma's body. Her gaze flew instinctively to the surrounding bush. The idyllic setting had suddenly assumed a brooding aspect. Was the person who had done this still around? Had Zac killed her and run off or was he himself lying dead somewhere? What could possibly have gone wrong? She heard the click as a gun was cocked behind her and spun around to find Fred holding the *Mary B*'s shotgun. The tension was palpable. Even the birds seemed to have fallen silent for a moment.

"Blimey," said Blue.

Emma took a shuddering breath and turned her attention back to the body.

"What do we do?" she whispered.

Daniel ran a hand over his head. "I guess we should bury her and report to the police when we get to Euston. And warn the stations about Zeller if he's on the run."

"Yes," Emma agreed. They were a hundred river miles from Euston. In this heat, especially, they couldn't transport a body "I want to prepare her for burial." Daniel gave her a look she couldn't interpret.

"How long..."

"I'll be as quick as I can, Daniel. Half an hour at most. It will take you that long to dig a grave anyway, won't it. Willy, can you get me a sheet of canvas from the stores to lay her on? And then I'll need several of you to carry her up to the shack."

"Sure, Boss."

"You'd better keep that shotgun ready, Fred. Just keep your eyes and ears open," Daniel told him.

"Aye, Capt'n."

Shorty and Daniel continued to remove more of the wood, Shorty's eyes darting nervously back and forth to the surrounding bush. Emma went back up to the shack to speak to the children feeling exposed as she did so. She didn't want to think about what sort of targets they made. She couldn't remember feeling so ill at ease in the bush.

Henry paled at the news his mother had died, but she didn't think it came as a great surprise. How much did they know of what had happened here? Erich just stared, not quite comprehending, while Gertie was too young to understand though she was unsettled that things weren't as normal.

"I'll take you down to the boat and you can wait there for a little while and then we will have the burial." She picked up Gertie and went to the door. "Do you understand, Henry?" she asked, when the lad didn't move from where he was standing, his arms hanging limply by his side.

"We have to wait for Father."

Emma could see a problem looming but decided to take it one step at a time. "Just come down to the boat for now Henry. You can have something to eat while you wait. We'll come back here afterwards, all right?"

He stared at her for a moment as if trying to assess how trustworthy she was. Their eyes met then he lowered his gaze and moved to follow her. The boys kept their eyes averted from the woodpile as they passed, though someone had thoughtfully put the canvas over Hilda's body. Emma left the children in the saloon with Ah Lo and a plate of bread liberally spread with dripping. Comfort food. She felt she could have done with some herself. What in heaven had happened here?

Chapter Four

EMMA COULD HEAR the men digging in the soft sand as she undressed Hilda on the bed in the tiny main bedroom. It would have been a lot easier with another pair of hands but there were none available, that were appropriate anyway.

She wasn't changing Hilda's clothes on a whim. She wanted to take what the woman was wearing to the police as evidence of what had happened to her. She studied the bullet wound. It was small and neat and in the area of the heart. The other wounds were minor, scratches on Hilda's arms and legs probably from when the wood was piled over her, and one cheek swollen and bruised.

Less than twenty-four hours dead but Shorty had been right about the odour. They might have taken more notice of it, but it wasn't unusual. Animals died in the bush all the time. As it was the ants had found the body. Emma washed them off using water from a bucket in the kitchen and a clean tea towel. She located several dresses in the large tin trunk in the corner of the room and chose the one Hilda had worn that Sunday. The German woman wasn't tall and more of an angular body shape and Emma was hot and short of breath by the time she had managed to clothe the inert body. At least rigor mortis had passed otherwise the task would have been impossible.

She knew that without a woman available Hilda Zeller would have been wrapped and buried unprepared for her final journey. She couldn't help the few tears that slid down her cheeks at the waste of a life and the thought of the children's future. Even after seeing the bodies of Sam and Michael and her grandfather she still found the sudden cessation of life, the empty shell, difficult to comprehend. Did one ever get used to it?

Finally, she pinned up the loose plait using some pins she found in a flowered dish on the small table beside the bed. Smoothing down some stray strands of hair she surveyed the result. Not as neat as Hilda would have done herself but it would suffice. When she had finished, she wrapped the canvas firmly around the body. She heard someone come into the shack.

"The hole is ready," Daniel announced.

"I'm done here."

He came in with Willy and they carried the body out. Emma sent Shorty down to the boat to bring the children up for the burial. Ah Lo came up carrying Gertie, the boys trailing behind. It was a sombre little group that stood around the grave.

Emma uncovered the face for the children to say goodbye before it was covered again, and the body lowered into the grave. Henry was stoical as he took his last view of his mother, but tears slid freely down Erich's face and Gertie let out one mournful 'Mama' and sobbed quietly on Emma's shoulder. Emma's own throat constricted in sympathy. She didn't imagine the men found the situation any easier. Daniel had to clear his throat twice before he could speak.

"For as much as it has pleased Almighty God to take out of this world the soul of Hilda Zeller, we therefore commit her body to the ground, earth to earth, ashes to ashes, dust to dust."

Emma wondered when he had learned the words. Was it a requirement of a Captain's certificate to be able to bury someone? Odd, when they couldn't perform a marriage. Did that say something about life? She picked up a handful of soil and tossed it into the grave, encouraging the boys to do the same.

"We should pack up a few of your belongings," she said to Henry as she shepherded them back to the shack, leaving the crew to close the grave.

"Why?"

"You will have to come with us on the boat, now."

"*Nein*," Henry announced. "Father said to wait. He will come back."

"Did he say how long he would be?"

The boy hesitated. Was he considering what she would believe? "*Nein*," he said finally.

"Do you know where he is, now?"

"*Nein*, but..."

"We can't leave you here, Henry." She put Gertie on the floor and bent down to him, eyes at his level. He was sturdy but not tall. She wanted to put her hands on him, comfort him, but had the feeling it wouldn't be welcome. "Something bad has happened here. We don't know where your father is, if he's safe or when he's going to come back." Or if he will be able to come back. "You can't look after your brother and sister here by yourself."

"Yes, I can," he insisted. Emma thought he probably could in the short term, but she continued to look at him without speaking. "You can take Gertie," he said finally, making the concession willingly enough it seemed. "Erich and I will stay."

"And if your father doesn't come back? What then?"

He thought for a moment. "Erich and I will get on a boat."

"But there's the problem, Henry. We are the last boat." There was the *Lisette* still to come, unless the Company planned to have it work the bottom end for now, but she didn't need to mention it. If anything, it would be barely a day behind and it wasn't a chance she was prepared to take. "The river is falling fast. It will be several months before there is enough water for the boats again."

"Father said we are to wait for him," he repeated, his voice almost breaking at the last word.

Emma was at a loss. Short of hauling the children on board and holding them captive she wasn't sure what to do but leaving them behind wasn't an option either.

"What if we leave a note for him, telling him where you are?" she suggested thinking fast. "That you are with Captain Daniel and Mrs. Berry on the *Mary B*. Your father knows us."

She could see Henry's mind working. He had to be frightened and worried despite attempting to appear in control.

"That would be all right…I guess," he said grudgingly.

"Good. We'll do that."

"I know," he said. "You could leave us at the next station, and he could come get us there. We could do that, *ja*?"

"That would be Kulkyne Station. You know the people there, don't you?"

"We stayed there last summer," he said eagerly. "Mr. Bell visits sometimes."

"Well, we can see about that when we get there."

The Bell family at Kulkyne had something like eight or nine children. She supposed another three would hardly be noticed. Henry found paper and pencil and Emma set about writing the note while Henry gathered their clothes, and anything else he wanted to take.

Her note was brief and to the point.

Dear Mr Zeller. We have found Hilda's body in the woodpile and have buried her behind the shack. We are taking the children with us on the Mary B fearing for their wellbeing here alone. I hope you understand.

She couldn't give an answer as to where the children would be. Finally, she wrote:

I will leave messages at the stations on the way, and with the police, as to the children's whereabouts. Emma Berry.

She read the note out to Henry who seemed satisfied with it, and then placed it on the kitchen table weighted down with an empty jam jar. Given the nature of things she thought it might be a good idea to have a quick look around the shack in case there was anything to indicate what had taken place. She needed to think like Mrs. Paschal her favourite fictional detective. Mrs. Paschal maintained that no detective, male or female, should be too nice. Emma had found that maxim useful in the past. The crew still had to finish loading the wood so there was time. Henry and Erich sat patiently on the bench beside the front door staring down at the river.

The shack was built of rough-cut timber boards unlined, the construction visible on the interior. It consisted of a main room that occupied the space down one side and functioned as kitchen, dining and sitting room while the other half was divided into two bedrooms. The main room was neat and tidy as Emma had always seen it, apart from the dishes on the kitchen bench. The dust had only just begun to settle over everything. Apart from some magazine pictures pinned to the walls it offered no decoration. The floor was bare packed earth.

There was a fireplace on the back wall, and a door that opened to the hen house and vegetable garden. Beside it was a bench hung with a curtain to hide the shelves beneath with the wash bowl on top. Several pots and pans hung from hooks on the wall above it. The first shelf under the bench held a collection of china and a tray of well-polished silver cutlery that spoke of better days, while on the bottom shelf were bags of flour and sugar, some tinned foods including milk powder, and a bowl containing three eggs. Hardly enough to keep the children for more than a few days at best, though she didn't know if Henry's skills were up to making damper or catching fish.

The unglazed window in the side wall had hessian tacked over it. Beneath it was a wooden table with a bare bench seat on each side and beside the front door a shabby two seat sofa. Gertie had climbed up onto it and was half lying, her thumb in her mouth eyelids flickering. A small bookcase in the corner roughly made from bush timbers held a collection of books. All were in German except for two of Trollope's Barchester stories in English and an English primer.

She looked at the flyleaf of each book. Most had no inscription, but on several the name Franz Krueger appeared, and Hilda Busch was written on two others. She imagined Busch could have been Hilda's maiden name, but the Franz Krueger was a puzzle.

One book was inscribed "*Um Hilda auf ihrem 10. Geburtstag von Mama.*" Grimm's Marchen was the title. From the illustrations, it appeared to be a copy of Grimm's fairy tales. On the bottom shelf of the bookcase were several recent editions of the *Melbourne Argus* newspaper. There was nothing in the room to give any indication of what had happened here. She called Henry in.

"Do you want to take any of the books?" she asked. "There's one here I think you should have in any case."

She handed him the Grimm's fairy tales, open at the flyleaf. He looked at it briefly before putting it in his bag.

"*Danke.*"

In the main bedroom, the bed pushed against the far wall consisted of a flock mattress on a bush timber base and a cotton blanket over white sheets. All that was needed in the summer heat. She smoothed out the rumples that had been made when she washed and dressed Hilda. There was a small gilt framed mirror hanging on a nail on one wall and the large trunk in the corner where she had found the clean dress for Hilda to be buried in. A rag rug covered part of the floor inside the doorway.

Zac's Sunday clothes were in the trunk with Hilda's dresses. That meant he must be wearing his work clothes at that moment, wherever he was. There were underclothes, worn but clean, and at the very bottom a patchwork quilt, yellow, pink, and blue in a chevron pattern. The quilt was old and beautifully stitched. Perhaps it had been handed down for several generations of Zellers or Busches.

Emma was tempted to take it with her for the children, but it felt like stealing. Perhaps if Zac didn't return, if he had been responsible for Hilda's death, she could arrange to collect it later. The uncertainty made it difficult to know if what she was doing was for the best. She packed the quilt carefully back in the bottom of the trunk and completed her search of the room with a quick glance under the bed. The space was bare. Nothing to help there either.

"We'll go down to the boat very soon," she told the boys and went to look in the children's bedroom. She didn't expect to find anything and wasn't proved wrong. The room held a double bed leaving little room for anything else. The covers had been roughly pulled up. There were no playthings and the earth floor under the bed was again bare.

A sharp toot on the *Mary B*'s whistle reminded her of the time. She picked up a half-asleep Gertie from the sofa, collected the bundle of Hilda's damaged clothes from where she had left them and made sure the front door was properly closed behind her.

"Ready?" she asked the boys.

"The chickens," said Erich. "Who will feed the chickens and the goats?"

She had forgotten the animals.

"*Vater wird*," Henry said to his brother.

"What was that, Henry?"

"I said, Father will feed them."

"They will be out of water in a day, Henry. And if your father doesn't get back in time they will suffer, and they may die. We'd best leave the door of the chicken pen open," Emma replied.

"But some animal will get them," Erich said.

"They'll die without food if we keep them shut in, Erich. They'll have to take their chances with the animals." Erich looked uncertain. "Hens can fly up and roost safely in the trees."

It seemed to satisfy him. They went around to the hen house which was a lean-to off the back of the shack. Emma propped the door to the pen open with a stick. The hens rushed out and made straight for the greenery of the vegetable garden. Emma sighed. A pecked-over garden wouldn't be well received if Zac returned but she didn't feel she could leave the hens in the pen any more than she could leave the children in the shack. The goats were another matter.

They were not her favourite animal. There were three billies and a nanny, a milker by the look of her swollen udder. She remembered being told sometime that keeping nannies and billies together made the milk taste bad. Perhaps they were normally separated. Daniel called to her from near the shack.

"Emma, where are you? We need to get on."

"Here, round the back. We have to do something about these goats," she said when he joined them.

"Just let them loose?"

"They belong to Father," Henry said. "They pull the wood cart."

"You're right, Henry," Emma said. "They're working animals, valuable for the woodcutting operation." She turned to Daniel. "We could take them to Kulkyne. Ask if they would take care of them there until, well, until they are needed here again. What do you think? I wouldn't mind keeping the nanny. I can milk her. Does Gertie drink goat's milk, Henry?"

"We all drink goat's milk."

"There you are, then."

"They smell, Emma and they make an even smellier mess," Daniel said not amused.

"Only the billies smell and we'll be at Kulkyne by dark. We can't leave them like this, Daniel. I don't think…" She didn't want to say in front of the boys that she was afraid their father wouldn't be back.

Daniel heaved a sigh. "No," he conceded. "It doesn't look promising. All right boys, grab a goat each."

"I'll take Whitey," Erich said, deftly undoing the rope of the smallest billy goat.

Henry and Daniel each took one of the larger goats.

"You'll have to take the nanny, as well," Emma said. "I can't manage her and carry Gertie and these things at the same time."

"I'll send one of the boys up," Daniel said.

Emma went back into the shack and added the information about the goats to the note. When she came out Blue was leading the nanny down to the *Mary B*. Shorty, on the boarding plank, was hauling on the lead of a reluctant billy goat with Daniel wondering where to put his hands to push from behind.

"You could lend a hand here," Shorty grumbled as Blue came up. Between the three of them they got the goat boarded. The other three animals followed tamely enough once the example was set. Fred and Blue pulled down some sheep hurdles that were stacked on the roof and created a pen at the stern, lashing the hurdles together. Despite their makeshift yard, the goats were tethered as well. They weren't as placid as sheep and Daniel wasn't taking any chances of them getting out and running amok.

"You know who's goin' to have to clean up after this lot, don't you?" Shorty complained, once the work was done.

"You can have a glass of goat's milk for your trouble," Emma told him.

Shorty looked disgusted. "Milk, Boss? Milk? That's for bebbies, milk."

Chapter Five

THE CREW SET ABOUT casting off and Emma was left with the job of settling the children. She had a choice of cabin as the *Mary B* wasn't carrying any passengers. Most people who were travelling at that time preferred an uncomfortable journey with Cobb & Co over the possibility of being stranded en route in a riverboat with the water levels so low. She chose the cabin next to hers that was fitted out with a double bed, thinking the children would feel more comfortable being together as they had back at the shack.

She brought up the tin bath to the cabin and helped Ah Lo carry up hot and cold water to fill it. She bathed Gertie first and then left the boys to bathe themselves. They would feel a little better once fresh and clean she reasoned. Gertie needed a fresh set of clothes which Emma got from the bag Henry had packed but the boys put back on what they had been wearing. They had one other set of everyday clothes as well as their Sunday best, but apparently what they were wearing had to last the week and Henry wasn't about to change their normal routine. Emma didn't argue. She wasn't in any hurry to do their wash. At least Hilda wouldn't have lacked firewood to heat her wash water.

That thought brought her back to Hilda's body in the woodpile. Why put her there, of all places? She put Gertie down for a nap, thumb in mouth and clutching a soft toy Henry had packed. Did she suck her thumb normally? The boys were quiet not speaking except in response to something said to them. Shock and grief would do that. That and being among strangers. But she would have to speak with them at some time. She was sure they knew more than they were saying about what had happened with their parents.

"We'll reach Kulkyne station in a few hours," Emma told Henry. He merely nodded. She left them on the lower deck at the bow where they could watch the men and the river. She went up to the wheelhouse, needing to talk to Daniel. The world seemed a little adrift, as if it had lost its moorings.

"The kids okay?" Daniel asked when Emma appeared at the wheelhouse doorway. Willy was sitting in the far corner.

"I've settled Gertie for a nap, and the boys are down below with Fred and Shorty," Emma told him. Gertie would sleep, lulled by the motion. She wasn't so sure about the boys.

"If you're staying for a while, Boss, I'll go and get myself a cuppa," Willy said, getting to his feet and stretching.

"Sure, Willy. I'll give you a shout."

"Bring one up for me when you come back," Daniel told him.

"Aye, Capt'n."

Emma moved to stand beside Daniel. In front of the wheel the linen chart mapping the river was stretched out, its drawn lines marking the river channel, the bank, rocks, and sandbars. As she watched, Daniel turned the chart further onto the roller at one end bringing the next few miles of the river into view.

"Have they said anything more about what happened?" he asked.

"No, but then I haven't asked. I was planning on leaving that until later. Henry was very reluctant to leave the shack. He only agreed when I left the note. He wants us to leave them at Kulkyne."

"They know the Bells, don't they?"

Emma nodded. "I let him think they could stay there so he would stop arguing about leaving but really, giving it some consideration, I'm not sure the Bells would want the responsibility. What would they do if Zac doesn't turn up to claim them?"

"We don't want to be responsible for them either, Emma. We should just hand them over to the police at Euston."

That didn't feel right. It wasn't like delivering a piece of cargo. And what would happen to them if their father had killed their mother? She shuddered to think of these children, of any child, being placed in an orphanage. However good the care it didn't replace the love of a family.

Daniel was probably right when he saw her as having a privileged upbringing on her family's sheep station. Wirramilla and its people had always been there for her. She knew Daniel hadn't been so lucky. His parents had died when he was barely old enough to work and he'd had his younger brother to think of. A bit like Henry now.

"They might have relatives somewhere in the colony who could take them in. I'll ask them about that too." She sighed. "What on earth could have happened? Bushrangers, do you think?" She didn't want to think that it could have been Zac.

He shook his head. "Haven't heard of any in the area lately. It doesn't look good with Zeller missing. Perhaps they had an argument? Perhaps Zeller – hmm, I don't know."

"Perhaps Zac what?" Emma asked.

"Perhaps he lost his temper about something," he said quickly. "Perhaps he didn't want her going away with the children. Did you consider Hilda might not have intended coming back?"

"I hadn't thought about it, but I guess that might be possible." Hilda and Zac had seemed comfortable enough with each other, but she couldn't imagine anyone wanting to live as they were. Despite the brief visits of the riverboats it would be lonely and only the company of men. Perhaps Hilda wanted a better life for herself and the children.

"It might have been an accident," Daniel said.

"She didn't get into the woodpile by accident."

"I meant the shooting."

Emma stared out at the water. A little ripple of current eddied around a fallen branch at the water's edge. A leafy twig bobbed into view, disappearing into the boat's wash.

"The whole thing is upsetting. I liked Hilda, and Zac come to that. I can't see him shooting her."

"I can almost see your mind working," Daniel said. "You're trying to play detective again, aren't you?"

"Well, it did work out last time, remember," she reminded him a little tartly.

"Leave it to the police, Emma," he said his voice firm. "We'll report it at Kulkyne station and have them send a telegraph to the police at Euston. If the Bells won't take the children, we can leave them with the police. It'll be out of our hands."

Emma supposed it was fortunate Kulkyne had the telegraph. Until recently the police had been stationed there. While Euston was only fifteen miles overland from Kulkyne, by river it was a ninety-mile journey around the Kulkyne Bend. And they had to collect wool at Pattin Downs on the way. It would be two days before they reached Euston. Best the police were alerted as soon as possible and started the search for Zac Zeller. Or whoever was responsible for Hilda's death.

Everything pointed to Zac, but Emma found it hard to accept he would leave the children alone for so long. Unless he wasn't able to return. Or if he knew someone else would be along to take care of them. He knew the *Mary B* would be calling in to collect Hilda. He'd have to know Emma wouldn't leave the children there alone. It made as much sense as anything.

What did one know about the lives of other people? Everyone had one face for the world and one for private she had found. Daniel rolled the chart on and Emma had a sharp image of seeing Sam do the same.

"I'll send Willy back up," she said and left the wheelhouse.

She could hear Erich's plaintive voice as she reached the bottom of the stairs.

"I can't do it." What were they up to?

"Now then, there's no need for that," she heard Fred admonish gently. "Try this one, see, you just put this piece under here and poke it through. Like that. There you are. Well done, lad."

Fred's favourite occupation, playing around with rope.

"That's just a granny knot," said Henry, his tone dismissive.

"Which is no doubt all you could you do when you were your brother's age," said Fred. "How are you doing with that reef knot?"

Emma stepped out onto the deck in time to see Henry hold up his completed knot. Willy, seeing her, hauled himself to his feet and went to the galley to see to Daniel's cup of tea. Nearby, Shorty was sitting on a barrel frowning over a piece of wood he was whittling, the inevitable roll-your-own clamped between his lips.

"Everything all right here?" Emma asked. She moved a chair closer to where they sat under the shade of the overhang.

"Sure, Boss. The young lad here's going to make a great little sailor when he puts on a few inches."

"I'm not going to be a sailor," Henry said, dismissing the idea as if it were beneath him.

Fred raised his eyebrows at Emma. Apparently, it wasn't the first opinion of Henry's he had heard. Emma asked the inevitable question.

"What do you want to do, Henry?"

"I'll be like, someone in business. And I won't live in the bush. I'll live in a house in a town."

"We used to live in a house in a town, didn't we Henry?" Erich said frowning over his knot. "Look, Mr. Fred." He held out his piece of rope. "I did it. Is that a reef knot?

"Almost, lad. You just need this end tucked through here."

"Oh."

"What was the town where you lived?"

"Melbourne," Henry put in as Erich hesitated. The younger boy may not have known the name. Emma wondered if that was where they had learned to speak English so well. Perhaps they had been in the colony for some time.

"But I liked Uncle Axel's farm at Kerang best," Erich said. "We lived there when..." Henry reached across and grabbed at his brother's piece of rope. "Don't, Henry. Now look, you made it come undone." There were tears in his voice which Emma suspected had nothing to do with the piece of rope.

"Hush, you can do it again, lad," Fred said. "Now, show me."

Emma watched as Erich concentrated on the rope. Had that grab been a diversion on Henry's part to stop his brother talking? She reached into the work bag that hung on her chair and pulled out a piece of needlework, a shirt of Daniel's that needed darning since he had caught the sleeve on a nail the week before. They all worked in silence for a few minutes.

"Is Uncle Axel your dad's brother?" Emma asked casually after a few minutes.

"*Nein*," Henry said.

"What is their family name. Perhaps I've heard of them."

Henry didn't answer. She recalled one of the names in the books she had seen at the shack.

"Is it Krueger?"

"*Nein*."

"Do they have a sheep farm, these people?"

"They milk cows, and make butter and cheese," Erich said. "I like cheese."

"*Halt's maul*, Erich," Henry ordered. "*Erinnern sich was Vater sagte*"

Erich looked as if he were about to cry and Emma's heart hardened toward Henry. She knew the word *vater* was father, and 'halt' would have to be stop, surely? Stop what? Talking about their father, their father's family? Had Zac told them not to talk? But why?

At least it wouldn't be hard to find a dairy farm at Kerang run by a German named Axel. And it provided an alternative of what to do with the children if, as she expected, the Bells at Kulkyne didn't want to take on the responsibility for them. Kerang wasn't on the river, but it wasn't too far from it, a little south-east of Swan Hill. If they were Hilda's family, they would want to know she had been buried properly even though her death meant that another family member may have been the cause of it. If they were Zellers, well, that might be a reason for more caution.

Chapter Six

IT WAS AROUND SIX O'CLOCK when the *Mary B* eased into the Kulkyne station landing. Daniel went up to the homestead to talk to Ted Bell the manager. Emma remained on the *Mary B* with the children. Gertie had woken from her nap and required constant attention as she couldn't be let wander around freely. There were any number of dangers for a small child: falling down the steep stairs, falling overboard, getting into the engine room with its blazing boiler fire, or into the galley. Emma could see herself being kept busy.

She set Henry to milk the nanny goat, not knowing if they would be keeping her. Henry gave Erich the milk bucket to carry and they both went off together spoiling Emma's chance of having some time alone with the younger boy. When they returned with the milk Emma found that the nanny had given half a gallon of creamy yellow liquid.

"But it doesn't smell right," Henry told her frowning. "It was fine this morning."

Emma sniffed at it. It wasn't pleasant. "You're right, Henry. It smells too goaty. Your father didn't always keep the billies and the nanny together, did he?"

Henry stared at her for a moment as if wondering how she could know that. "I didn't want to take them to the clearing, it was too far in the bush," he said words tumbling over his tongue, "and I couldn't leave Gertie and Erich. I had to look after them."

He looked at her with an element of defiance that didn't quite cover his fears. A lot seemed to have been heaped on his young shoulders. Had he been afraid of what he might find if he went into the bush? Or who might find him? Now was not the time to ask. She needed to gain his trust if she were to discover what had happened that day.

"It's all right, Henry. You did right. The nanny's milk will be fine in another day or so. It gets a bad taste when billy goats are kept nearby. In the meantime, we have powdered milk."

"What if Gertie doesn't like it? She might get sick."

Emma had seen a tin of powdered milk in the shack kitchen, but perhaps the goat's milk had been kept for the children.

"How does the milk get a bad taste if the billy goats are there?" Erich wanted to know.

"I don't know Erich," she said, not wanting to get into a discussion of animal mating. "I just know that's what happens. Let's go get us some powdered milk and we'll find out if Gertie likes it. It'll be time for your dinner soon anyway."

"Does she eat the grass where they pee?" Erich asked. "I bet that's what it is, isn't it?"

"You talk too much," Henry told him. Emma doubted Henry knew the answer either. She was sure he would have been pleased to display his greater knowledge if he had.

Behind the paddle box where the galley was housed a wet hessian bag covered some food items kept fresh in the spray from the paddles. It was a natural cool store. Emma picked up a gallon jar half full of white liquid from under the hessian cover. Erich stepped into the spray and waved his arms in the misty air. Gertie, held on Emma's hip with her free hand, squealed at Erich in delight. Henry looked on as if such childish behaviour was beneath him.

She fetched a mug from the galley and poured some milk into it. Gertie grabbed at it and drank eagerly. She stopped for a moment as the taste hit her tongue then

licked her lips and drank again before finally coming up
for air with a satisfied sigh.

"Gertie's got a white moustache," Erich sang.

"Well, Gertie likes it, Henry," she said, smiling at the
older boy. "And we all drink it as well so I'm sure she will
be just fine."

"*Danke*," he said quietly.

Emma heard voices and the *Mary B* rocked on its
moorings as several people came on board. Daniel
appeared with Ted Bell and a station hand.

"G'day, Mrs. Berry," Ted Bell greeted her. "Sorry to
hear about your troubles." He nodded at the children. "I'm
afraid we can't help you here," he said. "Ruth doesn't
think it's a good idea, especially if – ah – if he's around
somewhere."

Emma wasn't surprised at their reluctance. "That's
perfectly understandable, Mr. Bell. You have to look after
your own first."

"Bad business though. Really bad. We can take those
billies off your hands, anyway, and keep them til we know
what's what." It seemed Daniel had allowed the nanny to
stay on board which saved her having to argue for it. Even
if Gertie did like powdered milk, the goat's milk when it
was drinkable was better for her. "The missus will be
down later with a little something for you all."

"That's very kind of you." Compensation for not
taking the children? "You knew the Zeller's quite well, I
guess. Hilda told me they were here last summer, and
Henry said you called in to their shack on occasion."

Ted Bell shifted his feet as if uncomfortable. "Ah, yes.
Well, they were isolated there, so I rode up and checked
on them every few weeks. Took them some fresh meat.
Nice people, nice people," he repeated nodding his head.

"When did you see them last?" Emma enquired.

"Oh, it's a couple weeks ago now. Hilda was going
away, and Zac was going to be working here until the

steamers were back, so there was no point taking them any fresh food." He nodded to Emma. "We'll take those billies, now," he said, turning to Daniel.

Emma thought Ted Bell wasn't all that keen to talk to her about the Zellers. Could he have had anything to do with Hilda's death and Zac's disappearance? She thought it unlikely but decided to keep an open mind on the matter. Before he and his offsider left with the billy goats Ted Bell promised to send a bale of hay along for the nanny.

"It'll make her pen easier to clean, if you spread a thick layer on the floor," he told Daniel.

Emma thought Shorty would be pleased at that. When Daniel returned from seeing the goats safely off the boat, he told her he would be in the saloon writing up his logbook if anyone needed him.

"You just want to avoid Ruth Bell," Emma accused.

He grinned. "You would too, given the chance," he said and took the stairs two at a time.

"Coward," she called after him.

She caught Henry's eye and smiled at him, but the boy looked quickly away. Grief was a funny thing. One could smile and even laugh while carrying an underlying feeling of sadness. Henry would learn that in time just as she had. At least, she hoped he would. He didn't seem to be a boy who smiled much or saw the lighter side of life.

It wasn't long before Ruth Bell arrived. She was a woman of middling height and a little overweight with brown hair speckled with grey pulled back in a loose bun. She carried a plate of something covered with a cloth and was accompanied by a young black woman holding a basket of vegetables.

"We've recently killed us a cow, Mrs. Berry," Ruth Bell said, not bothering to introduce her companion. Emma smiled and said hello to her, anyway, earning a shy smile from the young woman in return. "I'm sure some good beef and fresh vegetables will help set you all up after your experience. What a dreadful thing to happen. We've sent a telegraph to Euston. It was only a year or so back the police were moved there, you know. Euston is going ahead in leaps and bounds I must say. Regular little village now. Wouldn't be surprised if the police turn up here tonight. They'll be keen to get on the trail as quick as possible I've no doubt.

"We're setting up sentries for tonight in case Zeller comes this way. One can't be too careful. May want to try stealing a horse, perhaps. How dangerous do you think he might be, though I suppose any desperate man can be dangerous, can't he? If he's already killed once he's not going to turn a hair at doing it again, is he. Nothing to lose now."

Emma was glad the boys were at the bow with Fred and Shorty and responded in monosyllables and nods as she unloaded the plate and the basket in the galley. Ah Lo eyed with pleasure the plump steaks. The meat had obviously been hung and looked dark and tender. The basket contained freshly picked Brussel sprouts, beans, and yellow squash. There was also a container of cream and some eggs. They had already used a lot of the green vegetables from Wirramilla. Only the root vegetables kept for any length of time in the hot weather.

"And how are the children?" Ruth Bell prattled on. "All right are they?" she asked looking around. "Poor mites. Bring them up to the homestead after supper, Mrs. Berry. My lot could entertain them while we have a good chin wag. I'm sure you have lots of news."

"That's very kind, but I'm not sure that would be a good idea," Emma managed to get in, putting her hand on the woman's arm to silence her for moment. "Not tonight. They've just buried their mother, after all."

The woman had a good heart but her children... Emma couldn't remember exactly how many there were, but they

were the rowdiest bunch she had ever come across. The
Zeller boys would be overwhelmed if she let them loose
with the Bell's lot right now. They'd be like exhibits in a
zoo.

"Well, I would have thought they could do with some
cheering up. But if you say so. And how are you managing
these days? We haven't seen as much of you since your
husband died. Still, I suppose you must be kept busy
helping run the steamer now and I'm sure you're a
comfort to one another you and the Captain, both of you
suffering such a tragic loss. Such a nice man..."

Emma wasn't sure if Ruth was referring to Sam or
Daniel as the nice man but pretended not to notice the
insinuation. She was almost tempted to invite her up to
the saloon for a cup of tea. That would teach Daniel to
leave her alone with the woman. Eventually Ruth's
chatter eased enough for Emma to make some comments
of her own.

"You must have known the Zeller's fairly well," she
said.

"As well as any around I suppose. Always wondered
why they took up that timber lease. It used to be worked
by Ben Trumble til he broke his leg. Nearly lost it he did
before he could get to a doctor. Just a young fellow he
was, in his twenties. Believe he walks with a limp now.
Lucky to be walking at all if you ask me. He's working at
Pattin Downs now, you know."

"Hilda told me Zac worked here during the last off-
season," Emma said, trying to get the woman back on
track.

"Yes, he did, and Hilda and the children stayed in one
of our cottages. Better there than that shack. Zac was
going to be working here again but she was off
somewhere this year. I wouldn't have been surprised if
she didn't come back. Used to something better I would
have said."

"Did she talk to you about having family in the colonies? At Kerang perhaps?"

"She wasn't the talkative sort, I'm afraid. She did speak a lot about Germany. Homesick, I think. Wouldn't have surprised me if she went back there."

Emma didn't learn anything else and eventually managed to thank Ruth Bell again for her generosity and saw the woman on her way.

"Those steaks do look tempting," Emma said to Ah Lo, "and the vegetables, we can always do with those. We have potatoes, don't we. Do you think Mr. Summers would let us bake potatoes in the fire box tonight?"

She hadn't thought of that for an age. Potatoes baked in the boiler's fire box had been a real treat on the *Mary B* before the accident. Perhaps Ruth Bell was right, and a good meal was just what was needed after the events of the day.

"On'y if you ask, Missus," Ah Lo informed her.

"Baked potatoes!" Jake Summers said when Emma spoke to him. He seemed somewhat put out at the thought as if it were an insult for his stokehold to be treated as a cook house.

"Just imagine, Mr. Summers. A beef steak, with green vegetables, squash, and a baked potato smothered in butter."

"Well, I'm not big for the green vegetables, but the beef steak sure sounds a treat. And I guess a baked potato would go down well with it."

"You'll let Ah Lo do that then, Mr. Summers?"

"Aye. I'll be here to keep an eye on it and all."

Emma thanked him and almost bumped into Henry as she turned away.

"Can we go now?" he asked. He seemed tightly wound. "We can stop here, *Ja*?"

"I'm sorry, Henry. The Bell's don't think it would be a good idea. You will have to go on with us."

He stamped his foot. "*Nein*. We need to stay here. How will Father find us?"

"He knows where you are, Henry," Emma said quietly. "It's in the note we left for him, remember?"

"It's not right. You can't take us away," he said, his voice shaking as it rose in volume. "He said to wait for him. I told you."

Footsteps sounded on the stairs. "What's the trouble?" Daniel asked, rounding the stokehold.

"Henry's upset because they can't stay here," Emma told him before the boy could start again.

"We can't do much about that," Daniel said.

"Father said to wait for him," Henry repeated but quieter now. Emma wondered if he knew better than to argue with a man.

"We can leave you with the police at Euston," Daniel told him. "That's not too far away and you will be safe there. They can arrange for someone to look after you until your father can collect you."

Emma didn't miss the brief flash of alarm on Henry's face at the word 'police.' She saw the boy's face close before he nodded and turned away. She was left feeling uneasy at his sudden compliance.

======

IT WAS ANOTHER HOUR before Jake Summers deemed the coals ready to bake and not burn, so the potatoes weren't ready for the children's supper. Instead, Emma gave them some of the peach preserves Lucy had provided topped with a little cream. They enjoyed the treat if their empty bowls were anything to go by.

After supper, she settled them in their cabin, the boys more tired than Gertie after her afternoon nap. She was restless and cried for her mother. Even her soft toy couldn't console. Emma's heart went out to her. She finally gave the little girl a spoonful of cough syrup which had a soporific effect and got her settled in the double bed between her brothers. She would check in on them later.

In the saloon, a cooling breeze tickled the gauze curtains and flowed across the room through the open windows. The Tilley lamp hanging from the ceiling created a soft enclosing glow while outside the *Mary B*'s navigation lights turned the water silvery. They had finished eating and were sitting over drinks, tea for Emma and a tot of whisky for the men when Blue spoke up.

"You think the police will want statements from us?" he asked. Blue had experience of police statements.

"They'll want to make sure our stories match I imagine," Daniel said.

"But they won't, not exactly," Emma put in.

She remembered herself and Joe, and Sal and Jacky Wirra, recounting something that had happened years ago and each having a different memory of events. They had argued about it and she had realised then that memories were coloured by who you were, and your opinions of the people involved and how the event affected you personally.

Daniel gave her a look. "What do you mean, they won't? We all saw the same thing."

"No one sees or remembers things exactly the same way," she said. "And shock can affect your memory, too."

"We all saw Hilda Zeller's body in the woodpile. I can't see how you can change that."

"What colour was her hair?" Emma asked.

"It were brown, like," said Willy.

"You must be half blind," Shorty scoffed at his fellow crew member. "It were definitely yeller."

"See?" said Emma to Daniel.

"What colour was it, then, Boss?" Blue asked.

"She had blonde hair, yellow as Shorty said."

"It didn't look yeller from where I was. She were wearing a grey dress though, that I know," Willy drawled in what was a long speech for him.

"Yeah," Blue said nodding at Willy. "That's right. It didn't show among the logs. Looked like bark."

"Those are just details. It doesn't change anything," Daniel argued.

"But it does illustrate my point."

The sounds reached them of galloping horses and the jingle of harness followed by splashing as the river was crossed. The *Mary B* rocked gently in the ripples amid the slosh of waves lapping the bank. The police had arrived.

Chapter Seven

VOICES FLOATED DOWN from the farm buildings a little distance off and lamps were seen moving around. Emma helped Ah Lo clear the table and carry the dishes down to the galley. They had barely finished when a voice hailed them from the bank.

"Ahoy, *Mary B*. Police. Lieutenant Forrester would like to come aboard."

A tallish man in his thirties, of distinct military bearing complete with bristling moustaches stood below on the bank. An armed trooper, rifle slung over his shoulder, stood behind him. Daniel greeted them from the upper deck and sent Willy to lay down the plank gangway which was always taken up at night.

"Come on up, Lieutenant."

Emma went to her cabin to fetch the bundle of Hilda's clothing and followed the police officers into the saloon. Daniel introduced himself and the crew, and the Lieutenant shook hands all round. He introduced his companion as Trooper Stark. While the Lieutenant took a seat at the table the Trooper stood leaning in the open doorway on the starboard side, facing the Lieutenant.

"Can I get you something to drink, Lieutenant?" Emma asked, still on her feet.

Lieutenant Forrester looked at the glasses on the table. "A whisky and water would be welcome, ma'am, thank you."

Emma collected two glasses from the dresser behind them and Daniel poured. Trooper Stark stepped forward to accept his with a nod.

"Pleasant little operation you have here, Captain," the Lieutenant observed. "Very cosy." His gaze rested for a moment on Emma as he accepted his drink. Emma looked steadily back at him. She wondered if Ruth Bell had had the Lieutenants ear.

"Mrs. Berry is part owner as well as the purser of this vessel," Daniel said coolly.

"And a fine job she does of it too," put in Fred Croaker.

"We're the envy of the fleet," said Shorty. "This is the best little working boat on the river."

"Aye," said Willy.

Ah Lo nodded vigorously while Blue glared and flexed his hand resting on the table. Jake Summers just looked on amused.

There was a moment of uncomfortable silence as the crew looked at the police officer and the police officer looked back, perhaps wondering what he had stepped into. A riverboat crew was like a family. They might fight and argue among themselves but let an outsider attack and it was one for all and all for one. The three musketeers had nothing on rivermen. Emma thought Lieutenant Forrester should have known that. But then he may not have anticipated the same reaction where a woman was concerned; may even have thought her presence resented. She sometimes wondered herself if she was barely tolerated.

The Lieutenant cleared his throat and became all business. "Right. I believe you have a death to report that took place on the Victorian side. Officially, my jurisdiction is in the colony of New South Wales and your body is rightly the problem of the Swan Hill station, but we co-operate where possible. So, what's it about?"

Daniel reached for the logbook on the dresser behind him.

"I've written out a report on the matter. I'll read it out if you like and you can ask whatever questions you want."

"Right. Go ahead."

Daniel did so, as the Lieutenant leaned back in his chair and listened without interruption, sipping occasionally on his whisky and water. Daniel's report was short and to the point, simply stating how Hilda's body had been found, noting the bullet wound, that Emma prepared her for burial, and they had buried her behind the shack. It also noted that the children found at the shack had been taken aboard the *Mary B*.

"That's your story then, is it? That she was already dead in the woodpile when you got there?"

Daniel stared at him. "That's right."

"You or your crew didn't have anything to do with her death?"

"Just what are you suggesting?" Fred Croaker growled amid murmuring from the rest of the crew. Behind her, Emma was aware of a movement from Trooper Stark.

"A woman on her own, something getting out of hand perhaps?"

"You've got a very nasty mind, Lieutenant," Daniel said.

"Do you really think we would all agree to hide such a thing?" Emma asked him, aghast at the suggestion. "That we would protect someone who would behave in such a manner? I can assure you we would not."

"Rivermen are a law unto themselves, I've found, Mrs. Berry. And you seem a particularly tight little group. What did you do when you arrived at Zellers? Were you party to discovering the body in the woodpile? Your brother-in-law's report hasn't mentioned that."

His cold gaze held hers. Emma wished he would choke on his whisky. Why refer to Daniel as her brother-in-law when he could simply have called him by name. As if being her brother-in-law had some unsavory significance. Was he deliberately trying to rile her? She reminded herself of Mrs. Paschal's words. If they were good enough for her, she couldn't blame the Lieutenant for applying them.

"I went straight up to the shack. Hilda and the children were going to be travelling to Echuca with us," she said, her voice sounding a little shaky even to herself. The events of the day were still too fresh in her mind and the Lieutenant's attitude was unsettling regardless of his motives. She gathered herself and went on. "I found the children and learned that their mother was missing. Then I heard Shorty call out about something in the woodpile and I went back down to see."

"Ah yes. The children. You have them on board with you I understand?"

"Yes."

"I'll want to speak to them."

"They're asleep. They buried their mother today and their father is missing. You can't be so callous."

"I have a job to do," he said but he didn't order her to fetch them. He turned his attention to Daniel. "You say there were signs the Zeller woman had been shot?"

"That's right. There was what looked like a bullet wound in the – er – the chest area. And blood of course."

"There was a clear bullet wound in the area of the heart," Emma said quietly. She picked up the bundle of clothes she had put beside her chair and placed them on the table. "Here are the clothes she was wearing."

Lieutenant Forrester gave her an apprising look before reaching for the bundle. He spread the grey dress out on the table, fingered the bullet hole surrounded by the dark stain. Emma looked away.

"Powder burns as well," he said. "Hmm. Did you see any other wounds?"

"Hilda had a bruise on her cheek. And there were scratches on her arms and legs most likely from when she was put on the woodpile and the logs were piled on top of her."

"I didn't remember the bruise." Daniel realised what he had said and pursed his lips. Lieutenant Forrester pulled out a notebook and began scribbling in it.

"And she had been hidden in the woodpile? You didn't know she was there until you began taking the wood?"

"Gave us all a right shock it did, I can tell you," said Shorty. "I'll be lookin' to see a face now whenever I pick up a piece of firewood."

The Lieutenant leaned back in his chair and swept his gaze around them. It was clear he hadn't given up the idea that they might be involved.

"What weapons do you have on the boat?"

"Only a shotgun," Daniel said.

"We'll search before we leave."

Jake Summers moved uncomfortably in his chair, his feet scraping on the timber floor. The Lieutenant fixed him with a stare.

"I have a pistol in my bag."

"Anyone else have a weapon?"

Heads were shaken.

"Go get it," he told Jake.

Jake Summers got to his feet and at a nod from the Lieutenant Trooper Stark accompanied him out. Lieutenant Forrester turned his attention back to those remaining.

"Odd place to put a body," he mused. "You knew these people well, the Zellers?"

"They took over the place from Ben Trumble about eighteen months ago, perhaps a bit less," Daniel said. "We knew as much about them as about any of the woodcutters along the river."

"We spent some time in their company one Sunday. It would be a little more than a year ago," Emma added. "Hilda was at the shack most times we called at the woodpile, but occasionally she was out, helping her husband, I guess. I visited with her whenever I could. Life could be pretty lonely for a woman in the bush."

The more she said the more she realised how unusual the Zellers were. Most of the timber leases were managed by a man or two. Some of the stations provided wood for the steamers as a sideline. They used a horse for hauling the wood to the river, while the Zellers had goats to haul a small cart. They were much less expensive to keep and the boys could manage them, she imagined.

"Why would he take a family into a job like that," mused the Lieutenant, clearly thinking the same. "Farm labouring would provide a better living. Something in their background perhaps?"

Emma wondered if she imagined the atmosphere that seemed to permeate the crew at his words. Fred pulled out his pipe and began to fill it. Blue, Shorty and Willy seemed to take that as a signal, and each began to put a cigarette together. They couldn't have looked more suspicious if they'd tried. Daniel, who surprisingly didn't smoke, kept his attention on his whisky glass.

Their behaviour wasn't missed by Lieutenant Forrester who fingers beat a tattoo on the table, but no one spoke.

Jake Summers came back followed closely by Trooper Stark carrying a pistol wrapped in an oily cloth which he handed to the Lieutenant.

"It ain't loaded," Jake growled as he took his seat again.

The Lieutenant ignored him, unwrapping the cloth in a leisurely fashion, and checking the breech. He held the muzzle close to his nose and sniffed.

"When was this fired last?"

"Haven't fired it in months. Only keep it for protection."

"Do you always keep it unloaded?"

Jake gave a sideways glance at his fellow crew mates. "Pretty much," he admitted reluctantly.

Shorty snorted around his cigarette, and Blue who, was sitting next to Jake, pushed his chair back sharply. Ah Lo muttered something in Chinese and topped up his cup of of black tea. What was going on? Probably nothing to do with Hilda Zeller but something she should know about before it caused trouble. If it hadn't already. She would talk to Fred about it later.

Lieutenant Forrester seemed to lose interest in the pistol.

"Well, now," he said, through the gathering smoky haze, "these children. What have they to say on the matter?"

Daniel looked to Emma.

"They say their mother wasn't at the shack when they came back from work the previous evening. They found Gertie on her own and their mother nowhere to be found. According to Henry, the oldest boy, their father went off into the bush and hadn't returned by late next morning when we arrived."

"Why did he do that?"

"Henry didn't say."

"Was he armed?"

"I don't know that either. He may have been. I didn't find a gun at their shack."

Lieutenant Forrester puffed thoughtfully on his cigar for a few moments.

"So, the woman was going off with the children without her husband. Was she not planning to come back?"

"If that was her intention, she didn't say anything to me about it," Emma replied.

"But not impossible," the Lieutenant said.

"No," Emma had to admit it wasn't. Ruth Bell had suggested the same. And there was the matter of the herbal Hilda was taking to prevent another birth. Did that reflect an unstable relationship or was it just, as Hilda had explained, their way of life wasn't conducive to another infant difficult enough as it was with Gertie?

When Hilda had asked for something, Emma had been firm that she wouldn't provide anything to end a pregnancy. It had to be a preventative only. Children were a blessing but too many could be a curse, was her grandmother's mantra on that subject, but she would not destroy a life already begun.

"Zeller. That's German?" the Lieutenant was saying.

"Yes, but they spoke English," Daniel put in.

"Hilda better than Zac," Emma added. "They talked about a farming area somewhere near a place called Weiden, I think it was."

They had been happy to talk about Germany and life there but had not said a word about what had brought them to a woodcutter's shack on the Murray River on the other side of the world.

"Right. Would you describe Zeller, please?" the Lieutenant asked of Daniel, his pencil poised over his notebook.

Daniel shrugged. "Typical German I suppose, blonde, blue eyed, well built. A good-looking bloke."

"Any distinguishing features?"

No one could think of any.

"Clothes?"

Daniel shrugged again. "The usual work clothes. He was wearing his Sunday best when we met him. Duck trousers, white shirt, vest and jacket."

"His Sunday clothes were still in the trunk at the shack," Emma said.

The Lieutenant turned his eyes on her. He had an uncomfortable habit of looking and pausing before he spoke. It was probably part of his questioning technique to unsettle people he was interviewing. It worked.

"You checked his clothes?"

"I had a quick look around the shack in case there was something to indicate what had happened or some reason for it," she told him trying not to sound defensive. "It seemed like the sensible thing to do under the circumstances. I didn't know when Zac or someone might be back and remove something."

"And was there anything?"

"Not that I could see," she had to concede. "There were no papers of any sort, just clothes, some books, and the usual household items. It was quite basic."

"Right. I'll need to speak to the children, the older boy anyway."

"They're asleep, as I told you, Lieutenant. Couldn't it wait til morning to question them?"

"No, afraid not. I want to be away at daybreak tomorrow. See if we can get on his trail. He's already at least a day ahead."

Emma nodded. She could see the sense of it. Henry was awake when Emma entered the children's cabin. He looked to Emma like a boy with a great worry on his mind, hardly surprising in the circumstances.

"There's a police officer here. Lieutenant Forrester. He wants to speak to you about what happened yesterday, Henry." She spoke quietly so as not to wake the other two who seemed to be sleeping soundly.

"I don't know anything."

"Don't worry. Just answer his questions. It won't take long," Emma said trying to reassure him.

Even if his father had killed his mother, it didn't follow that the boy wanted his father captured and hanged for the offence. What a position to be in. She waited outside the door while he put on his trousers and shirt. She put her hand on his shoulder as they entered the saloon, but he shrugged it off. Not letting anyone get close. Not letting his guard down.

Lieutenant Forrester turned his chair to face Henry who remained standing. "Now then, lad. Tell me what happened yesterday."

Henry shook his head. "I was not there."

His words were clipped and correct, more pronounced than when he was speaking to her.

"Where were you?"

"In the bush, getting wood with, with *meine vater und bruder*."

"Your father and your brother?"

"*Ja.*"

"Where was your mother while you were in the bush?"

"She was home with Gertie."

"Gertie?" He looked at his notes. "Your sister?"

"*Ja.*"

"How old is she?"

"Not yet two-year old."

"And how old is your brother?"

"Seven."

"And you?"

"Almost twelve."

"So, what happened when you finished cutting wood and went home?"

"Mother was not home. Gertie was alone. Father went into the bush and said we were to wait for him."

"He went looking for your mother?"

"He heard something. In the bush."

"What did he hear?"

"Someone. Someone was there."

"Are you sure it wasn't your mother he heard in the bush?"

"*Nein.* Mother would not go into the bush and leave Gertie alone."

"When did your father go into the bush?"

"Yesterday. We stay one night on our own."

"When did he come back?"

Henry shook his head.

"He didn't come back?"

"*Nein.*"

"Did he take a gun with him?"

Henry paused for moment. "He had his axe."

The Lieutenant had been firing the questions in quick succession, but now paused. Henry wasn't telling the whole truth and he sensed it.

"Your father must have had a gun," the Lieutenant said sharply trying to shake the boy.

"*Ja.* For birds, ducks, sometimes snakes."

"A shotgun?"

"*Ja.*"

It hadn't been a shotgun that killed Hilda.

"Did he have any other gun? A rifle or a pistol, perhaps?"

Again, a slight hesitation. "*Nein.*"

"So, you were alone during the night and today?"

"*Ja.* Until the boat comes... and they find..." Henry's voice faltered.

"Is that all, Lieutenant?" Emma asked.

The boy had been through enough in the last twenty-four hours. It was clear Henry was trying to create the impression that Zac had been chasing after someone when he went into the bush. He hadn't mentioned that to her, before. Had he just invented it?

It was also clear he wasn't telling the whole story, but was he actually lying? Emma wasn't sure. The questions remained. Who had taken the shotgun? Did the Zellers have a rifle or pistol as well? Someone had, according to Hilda's injury. Lieutenant Forrester gave Henry a long calculating look, but the boy stared straight ahead and didn't flinch. He dismissed him and Emma took the boy back to his cabin.

"Try and get some sleep." There wasn't a lot else she could say. When she returned to the saloon the Lieutenant was taking his leave.

"No, there's no need for you to stay," he was saying in response to something Daniel had asked. "We'll be leaving at dawn ourselves. But I want you to call into the station when you get to Euston. We'll get you to make a formal statement there if you wouldn't mind." He took a step onto the plank gangway, then stopped. "Oh, by the way, what are you intending to do with the children?"

"I thought the police..." began Daniel.

"They have family at Kerang," Emma interrupted him.

"They do?" Daniel asked. "When did you learn that?"

"This afternoon. I haven't had a chance to tell you." Truth be, she had forgotten she hadn't told him. Daniel looked annoyed.

"I'd like that information if you please, Mrs. Berry." The Lieutenant stepped back onto the boat and pulling out his notebook.

"Erich told me his Uncle Axel has a dairy farm at Kerang," Emma explained. "I couldn't get any other information. Henry told his brother to be quiet, or words to that effect and he wouldn't tell me the family's name."

"Interesting. That should be enough anyway. I'll pass that on to Swan Hill and they can get in touch. I take it you will transport the children to Swan Hill and hand them over to the police there?" Emma assured him they would. "Good. At least it means the children aren't our problem."

"Nice of you to offer our services. For free, too," Daniel grumbled when the Lieutenant had finally left.

"We could hardly do anything else, Daniel."

"I suppose not, but it would have been nice to know about the Kerang connection beforehand."

"I'm sorry. I wasn't holding it back deliberately. Did the Lieutenant have anything to say after I took Henry back to bed?"

"Not much," he said shortly. She was sure there had been. Something was being kept from her.

Emma found she was wide awake when she'd prepared for bed. She pulled out her notebook and sat propped against her pillows, knees drawn up, glad of the slight breeze that came in through her open window.

She wrote a brief outline of Henry's answers to his interview and tried to fit them with what she already knew but was left with as many questions as before. Was the boy telling the truth about his father hearing someone in the bush and going in pursuit or was that a ploy to avert suspicion? What happened to Zac's shotgun if he went off with only his axe, and what had happened to the gun that killed Hilda? None of it added up. Henry, she was sure, knew it all. If he were protecting his father, it could only be because Zac had killed Hilda. What other reason could there be?

Chapter Eight

THE SUN WAS BARELY UP next morning when Emma woke to the voices of Blue and Shorty shouting back and forth between the *Mary B* and the *Owen*, as the boat and barge pulled away from the bank. Sounds in the distance suggested the police were getting ready to start out as well, the activity overlaid with the smell of bacon cooking.

She dressed and went to check on the children. The air was already hot, even though the sun wasn't yet over the trees. The boys were still asleep, but Gertie was awake and lying wide-eyed. She made one whimpering "Mama" and Emma gathered her up in a hug, tears forming in her own eyes at the little mite's confusion. She hoped the presence of her brothers was some comfort.

"Let's go milk the goat," she said, taking Gertie's hand. The milk would probably still be undrinkable, but it was something to do. It wasn't long before the boys woke, and Emma helped Ah Lo prepare porridge for their breakfast with toast and jam. At least their appetites weren't impaired. They ate in the saloon and had almost finished when Fred Croaker's grey-whiskered face appeared around the saloon doorway. He winked at Emma.

"Thought I might give these lads something useful to do, Boss," he said. "They need to earn their passage. Can't have 'em eating us out of house and home for nothing, now, can we?"

"Certainly not, Fred. What did you have in mind?"

"A spot of fishing, I'm thinking. Ah Lo has ordered some cod for lunch."

"I like cod," said Erich. "But not smoked."

"Oh, it'll be fresh and kicking right enough," Fred assured the boy. "We just have to catch us some. Come along, now."

The boys followed Fred out leaving Emma with Gertie. She heard Erich telling Fred they used nets to catch fish back at the shack, and Fred's response about using fishing lines, which needed some skill. Emma remembered Hilda telling her she smoked a lot of the fish they caught. Given Erich's response it may have been a major part of their diet.

The image of fish hanging over a smoky fire brought another thought to Emma's mind, startling her. A funeral pyre? Was that what Hilda's killer had been planning to do? Set fire to the woodpile and burn all evidence of what had happened to her? It was an explanation that made as much sense as anything. The body wasn't on top of the woodpile though. Perhaps it was in the middle to hide from view as it burnt, with enough wood below and above to destroy all evidence of it ever having been there.

With the boys occupied, Emma took Gertie along to the wheelhouse. Willy lounged in the doorway on the far side. She pointed out the ducks flying up from the water below them, a different view from what one had at water level. When Gertie became restless, she took her down to watch the boys as they dangled their rods off the side of the boat behind the paddle box. No one seemed to be catching anything but there was a lot of hauling in of lines and baiting of hooks. And a lot of chat, especially from Shorty who was telling tales of sea monsters.

Shorty had plenty of stories from his days as a sailor. He was suspected of jumping ship at some colonial port, perhaps to try his luck on the gold fields but unable to stay away from boats.

Erich was hanging onto every word while Henry was trying to look disinterested and only partly succeeding. Even Ah Lo had been drawn out of his galley to watch and listen. Fred sat quietly smoking his pipe and helping the boys with their lines while Blue piloted the barge following behind on its hundred-foot towline.

Emma recognised their location as the *Mary B* turned sharply into a section where the river course was shaped like a bowtie with five miles of twisty river for only a hundred yards of real distance. An hour later they were back at the other side of the 'knot' and still no fish caught.

A signal rang down to the stokehold.

"Hello, what's up now," said Fred as the engine was cut back to slow. The *Mary B* eased toward the bank. A dog could be heard barking.

"Haul your lines in, quick now," Fred told the boys.

Emma moved around to the starboard side to see why Daniel was pulling in. The barking materialised into the shape of a little dog running up the bank and back down again to the water's edge. She recognised it as a Jack Russell, sporting the usual colouring of its breed; brown ears and eye patches and several brown splotches on an otherwise white coat.

Fred came to stand beside her. "Now there's a dog with a message if ever I saw one," he said as the Jack Russell continued to bark at the boat and make its little runs. "Something's up."

He and Shorty went over the side to investigate following the dog up the bank. They disappeared over the top into the bush. A few minutes later Fred reappeared.

"It's an old fella, Capt'n," Fred called down. "Looks like he went to sleep and never woke up again. Still in his swag."

"Been there long?"

"Couple of days, I reckon."

A natural death? Emma hoped so. Surely there wasn't someone going along the river killing people.

"Well, we'll have to bury the poor bloke, I suppose," Daniel said.

For the second day the shovels were brought out. Daniel and Willy went up and Blue brought the barge into the bank and followed, not wanting to miss anything. Jake Summers and Ah Lo stayed onboard.

"Are we going to take the dog?" Erich asked, a concerned look on his face. "He'll get hungry."

"I think we might have to," Emma said.

This was turning into a journey of death and rescue. Just in case the dog proved wary she had Ah Lo cut a small piece of the beef left from the previous night as a tempter. The little fellow would have had all he needed to drink, but possibly nothing to eat for several days.

It was a quiet group that came back to the *Mary B* sometime later. It would not have been a pleasant task in the heat. Blue was carrying a billy and a pan and Willy and Shorty had several cans of beans and a small bag of flour between them. The Jack Russell followed. It stood on the bank and watched as the men went aboard, looking back now and then. Was he waiting for an invitation?

"Here, see if he wants this," Emma said, giving Henry the piece of meat. He knelt at the top of the plank gangway, holding it out.

"Here, come on. Are you hungry?"

The dog sniffed the air and came forward, hesitantly onto the plank, nose quivering. Then hunger got the better of him and he ran forward and lunged at the meat. Henry hung onto it and grabbed the dog with his free arm, swinging him onto the boat. He let the dog have the meat and Fred quickly slipped a leather strap around his neck and hitched a length of cord to the makeshift collar. The children sat and watched as the dog wolfed down his meal. He sat back on his haunches, licking his chops, and looked at everyone as if to ask, "So, what now?"

"What's his name?" Erich wanted to know.

"I wonder if he was called Jack," said Emma, "because he's a Jack Russell."

Daniel snorted in disbelief, but the dog looked at Emma, his ears perked at the mention of the name.

"You could be right, at that," said Fred with a grin.

"Jack, here," Erich called, standing a little way off and patting his knees.

The dog hesitated for a moment and then trotted over to the boy. Erich hugged him. Gertie squealed and wriggled in Emma's arms. She put the child down and Gertie joined her brother, throwing herself on the little dog.

"I think he's been adopted," drawled Willy.

"Now you lot we need to make 'im safe on this here boat," said Fred. "He's a landlubber. He has to learn what he can and can't do." He proceeded to show the boys where to tie Jack's lead, so he didn't have enough length to jump overboard and hang himself. "It's just til he gets used to his new life," Fred explained. "He looks a smart little dog. It won't take him long."

Daniel went back to the wheelhouse, Shorty trailing him, and the *Mary B* was once more underway. Jake Summers, the engineer, came out of the stokehold and stood watching the children with the dog. He wasn't the most sociable of men, preferring his engine and his books. As often as not he took his evening meal on the deck rather than join the rest of the crew in the saloon. Even when he was there, he said little.

"Do you like dogs, Mr. Summers?" Emma took the opportunity to ask.

"Had a Jack Russell when I was a boy," he said. "Back home."

"England?"

"Aye."

He hooked his thumbs in his vest pockets, not taking his eyes off the dog and children.

"The children have named the dog Jack," Emma went on conversationally. "It may have been his name already."

"Huh." He nodded to himself seeming to enjoy the notion. "My Jack Russell was called Tiny."

"Perhaps you could help get the dog accustomed to the boat, Mr. Summers? Considering you have experience with the breed."

"They need a lot of exercise. Good dog for lads, though." There was something wistful in his last words. Seeming to collect himself and remember his proper task, he nodded briefly and went back to tend to his engine.

Emma was curious about the old man the crew had just buried. She picked up Gertie to take her up to the wheelhouse, but the little girl screeched and struggled, twisting in Emma's arms her eyes on Jack.

"You can leave her for a few minutes, Boss," Fred said. "We'll keep an eye on her."

"Are you sure?"

"Aye. I've got grandchildren the same age, you know." Emma did but it didn't make her feel any easier. A moment's inattention and the little girl could be in the river.

"Well, all right. I won't be too long."

She set Gertie back on her feet, relieved as the child stopped her noise. Gertie grabbed at Jack, pressing her face into his side. The dog turned his head and Emma reached down to pull her away again, afraid he was going to bite but Jack just licked her face. Feeling relieved of responsibility for a few minutes Emma took a cup of tea up to the wheelhouse for Daniel.

"I hope there wasn't anything suspicious about the death of that fellow?" she asked him.

"No. Like Fred said. Just went quietly to sleep by the look of him."

"He was old then?"

"Could have been sixty I suppose. Bit hard to tell. There was an envelope in his coat pocket addressed to Jim Franklin at Pattin Downs Station. I think I've seen him about there. Did odd jobs."

Emma had no recollection of him. "Well, he wasn't too far from home then," she said. "Was there a letter in that envelope?"

Daniel pulled it from his shirt pocket. "Here, I haven't had time to read it."

Emma held it for a moment feeling she was prying into someone's personal affairs. This is what we all come to eventually, she thought. She opened the envelope and pulled out a much-thumbed sheet of cheap writing paper. The words 'Dear Pa' jumped out at her. She quickly scanned the brief message.

"He might have been on his way to Wentworth," she said. "The letter appears to have been from his daughter announcing a new grandchild. How sad. Perhaps he was heading for Kulkyne and the coach road. Another matter for the police to deal with. But I do hope that's the last body we find." She didn't want to consider the adage of things coming in threes. "What did you do with the rest of his swag?" she asked, remembering the odds and ends they had brought back to the boat.

Daniel gave her a look. "Buried him in it."

"Ah." She was silent for a moment or two. "About the children…" she said.

"What now?"

"I was thinking, I want to deliver them to their relatives at Kerang myself. I know the police would take them, but I'd like to make sure they're safe and that these people know Hilda was buried well. It makes sense for me to leave the *Mary B* at Swan Hill in any case to take the coach back home. I will just have to make a detour."

"But you don't know if they're Hilda's relatives or Zeller's, do you?"

"I can't see that it matters. Hilda must be related by marriage at least if this Axel is the children's uncle."

"And what if they are Zeller's relatives?" Daniel insisted. "They could be more intent on protecting him if he reaches their farm. It might not be safe."

"But it's hardly anything to do with me, is it? All I want is to deliver the children to their family."

"But if he's there and he sees you?"

"Really Daniel. You are making much of nothing. The chance of that happening are extremely remote. I would imagine the Swan Hill police are already keeping an eye on the family at Kerang."

"Anything is possible, knowing how you rush in first and think later," Daniel grumbled.

"I don't do anything of the sort," Emma retorted. She picked up his empty mug and left the wheelhouse. Just as well this was the last trip of the season. They were all in need of a break. Whatever happened though, she wanted to see the children settled and she wanted to find out more about Hilda from whoever the family was at Kerang. It seemed the least she could do for her friend.

Chapter Nine

AN HOUR LATER, the *Mary B* pulled into the bank at Pattin Downs on the New South Wales side of the Murray. Station owner Stan Gartner, a tall figure somewhere in his fifties and burnt brown from his work outdoors, came across from one of the farm buildings to meet them, his legs covering the ground in long strides. An aged sheep dog followed.

"Berry how do. Mrs. Berry." Stan Gartner stuck out his hand to Daniel and nodded to Emma. "Enough water for you?"

"Just," replied Daniel, shaking the proffered hand. "We should make Echuca without too much trouble."

Men, Emma thought, never admit to one another that they might not be in complete control. Though she had to admit it was good business not to complain about water levels. The squatters wanted their wool delivered safely after all. No need to give them cause to worry. They might take their transport business to the McCulloch Company whose boats dominated the rivers.

"Good, good. The wagon is loaded and I've another standing by as soon as the horses are free. I've just sent a man along to the woolshed to get it on its way. Should be down within the hour. And then we'll load the empty wagon and do it all again."

"We'll get it done as quickly as possible," Daniel assured him. He might appear relaxed, but Emma knew he would be feeling frustrated at the casual manner some station owners dealt with the riverboats. One of the wagons should have been waiting on the bank, cutting down the wait time. But speed wasn't a priority for them out here. "We've got stores for you too, from John Egge."

"Excellent. Ben," he called, "here, Ben." A man in his twenties, with a pronounced limp, came from around a building. "There's stores to be unloaded. Here," he pulled some keys from his pocket and tossed them to him, "put them in the storeroom and make sure you check everything against the cargo list."

"Sure, Mr. Gartner. Howdy, Captain." The young man saluted Daniel.

"Good to see you up and about, Ben."

"Yeah, thanks, could be worse," the young man drawled and limped away on his task.

"Is that Ben Trumble?" Emma asked, remembering what she had learnt at Kulkyne about the previous owner of Zeller's timber lease.

"Good of you to give him a job," Daniel said to Stan. "He's not exactly fit for a lot of things."

"No, but he's not going to go running off anytime soon, either. And he's trustworthy. Come on up to the house, now. Have some tea while you wait. Ann will be pleased to see you, Mrs. Berry. Say, whose is the young un? I thought..." His voice tailed off, suddenly embarrassed. It was well known along the river that Emma had lost the child she was carrying following the accident to the *Mary B.*

"This is Gertie Zeller. Hilda and Zac's little one. They have Ben's old timber lease," Emma explained, smoothing over the man's embarrassment.

Stan looked surprised. "The Zellers are with you?"

"Only the children."

"What? Are they sending them away for schooling or something? I could understand with the boys, but I would have thought Hilda would want to hang onto this little one."

"Do you know the Zellers, Mr. Gartner?" Emma asked, surprise tinging her voice. First Ben Trumble, now the Zellers. It was a small world for all its size.

"Know them. I should say so. They were here for some three or four months. This young un was born here if she's theirs, Mrs. Berry," Stan Gartner looked for a moment at Gertie. "Yep. Looks like her mother."

Emma and Daniel exchanged glances.

"I'm afraid we have some bad news," Daniel said. "Hilda has died, and Zac is missing."

Stan stared at them both for a moment, then glanced briefly toward the homestead. Emma wondered if he was thinking how such news might affect his wife. She knew Ann Gartner suffered from nerves. Stan pushed his hat back and scratched at his head.

"What happened?" he asked. Daniel told him what little they knew. "That's incredible. And the police are already out looking for Zac?"

"Yes. They set out from Kulkyne early this morning," Daniel replied.

"Incredible," he repeated. "I would have said they were the last people to...seemed devoted to one another."

"We thought so too," Emma agreed.

"There's another matter..." Daniel began.

"Stanley." Ann Gartner called from the homestead door. "Don't stand out there. Bring the people up."

Stan waved a hand to acknowledge his wife. "Come in," he said turning toward the building.

Emma and Daniel followed. The Pattin Downs homestead was a timber-clad building, with a small covered porch over the front door. Like many, it had started out as two rooms and been added to at various times giving it an odd shape with multiple roof lines. Ann Gartner stood waiting for them. She was as tall as her husband; a thin, redheaded woman, as pale as her husband was brown.

"Mrs. Berry, Captain. How lovely to see you. Do please come in."

"Thank you. We have your order from Wirramilla," Emma said indicating the parcel Daniel was carrying.

"Oh, wonderful. I am running low on some things." Ann Gartner put the parcel on the hall table and asked after Emma's grandmother. "So wonderful the things she does. Now, I ordered tea in the drawing room when I heard the boat," she said leading the way. "I was sure it would be the *Mary B*. Are there any other boats on the river still?"

"The *Lisette* was still at Wentworth when we left," Emma replied.

The drawing room was a comfortably shabby room without ostentation. The kelpie followed them in and made himself at home on the rug which explained the slight doggy odour that prevailed. Emma, trying not to wrinkle her nose, was reminded of the clean floral smells of the Wirramilla drawing room and her mother's insistence that Emma's fox terrier Floss be bathed regularly. Gertie wanted to be let down.

"She'll be all right, Mrs. Berry. Barney will move if he gets bothered."

Gertie happily went and patted the dog rather warmly on the head. Barney was bothered enough to immediately get up and go out into the hall. Stan Gartner shut the door on him as Gertie made to follow and the child set up a wail.

"She's missing her mother," Emma said. "Perhaps I should take her back to her brothers. She's happier around the boys."

"Who is she?" Ann Gartner asked, getting to her feet and picking up the child. A maid came in with the tea tray at that moment and Ann gave Gertie a biscuit which quietened her for the moment.

"She's Hilda Zeller's young un," Stan Gartner told her.

Ann Gartner stood very still for a moment. There was a sharp edge to her voice when she responded.

"Where is Hilda? Why hasn't she come up to see me?"

"Hilda has died, Mrs. Gartner. We are taking the children to their family in Kerang," Emma said accepting a cup of tea from the maid.

"They have family at Kerang? Hilda never spoke of them." She looked at Emma. "Did you say she has died?"

"She was shot, Ann," her husband answered. "The police are looking for Zac."

"No." She sat down with Gertie on her lap and looked around at them all eyes wide. "Are you serious? Zac shot Hilda? But that – no – that's – when did this happen?"

"We found her at their shack," Emma said wondering how much detail she should give. "The boys say their father went into the bush and didn't return. That's all we really know. We thought it best to take the children with us."

"Well, of course, you couldn't very well leave them there, could you." She gave a shiver. "I never did understand why Zac insisted on getting that timber lease and shutting them away by themselves in the bush."

"He was a good worker," put in Stan Gartner, "though he didn't care much for sheep. Preferred horses and growing things."

"You don't know anything about their family at Kerang, then?" said Emma. "We don't know if they are Hilda or Zac's relatives."

"No, no, they didn't talk much about themselves, did they Stanley? Strange really. I helped Hilda when her time came, had her here in the house. Well, the cottage only has two rooms, hardly suitable, what with the boys."

"Hard to credit. They seemed close," Stan murmured.

"Too close perhaps, Stanley. I don't think it's entirely healthy to be too devoted to someone. I mean," Ann Gartner said, looking at her husband, "you need to be able to rub along together but not be too entirely wrapped up to the exclusion of everyone else. I don't think that's healthy at all, do you, Mrs. Berry?"

"Is that what Hilda and Zac were like when they lived here?" Emma asked, not wanting to give an opinion.

"He was, more than her I would have said. I always felt he didn't like letting her out of his sight. What do you think, Stanley?"

"He was concerned about her condition at that time, I'll say that much. Don't know as it was more than that."

"Well, you aren't so observant about people, are you. It wouldn't surprise me if Hilda wanted more than life in a woodcutter's shack. It must be nearly a year and a half since they left here. Perhaps she wanted to leave the bush and Zac didn't want her to." There was that suggestion again. "But to shoot her. Can you credit that, Stanley?"

Stan shook his head.

"We don't know for certain that it was Zac who shot her," Emma said, disinclined to have Hilda's husband condemned out of hand. "Henry says his father went off after someone in the bush."

Ann Gartner's eyes widened. Her hands, holding Gertie, were scrabbling at the child's clothes.

"You mean there's a killer out there? Stanley, I won't be able to sleep a wink tonight. We must take precautions, have some of the men patrol the grounds, make sure everyone is armed..."

"I'll take care of it," Stan spoke calmly, but he sent a warning look to Emma to say no more on the subject.

"The police are already out searching, Mrs. Gartner," Daniel put in reassuringly. "Whoever did it won't get far on foot. You really don't have anything to worry about here."

Zac might be on foot, but if someone else was involved they could be on horseback. This wasn't the time to mention that idea, though.

"Well, if you say so, Captain Berry," she said, suddenly calm. How much of the woman's behaviour was put on for effect Emma wondered?

Ann began to talk to Emma about the garden and how difficult it was to get someone who knew what they were doing. "Zac was very good," she said, and Emma remembered the thriving vegetable garden at the shack. She became aware of Daniel speaking quietly to Stan. There was a rustle of paper and the letter Daniel had found on the old man was passed over.

"Ann, Ann listen, girl. Old Jim has died," Stan announced.

"What?" Her voice rose shrilly. "Not someone else murdered?"

"No, no. He seems to have died in his sleep, poor old chap," said her husband.

"Well, he would insist on walking to Kulkyne to get the coach. Who am I going to get to tend the garden now? You know I can't bear the sun."

Stan Gartner got to his feet and went to the sideboard where there was a collection of bottles and jars. Emma recognised them as being from the Wirramilla stillroom.

"Jim was our odd job man. Worked here on the station for years, but past doing the heavy work," Stan explained as he spooned one of the mixtures into a cup and carried it back to the tea tray. He filled the cup from the jug of hot water and stirred it for a moment before handing it to his wife. She took a sip, wrinkled her nose, and set it back on the tea table.

The whole thing was surprisingly off hand, but then he must have had years of experience dealing with his wife's histrionics. Unfortunately, the tea needed time to steep and to be sipped slowly to be effective. Emma wondered if Ann Gartner followed the instructions, or if the calming result was merely another part of the act. Gertie was wriggling on the woman's lap, but Ann seemed oblivious to the child though she still held Gertie with one arm. Emma stood up.

"Let me take Gertie for a moment, Mrs. Gartner. She'll crease your frock if she keeps wriggling in that way."

Ann looked up at her suddenly. "What's happened to Jack?" she demanded relinquishing Gertie.

"The little dog? The Jack Russell? Is that really his name?"

"Yes, Jack, Jim's dog."

"We have him with us on the boat."

"Do you have a use for him?" Stan asked. "It's not as if he can work sheep, and he's still a young dog, about four years old I seem to remember. Jim got him at Wentworth as a pup. Followed him everywhere it did."

"Well, he seems to be a friendly little fellow and the children have certainly taken a liking to him. What do you think, Daniel?"

"But I would like Jack, Stanley," Ann Gartner said quickly, a pout in her voice.

"He's too lively, Ann, he's not a lap dog," her husband said patiently. "Jack needs to be outdoors, running around, you know that."

"But I like Jack."

"He won't suit, Ann. If you want a lap dog, we'll get you one. Think of what breed you'd like. A Jack Russell won't do." Ann sighed and shrugged. "Good girl. He's yours if you want him, Berry."

"Well, if we don't keep him ourselves, I'm sure we could find a good home for him somewhere if you have no need of him," Daniel said.

"No, no. We've enough dogs here as it is."

"Thank you, both," said Emma. "Jack will make it easier for the children. I'm sure Hilda would thank you for that, as well, Mrs. Gartner," she couldn't resist adding.

"Well, we do what we can," Ann said, seeming to have completely forgotten her petulance of a moment before.

"And thank you for burying old Jim," Stan added. "I'll have to write to his daughter, now." He shook his head. "Pity he had to go like that, though, out there alone."

"Better than being shot," Ann said with a tight laugh.

Chapter Ten

WITH THE PATTIN DOWN stores unloaded Emma had to leave Gertie in the saloon with her brothers and Jack as she figuratively put on her loadmaster's hat and went to work. With two layers of wool bales already on the barge, the upper three layers needed careful positioning, edged a little further in, each layer tied around and down, ropes fastened to the rings set into the edges of the barge.

"Phew, it must be time for lunch?" Shorty said, swiping an arm across his sweaty brow when they had emptied the first wagonload. "My stomach thinks me throat's been cut."

"I'll see how Ah Lo is getting on with lunch," Emma told him, feeling it had been a long time since breakfast and she wasn't humping two-hundred-pound bales of wool. "Blue, make sure those last bales get tied down real firm. We've got another two wagonloads to get on."

"Aye, Boss."

The *Mary B*'s lower deck was deserted and there were no enticing smells of cooking coming from the galley as Emma stepped aboard. Where was Ah Lo? The sound of pattering feet and a child's laughter reached her as she made her way along the upper deck to the saloon. She opened the door.

"Watch out, Missus," Ah Lo cried as a white flash darted past her feet. Gertie tried to follow, and Emma scooped her up. The little girl set up a wail as Jack disappeared down the stairs and a moment later, she heard Shorty yell, "Hoy, Jack." Gertie continued to cry, working herself into a fine taking thrashing in Emma's arms. She wondered how women who lived on riverboats with their families kept the children occupied and out of trouble.

"Where are the boys?" she asked, as she realised Ah Lo was the only other person in the saloon.

"Boys run off. Little girl cry. I stuck here. No cook lunch."

Run off? What was Henry up to? Before she could deal with that, she needed to settle Gertie as the little girl continued to wriggle and cry.

"Do you have any biscuits?"

"No biskit," Ah Lo said, looking most put out. "I cook lunch now. Very late. Everyone hungry. Yell at me."

Emma followed him down to the galley and quickly put together a slice of bread and dripping for Gertie, then got out of Ah Lo's way as he began banging pots about and muttering. Gertie cried and hiccoughed but finally settled into sniffling between bites. She wasn't sure how Ah Lo had come to be caught up in minding the child, but it couldn't happen again. They didn't need an upset cook. But where had the boys got to?

Daniel was coming back from the barn with Stan Gartner. "We just saw the dog run past," he said, speaking to her from the bank as she stood looking up from the foredeck with the child.

"You've got to take him," Stan said. "You said you would. Ann will try and make a lapdog out of him and it won't work." He looked as if he didn't want the extra stress of dealing with that. The poor man must have his limits where his wife was concerned.

"Jack might have gone looking for the boys," Emma told them. "You didn't happen to see them as well by any chance?"

"Hilda's boys? What have they done?" Stan jumped in as Daniel opened his mouth to speak. Emma wondered if his wife's nervous habits were catching.

"They've run off, Mr. Gartner."

"They can't stay here, Berry," Stan said turning to Daniel.

"We won't be leaving them," Daniel said. "They can't be far away."

"Perhaps they're visiting places they remember," Emma suggested. Though she wondered if Henry thought they might be able to stay here and wait for their father, after being denied that at Kulkyne.

"I can get a couple of men to look them out," Stan offered.

"I might take you up on that later, Stan, if we need to but I think we'll leave it for now." Daniel told him. "We're going to be here for some time loading this wool. The boys will be easier to pick up when they're hungry and tired of hiding."

Emma looked at him with interest. Had he run away as a child and been through such a situation? She must ask him about that someday.

"As long as they don't get up to any mischief in the meantime," Stan Gartner grumbled before striding back to the homestead.

Daniel shook his head but was distracted by the empty wagon being hauled off again to the woolshed.

"Come and get lunch," he said to the crew. They had at least an hour before another wagonload would be down, probably longer.

"Ah Lo is a bit behind with lunch. I'd tread carefully," Emma warned. "Henry left him looking after Gertie."

Daniel's grunt of frustration echoed her own feelings. Ah Lo eventually served up a more than passable lunch. At some time during the meal they heard a dog barking down among the farm buildings.

"That's a Jack Russell," Jake Summers said with assurance.

"Perhaps he's found the boys," Shorty said not looking up from his mutton chops.

"He'll have found them a long time ago," Jake said.

Fred nodded knowingly. "Not a boy alive hasn't run away at some time," he said sitting back with a satisfied sigh. "Great lunch, Charley," he said to Ah Lo. Thanking the cook was good policy. Fred began an 'I remember when…' and they finished the meal with one of his stories before the next wagonload of wool arrived and they had to get back to work. Daniel took on overseeing the loading and left Emma to deal with Gertie. The child slept for part of the afternoon allowing Emma to catch up her bookwork. The men were still working when a temporary halt was called for supper.

"When are you going to look for the boys?" Emma asked. "It's almost dark now."

"In the morning is soon enough, I reckon," Daniel said. "They'll be hungry enough by then, and probably not slept well. They're not in any danger."

"You don't think they might have started back for home?"

"Good lord, I hope Henry isn't as stupid as that. No. We've heard Jack bark a few times if Summers is right. I reckon the dog will stay with them."

Emma found her sympathy for Henry running low. She was sure his little brother had been bullied into joining him in this escapade. Gertie was missing them too. Henry might think she was safe on the boat, but it was just another abandonment to the little girl and Jack wasn't there to distract her.

"We won't get an early start in the morning if we have to search for them before we can leave."

"I suspect it won't take too long to find them," was Daniel's prediction.

After supper, the crew continued to work, emptying the last wagon under the boat's lamps. It had been a long day. The barge was fully loaded, and the final layer of bales tied down. Emma didn't waste her time putting

Gertie into the children's bed. She was sure the little girl wouldn't settle on her own and took Gertie into her own bed. At midnight, all was quiet except for some snoring coming from several piles of bedding on the fore deck where the crew were sleeping in the cooler air.

Emma woke early next morning to the usual scent of bacon cooking. She immediately wondered if the boys could smell it. Would it draw them out? She dressed quickly eager to get the day's problems dealt with, leaving Gertie still asleep. When she went downstairs, Ah Lo was handing out loaded plates of bacon, eggs, and beans with slabs of fresh bread thickly buttered to a bunch of yawning men.

"Well, lookit there," said Willy.

Erich was coming across the yard toward the *Mary B* with Jack in his arms. Blue put down the plank and Erich came aboard. He looked as if he hadn't slept much, his hair mussed, his eyes merely slits. He didn't say anything as Fred slipped Jack's collar on before the dog was put on his feet. Not that the collar appeared necessary. Jack was obviously more interested in food than anything else. So was Erich.

"You okay, lad?" Fred asked as Ah Lo handed him a plate.

Erich just nodded and found a space to sit on the deck before quickly shovelling food into his mouth. Jack was treated to some bacon and a bowl of water as the crew finished their own breakfast. Daniel came down a few minutes later. He raised his eyebrows at Emma when he saw Erich.

"Only the one, so far," she said.

"I suspect we'll have to retrieve the other one ourselves."

"Shouldn't be too hard to find," Fred said. "The dog will lead us there. No need to trouble the lad."

Daniel and Fred headed across the yard with Jack on his lead. Erich watched them go. Five minutes later they were back herding Henry in front of them looking as rebellious as ever. As he came up the plank, he gave Erich a hard look.

"*Verräter*," he hissed. Erich shrank into himself.

"If you're blaming Erich for giving away your hiding place, forget it," Daniel said sharply. "He didn't tell us anything. It was the dog found you." Henry didn't look at anyone and started for the stairs. "Breakfast first. Some food might improve your attitude. We don't put up with bad behaviour here."

"I didn't ask to be here," Henry said sullenly, but he took the plate of food Ah Lo handed him.

"Yes, we could have left you to slowly starve, I suppose. Such bad people as we are," Daniel said. Emma was surprised but pleased Daniel had stepped up his involvement. A firm hand was what Henry needed. "If your father returned to the shack as he said he would he knows where you are and knows you are safe. If he didn't, well you and your brother and sister are better off, aren't you?"

Henry stared at his plate and didn't answer. Slowly, as if to prove it didn't matter either way, he ate. While he was doing that Emma took Erich off with her to milk the nanny goat and make sure it had its own food and water. She longed to ask Erich some questions about their last days at the shack, but he seemed fragile, so they just talked goats instead. Erich proved himself knowledgeable about their likes and dislikes. When Gertie woke, there was fresh goat's milk for her as well as a soft egg and toast. She greeted the appearance of Jack and her brothers with squeals of delight.

Chapter Eleven

THE NEXT STAGE OF their journey was through one of Emma's favourite sections of the river. It was a six-mile long semicircular reach. A steep bank confined the river's wanderings on the outside of the curve while the inner bank was low with swamps and noisy bird life. Flocks of moor hens, long legged ibis and spoonbills and graceful black swans inhabited the area. Emma stood beside Daniel in the wheelhouse as the *Mary B* steamed straight on for over an hour, no bends, no sharp turns just a smooth curving run. She imagined this was what it must feel like to sail on the sea.

Gell's Island, a large rocky ledge that split the river into two streams, was a feature of the next section of river. The channel on the Victorian side of the island was navigable, while on the New South Wales side the narrow stream was restricted by the steep, high bank where the river cut its way through the side of a rise. Emma stood on the lower deck checking to see how the barge managed the narrow way, Gertie playing at her feet. The *Mary B* had begun to move past the island when Emma saw the top row of bales on the barge begin to move.

"The barge is going," she shouted to the wheelhouse.

At the same moment Blue, feeling the shift, let out a great yell and released the tow rope. The taut rope, as thick as a man's arm, whumped against the *Mary B*'s stern causing Emma to duck involuntarily. As if in slow motion, bales slid toward the water and the flat-bottomed barge tilted with the shifting weight. Blue threw himself over the far side. As the wool bales hit the shallow water, they provided a wedge against the barge and prevented it tipping further. It rocked and righted itself. Emma let out the breath she hadn't realised she'd been holding.

On the *Mary B*, the half slow signal had sounded stridently in the stokehold at Emma's shout. The boat slowed but continued its way past the island as Jake Summers at the engine and Daniel at the wheel kept it from swinging in the current and hitting the rocky island. The *Mary B* eased toward the lower bank. Jake Summers let off the steam and Willy leapt over the side. Running and hauling, he got the stern mooring rope several turns around a tree and tied off with a half hitch. Shorty threw him the forward rope which he ran around another trunk. With the *Mary B* secure, Daniel dashed down from the wheelhouse.

"Is everyone all right?"

Blue, hauling himself out of the river onto the bank, waved his hand to signify he was fine. Shorty put down the plank and Blue trudged up, dripping, his red hair plastered to his head instead of standing on end. He looked shaken none the less. Ah Lo poured him a cup of tea which Daniel laced with a little whisky.

"What the blazes happened there?" he asked Blue. "Why did the load shift? Did you hit the bank? The ties give way? What?"

Blue took a long draught of his tea, and gasped. "Didn't hit nothing," he said when he got his voice back. "She was following fine in clear water."

"She was," Emma said. "The top bales just started to slide of their own accord. A tie must have given way, Daniel. Nothing should have moved."

"Did you check those ties this morning?"

"No, Capt'n, I checked 'em last night when we finished loading," Blue told him. "They were tight as need be then. Should have been the same today."

"We'll check that out later," Daniel said. He couldn't complain at Blue too loudly as he had been the one overseeing the last of the loading. "We're going to have to salvage those bales now and get them onto the bank to dry. They're blocking the channel as well. The *Lisette* is somewhere behind us, possibly catching up after our stop yesterday so we need to get a move on. We'll have to move the barge out of the channel as well. I want all hands to the task, Jake, so that means you too."

The engineer scowled. Deckhand work wasn't his job. "Daniel, you can't dry them out on the Victorian side. They came from Pattin Downs." Pattin Downs being on the New South Wales side of the Murray and effectively another country as far as customs duties were concerned.

If a customs officer happened along and found them with goods unloaded on the wrong side of the river without duty being paid, they could be fined, and the goods confiscated. Permission could be obtained to unload temporarily on the wrong side of the river but with no idea where an officer was at that time it was an unreasonable expectation. Just another issue of the bureaucracy that plagued rivermen.

"Blast and damn," was Daniel's response, earning a look from Emma for his language though she understood the frustration. To get the wool to the New South Wales bank meant skirting Gell's Island and hauling them up a small cliff face. Totally impractical. "We'll just have to take our chance."

"If we put a guard at each end, say half a mile away, we can say we were sending someone to get permission if a customs officer comes along," Emma suggested.

Daniel grunted. "We'll see. We'd be unlucky to get caught here in any case. This is turning into one hell of a trip," he muttered.

A movement above caused Emma to look up. Henry was standing on the upper deck peering out at the barge. His face looked a little more animated than usual. He glanced down to the lower deck and caught Emma's eye.

Looking away quickly he stepped back and went into their cabin. Emma thought he had looked rather pleased.

The crew went to work. First, the barge was floated back past the island and moored out of the way of the narrow channel. Then the *Mary B* was turned so the winch on the foredeck could be put into use. A rope was thrown over a convenient tree branch and Blue, already wet, attached the rope one at a time to the thirty or so bales that were in the river and they were winched out and manhandled onto tarpaulins laid on the bank where they could dry in the sun. It could have been far worse. At least it was high summer. The bales would soon be steaming in the heat.

Emma was occupied looking after Gertie. She sat with the children in the saloon at morning tea time. Henry talked to Erich in German, though it was more of a monologue as Erich didn't say much. Emma was sure Henry was doing it on purpose to shut her out. She decided to ignore it. Her feelings toward the boy were ambivalent, one moment feeling sorry for him and the next annoyed.

"We're going to be held up here all day while the wool bales are dried out," she explained to them. "You can go off the boat, but you must stay in sight of the river. We don't want you getting lost."

"We know our way in the bush," Henry said his tone indicating disdain.

"Better people than you have gotten lost in the bush, Henry," she said. "There could be blacks out there as well. Would you like more to eat?" she asked Erich.

"May I have another scone?"

"You may," she smiled at the young boy. He smiled tentatively back. Henry said something to him in German and Erich stared unhappily down at his plate. Had Henry learnt this behaviour from his father? Had Zac behaved this way in private behind his pleasant public face?

"Bullying is very unattractive, Henry," Emma said quietly, "in any language," and was rewarded with seeing a slight flush on the older boy's face. He might wonder now how much she understood.

After they had eaten, the boys went out to watch the men at their work and poke around in the bush the way boys were wont to do. They took Jack out on his leash with strict instructions not to let him run off. Henry tied the leash around his waist. Seeing that gave Emma an idea.

She had been wondering what to do with Gertie to keep her safe on the boat without having to carry her everywhere or lock her up. Following Henry's example, she searched out some fine cord and plaited a harness for the child. To this she attached another length of cord that she could fasten to anything solid. Gertie seemed perfectly happy to be tethered. Emma scavenged a tin plate and spoon for Gertie to play with. It was noisy but it kept the child occupied. When she tired of hitting the plate with the spoon, she tried banging both on whatever part of the boat her harness let her reach.

"You tie up like little pet, Missus," Ah Lo said, laughing his high-pitched cackle. He was probably glad not to be called into babysitting duties.

It took the crew the best part of two hours to retrieve and lay out the bales that had fallen in the river. Blue and Daniel went to check on the ties that had been holding down the wool bales.

"They can't have come undone on their own," Emma heard Blue complaining, as they came back along the bank. "Not possible. Those knots tighten 'emselves with the strain, you know that, Capt'n."

"Well, it's either that or you missed tying them off properly in the first place," Daniel replied. "Seems more like the latter to me."

"I didn't forget nothing. I double checked 'em all round twice when we finished loading." Blue, normally laid back and laconic, was getting upset.

"It's done. We just have to deal with it," Daniel said.

He didn't look at Emma as went past to the stairs. Blue flung himself down not far from where Emma was sitting and started to roll a cigarette, fumbled, and threw the makings away from himself in disgust.

"What happened, Blue?" Emma asked, quietly.

"Two ropes had come loose on the far side, Boss. They can't of, but they did. I checked 'em last night. They were tight as need be."

"The Captain didn't check them himself?"

"Nah. Mr. Gartner came out and the Capt'n was chatting to him. I told him everything was shipshape before I went to bed." Emma knew if she had been lax in that way, she would never have heard the end of it. "He thinks I've been careless. I knows I haven't."

"Could they have caught on a branch or something, perhaps?" Though even as she spoke, she knew it wasn't the cause, not with two ropes letting go anyway.

"Couldn't. The river's so low, the barge is way below any branches. Anyway, I'd have felt it if something had caught, and it didn't."

"All right. Tell me..." she hesitated for a moment, "...how do you think the ropes came loose, then?"

"If I didn't know any better, I'd of said someone loosed 'em off. Someone playing a practical joke. I'd like to know who. They'd get more'n just a piece of my mind, I can promise 'em that."

"You don't think Shorty or Willy, or Mr. Summers would do that do you? Or Ah Lo, perhaps?"

Blue shook his head. "Nah, wasn't thinking of them."

Emma wasn't either. She was thinking of Henry looking at the barge just after the accident. He would have had time late last night or early this morning under darkness before he was brought back on board.

"Ah Lo, can you bring some tea up to the saloon for the Captain and me?"

"Yes, Missus."

"I'll sort it out, Blue. Don't worry about it. Have yourself some tea and something to eat and then go help the rest of the crew turning the bales." Best he kept busy instead of sitting around getting worked up.

Emma checked on the whereabouts of the boys and saw them hanging around with the crew. She went upstairs, taking Gertie with her, and found Daniel in the saloon updating the logbook.

"And what's your excuse?" he asked before she'd even sat down but she took heart that his tone was tired rather than annoyed.

"My excuse? You oversaw the last of the loading, remember. Blue said Stan Gartner came out and spoke to you and you didn't do the final check."

Daniel put his elbows on the table and pressed the heels of his palms against his forehead.

"I did, didn't I." He sat back. "I'd intended to check this morning or get you to do it. Then Erich came back, and it completely went out of my mind. Blue should have known better, just the same."

"I don't think Blue made a mistake. There was no reason for the load to shift, for any pressure to be put on a tie. I'm wondering if it was sabotage by young Henry."

"Why would...?" He hesitated. "He can't possibly think Zeller will catch up to us."

"I'm not saying it's a sensible idea but he's just a child. I saw him come out on the upper deck and look at the barge. He seemed rather pleased. He could have loosened a couple of ropes during the night. You know as well as I do Blue Higgins is a better than average bargeman. He's quite upset that you think he was careless and let this happen. We need to consider that it was deliberately done."

Ah Lo came into the saloon at that moment with a plate of oat biscuits and two mugs of tea. Gertie popped up from under the table and was given a biscuit.

"I'll give you the possibility," Daniel said when Ah Lo had gone. "What do you think we should do about it?"

"I'm not sure. Do we let him know we suspect him or not?"

Daniel shook his head. "I don't fancy telling him personally. It could make him more determined and he could do some real damage the minute we take our eyes off him."

"And he could do that anyway," Emma said gloomily. "I'm thinking we just watch him, tell the crew. Seven pairs of eyes should be enough. And I'll give some serious effort to see if I can talk to Erich on his own. Though I suspect Henry's warned him pretty strongly about telling me anything." She took a sip of tea.

"Well, I'd rather think it was that German brat than Blue, in any case," Daniel conceded. He paused for a moment. "Have we made a mistake in bringing them with us, Em? Should we have left them where we found them?"

"I was thinking that very thing the other night, and no we couldn't have left them, especially Gertie but none of them. How would we be feeling at this moment if we had? We'd be worried sick. Even now we don't know if Zac has come back. Henry may be hoping he has but that's likely just wishful thinking."

"I'm leaning toward leaving them with the police at Euston if we have any more trouble," Daniel told her.

Gertie popped out from under the table again and grabbed at Emma's skirt with her biscuity hands. Emma brushed her hand over the child's head. "We'll see. Did you send anyone along the river to look out for a customs officer?"

"No. It'd be a waste of time, especially if someone comes along when the bales are almost dry. It would be obvious they haven't just been landed and that we've had no intention of seeking permission."

Emma shrugged. "It was just an idea. All the wool we have on the barge is from the other side. We can't afford to lose it." The stations who owned it wouldn't be impressed if they did either.

Chapter Twelve

"THERE'S ANOTHER BOAT coming up behind," Shorty announced part way through the afternoon, looking up as flocks of ducks started appearing overhead. The crew were taking an afternoon tea break in the shade on the foredeck between stints of turning the wool bales in the sun. Fred cocked his head and listened for a moment.

"It's the *Lisette*," he said calmly.

"No way can you tell that," said Shorty.

"Course he can," agreed Blue. "Everyone knows the *Lisette*'s engine. We spent enough time on her."

"What? Her engine?" He looked from Blue to Fred. "Aw, cut it out. You knew the *Lisette* was behind' us. It was at the wharf when we left Wentworth. You can't kid a kidder, boyo."

"Had yer goin' there for a minute, though," Blue said.

"Nah."

The sound floated intermittently through the air, until it became a constant. The ducks continued to fly as they left the water ahead of the approaching boat. Rounding the far curve, the *Lisette* came toward them down the last mile and pulled alongside.

"What ho, lads," Captain Mallory hailed them from the wheelhouse doorway. "Having some trouble?"

"Just a few wet bales," Daniel replied. "Nothing we can't deal with. We'll be on our way later this evening."

"Righto."

"Did you call in at Zeller's, Captain?" Emma asked, thinking he may have an update on the situation.

"I did, ma'am. I heard at Kulkyne you're rather involved in that bad business."

"You have time to stop for a tot, Mallory?" Daniel added.

Captain Mallory looked up at the sky. "Sun's over the yardarm and I never refuse an invitation to be sociable, Berry," was the reply.

Captain Mallory came aboard, and Emma went up the stairs with them. Gertie having her afternoon nap and the boys were laying on the bank in the shade of the trees, it being too hot even for them to run around. Emma wondered when they would have had this amount of free time at home and thought of idle hands making mischief. The crew of the *Mary B* and the crew of the *Lisette* were giving experienced eyes to the drying wool bales.

"You won't want any more hold ups, not on this water," Mallory said as Daniel held the saloon door for them.

"I hope we've had our share already."

"Yes. Heard the details from Mrs. Bell at Kulkyne, interminably."

"What did you see at Zellers?" Emma asked as they sat down. Daniel brought out the whisky bottle and two glasses.

"The place looked the same. We were just about to leave after loading up with wood when I saw a hen jump out the window of the shack. Went to investigate, found the grave behind the shack, and decided to check inside. More hens. You found her and buried her I believe?"

"We did," Daniel said.

"Bad business."

"Did you happen to notice if there was a note on the table in the Zeller's shack?" Emma asked Captain Mallory.

"A note? Can't say I did, ma'am. What's that about?"

Emma explained about Henry insisting their father had told them to wait for him and how she in turn had insisted they leave, with the compromise being a note to let Zac Zeller know where the children had gone.

"Well, of course you couldn't leave them there, could you? As far as I know, we're the last boats heading upriver right now. Like you, I'm just picking up some produce to make a paying trip. One doesn't want to stop anywhere for long."

"And you didn't see a note on the table?" Emma asked again.

"I think I should have noticed it, had there been one, ma'am. Would have checked it to see if it were anything relevant. Does it signify?"

"Well, it could mean that Zac Zeller came back to the shack and found it. Or I suppose it might only mean that it's fallen on the floor, or perhaps the hens have eaten it. Anything I suppose."

Captain Mallory was looking at her quizzically. "I see. Bit dangerous for him to come back, though?"

"But he would want to check on the children, one would think."

"Hmm. Well, I guess the police will sort it out eventually," he said comfortably. "No need for us to worry ourselves over it."

Emma felt she had been patted on the head like a good girl and told not to worry, everything would be just fine. Captain Mallory was clearly lacking in imagination and a sense of curiosity. The talk turned to river levels, engines, and crews, and it was agreed they should continue together in case one or the other of them got into difficulties.

Before supper, the *Lisette*'s crew helped the men of the *Mary B* reload the barge. Albert Fryling, loadmaster for the *Lisette*, checked the tie ropes with Blue as if Emma weren't capable. She could see that Blue wasn't overly impressed either. Emma wondered when Mr. Wilson, the *Lisette*'s previous loadmaster, had left the boat. She saw the engineer, Mr. Shankton but if he saw her, he gave no indication.

After a quick supper, both boats set off to put a few more miles behind them. The *Lisette* led the way and her headlamps lit up the river ahead of the *Mary B*, past Success Reef, and the S-Bend until they reached Nowlong station thirty miles on where they moored for the night.

In the morning, Emma had a word with Fred about keeping an eye on Henry and asked him to pass it on to the rest of the crew when the opportunity arose.

Fred nodding knowingly. "There's something not quite straight about that lad, if you ask me," he said. "Got a load of something on his mind. And all that chat in German to young Erich. It's like he's warning him or reminding him of something all the time. The young lad's afraid to say boo to a goose right now."

"He's been doing that around you and the crew as well? Were you asking about their family?"

"Not really. Mostly it's just the young lad wanting to talk, but his brother keeps shutting him down."

Emma sighed. "Poor little fellow. I do feel sorry for him. I would like to know what it is that Henry is trying to hide. Perhaps he knows where his father has gone. I don't know, but it would seem Erich must know what it is too, wouldn't you say, otherwise Henry wouldn't be trying to keep him quiet?"

"Seems reasonable."

"I need to get Erich alone so I can talk to him. But in the meantime, do we need to watch both? Do you think Henry might tell Erich to do something?"

"Well, it's possible. We would never know what they're saying."

"No. All right, we'd better keep an eye on both boys, then. It's all we can do at this stage."

Fred nodded.

A little later, Emma was sitting in the shade on the rear upper deck with Gertie, keeping an eye on the barge which Willy was piloting today, when Jack joined them. He was quickly followed by Erich, clutching the dog's collar and lead. As Erich tried to put the collar on Jack the dog took refuge under Emma's chair.

"Perhaps Jack doesn't need to be tied up now Erich," Emma suggested. "He certainly doesn't think so, does he?"

The boy shrugged glumly and turned away. Jack stayed, seeming to have taken a liking to Gertie's company as if sensing she needed him more than the boys did. Erich had gone back to the lower deck and Emma could just see him sitting, a sad bundle beside the galley door. Emma's heart went out to him. Shorty must have noticed the boy as well as he soon sat down beside the lad and started talking. It wouldn't matter to Shorty if Erich didn't say much, he'd just keep on with his stories of his sailing days.

Henry stomped along the lower deck from somewhere up front, Blue sauntering after him making no effort to hide the fact he was keeping an eye on the boy. Henry said something in German to Erich. The younger lad didn't respond. Henry shouted and Erich began reluctantly to get to his feet.

"Leave your brother be," Blue said sharply for him. "He's not doing any harm unlike others I could name."

Henry turned to look at him, decided perhaps that he didn't care for what he saw and hurried up the stairs without another word. Emma heard their cabin door close. Well, he'd know now he was under suspicion for loosening the tie ropes on the barge. Not that she could blame Blue for letting that out. He'd been sorely tried.

"Let your brother cool off," Blue said to Erich. The boy hesitated and then sat down again. Shorty and Blue began to chat, drawing Erich out until the three of them were soon nattering on like old mates. Emma was reminded what good men they were. Perhaps Erich would talk to her soon.

=====

THE LITTLE TIMBER COTTAGES that marked the town of Euston appeared as if out of nowhere later in the afternoon. Lining each side of the river, they were incongruous after the miles of empty countryside. Heads appeared out of windows and doors and children escorted them laughing and shouting along the bank as the *Mary B* and the *Lisette* steamed up to the wharf in the centre of town. The boats were the only contact the town had with the wider world and an important part of its commerce and its position in the surrounding pastoral region.

After making sure the barge was pulled alongside and tied off, Daniel and Emma went to call in at the police station opposite the wharf to leave their statements about finding Hilda Zeller's body. There was also the added report of the death of Jim Franklin from Pattin Downs station.

Daniel was keen to get the official business done so they could be on their way. Captain Mallory wasn't interested in staying long at Euston either. The only business he had was to send a telegraph to the Company office in Echuca reporting his progress.

Emma took Gertie with them and left the boys and Jack with the crew who were going to 'stretch their legs' around the town. Emma figured that would take them all of ten minutes. The place only had a hundred and fifty inhabitants.

The police station was a timber building, a one room affair with attached residence and a lockup in the yard next to the open tin shed that was used for stabling. The office door was locked. Daniel knocked anyway, but no one responded.

"We'll try the post office," he said.

It was another one room place of business with attached residence a little further down the street, and older than the police station. They found Captain Mallory inside, his telegraph report to the Company in the process of being sent by Mr. Mudge the postmaster, tapping away in the corner. Hardly private if you understood Morse code, Emma thought. She wasn't sure how many people would. She certainly didn't, but perhaps it was something she could learn. It was a job a woman would be able to do. Something to consider for the future if her time on the riverboats came to an end. Everything did, after all. She could picture herself running a post office. Not here at Euston, but in a bigger town. A place like Wentworth perhaps.

They waited while Captain Mallory's message was sent, and a reply received.

"I have to pick up wool at Merrim station," Captain Mallory told Daniel, "so I'll be getting on. You'll catch us up there."

"Right." They shook hands and Mallory left.

Mr. Mudge, tall and thin, of middling age with shoulders stooped no doubt from sitting over the telegraph, turned his attention to Daniel.

"Captain Berry," he greeted, pushing his glasses up on his long nose. "Haven't seen you in a while."

"Afternoon, Mr. Mudge," Daniel responded, shaking the man's proffered hand over the counter. "No, I have no need to send off water level reports to the Company now I've got my own boat under my feet again. I don't think you've met my sister-in-law, Mrs. Berry?"

"A pleasure to meet you at last, ma'am. You're the talk of the river." Emma didn't want to think what the talk might be about. "I don't know of any other boat that has a female officer."

"Indeed," she said with a nod and a smile. If that was all they were saying.

"Besides, I have a telegraph for you. Was about to check and see if it was your boat just arrived at the wharf and deliver it if so."

"Oh." She wasn't expecting any news. Was something wrong at home? She tore open the envelope and unfolded the yellow sheet of paper.

"It's from Joe."

"Nothing wrong?"

"No." Emma refolded the paper and put it in her reticule. Mr. Mudge let his eyes rest on her for a moment. He was probably curious about what it meant, but she wasn't about to share it.

Chapter Thirteen

"HOW CAN I BE OF SERVICE?" Mr. Mudge asked.

"Lieutenant Forrester asked us to call at the police station and leave statements but there's no one there," Daniel explained. "I hope you can deal with it as we need to be getting on."

"I can. Constable Fogarty should be in the office but he's more than likely slaking his thirst in the hotel. I wouldn't bother chasing him up. This have anything to do with that woodcutter who shot his wife?"

"It does."

"Come into the parlour and we'll deal with this in comfort. Be on your way in no time." He led the way into the adjoining room. "Patricia," he called. "Tea for three." A female voice answered from somewhere further back. "Sit at the table here," he said, pulling a chair out for Emma at the small round dining table.

"This is very kind of you," Emma said. "Do you mind if I put Gertie on the floor?"

"Of course, of course. Patricia," he called again. "And something for the child."

Mr. Mudge produced paper and pens and fussed around filling an inkwell for them. A small woman came in with tea and fruit cake. She looked sideways at Gertie.

"May I take her into the kitchen?" she asked Emma. "I could give her some milk and cake there."

"Thank you, that's very thoughtful of you," Emma said, though she imagined Mrs. Mudge was more concerned about Gertie's effect on her pristine upholstery and floor rugs than anything. "Go with Mrs. Mudge, Gertie." The child looked at her but didn't move. "I won't leave without you," Emma said, with a reassuring smile. Was the child becoming attached to her? It gave her a warm, but wary, feeling. How attached was she herself becoming?

"As if your mama would leave without you," said Mrs. Mudge, addressing the child.

"I'm not her mother, Mrs. Mudge. She has just lost her own mother. I believe her family usually spoke German in their household and I'm not even sure how much she understands of what I say."

"How terribly sad. Well, let's see what we can find for you in the kitchen, eh?" She took Gertie's hand and the child toddled off.

There was silence in the little parlour save for the scratching of pens and the occasional clink of china. Daniel had produced his logbook from his jacket pocket and was copying out his original reports on Hilda and Jim Franklin. Emma's report on the finding of Hilda's body was always going to be more thorough. It was she who had prepared the body for burial, searched the shack and spoken to the children.

She added in the information gleaned from the boys about relatives at Kerang and what the Bell's at Kulkyne and the Gartners at Pattin Downs had told them. In half an hour both she and Daniel had finished.

"Patricia, our guests are leaving," Mr. Mudge called. His wife came out with Gertie who was clutching a paper bag.

"We've been baking cookies, Mrs. Berry so Gertie has some to take with her. She's eaten two pieces of cake and had a glass of milk so don't be surprised if she has no appetite for her supper tonight."

"She looks as if she's enjoyed herself, Mrs. Mudge, thank you."

They said their goodbyes.

"That's done," said Daniel. "But I would have liked to speak to Forrester and get an update in case we could leave the children here. It looks as though we're stuck with them now until Swan Hill."

"Do you really want to just dump them like that?" Emma asked feeling he was being heartless.

"We don't need any more delays like that barge accident and the boys running off. Who knows what Henry might get up to next. I'm concerned enough about the water levels at the Bitch and Pups as it is. Seems the levels here are already lower than last year."

Emma's concerns rose also at the thought, although being stranded there wouldn't be the end of the world. It was only thirty miles from Swan Hill. They could find some transport from nearby Tooleybuc to get to the town, but Daniel would not be pleased if he and the *Mary B* had to sit out the off-season at what was little more than a shepherd's fold.

"What was the telegraph? News from home?" Daniel asked. Emma handed Gertie to him while she took the telegraph from her reticule, and then exchanged it for the child.

"Commercial traveller. China tea in 4oz packs?" Daniel read. "Is this some family code or something?"

Emma laughed. "No. Apparently Joe's discovered a commercial traveller on the coach carrying four-ounce packets labelled as China tea but in reality, containing opium."

"And you need to know about it, because...?"

"Beware China tea? No, Joe was considering the possibility of the opium being brought across from South Australia by coach when the riverboats aren't running."

"I thought I told you not to get involved in that."

"I'm not involved, despite the fact you have no right to tell me what I should or shouldn't get involved in,"

Emma said evenly. "I suppose Joe was just letting me know to keep an eye out for four-ounce packets of China tea in case we are asked to carry some as cargo."

"Hmph. Smuggling's the least of our worries," Daniel said, fortunately not commenting on her statement about her right to do as she wanted. "It's more important we get on. We can get another six hours of steaming tonight. It's a full moon."

They had reached the wharf. The *Mary B* was deserted, the only sign of life being the nanny goat chewing on some hay. And the *Lisette* hadn't moved despite Captain Mallory claiming he would be leaving immediately when he left the post office. The street was also deserted though in the heat of the day she supposed that wasn't surprising.

She looked at Daniel. "The hotel?" Both crews had gone off together. "They've got the boys with them too."

Daniel frowned. "I'll go and look. They can't have done too much damage in half an hour."

The hotel wasn't far from the wharf, the building jutting out a little over the river for ease of delivery. Beneath it was a secured space used to cool the beer and aerated drinks. As Emma put her foot on the plank to board the *Mary B*, she heard shouting.

A crowd of men erupted from the hotel. In front were Blue Higgins and another man being escorted along the street, none too gently, by a police constable and another man. The crowd behind, made up largely of both riverboat crews was shouting and waving fists at the policeman. A dog was barking. Blue and his companion were hustled past the wharf into the police station yard and into the lockup, the door clanging shut, and the bolt pushed to.

"What the devil is going on?" Daniel demanded of his men as they stood in the middle of the street like naughty schoolboys caught out in some mischief. The *Lisette* crew edged away toward their own boat.

"Just a bit of a disagreement, Capt'n," said Shorty quickly. "Blue and one of the *Lisette* men just had a little disagreement."

"A little disagreement that's broken up my saloon," said a large man following along the street from the hotel.

Emma knew him as Charles Penton, the owner of the hotel. He was a navy man. He had named his hotel The Admiralty Arms and was himself known locally as the Admiral. He was tall, well over six feet, and wide to boot. She was surprised that he hadn't been able to stop the trouble himself before it got out of hand.

"I'll be wanting compensation for the damage," Mr. Penton announced in Daniel's direction.

"Get on board the lot of you while I sort this out," Daniel ordered his crew. "You're confined to the boat for the duration of this stop."

"Blue was severely provoked, Capt'n," Shorty said somewhat unwisely. "He was defending the honour of the *Mary B* and its officers."

"What rubbish," roared Daniel. "Blue Higgins never needed an excuse to get into a fight yet, especially after a drink or two. Get on board and stay there or you can swim home. Do I make myself clear?"

"Aye, Capt'n."

They walked past Emma avoiding her eye. She was surprised to see that Fred had a grazed cheek. He didn't normally get into fights. Collateral damage while trying to contain Blue Higgins perhaps. Captain Mallory came up the street carrying what looked like a bag of vegetables, if the lettuce poking out the top was any indication. He hadn't been in as big a hurry to get on after all. Emma wondered what else he had been purchasing. She chastised herself for thinking meanly of the man, but life on the river had left her with few illusions.

"One of your crew get himself into trouble with the locals?" Captain Mallory asked.

"No, Mallory, with one of your men," Daniel told him with some relish. "They're both in the lockup now and Mr. Penton wants compensation for damage done."

"The deuce he does."

Captain Mallory went to talk to his crew who had disappeared into the *Lisette* and Daniel went to talk to Mr. Penton. Whatever the outcome any damages would come out of Blue's wages, or at least fifty percent of them. But how long would he be held in the lockup? Emma saw Henry and Erich on the side of the street with Jack and called them over.

"You didn't go inside the hotel, did you?" she asked.

"No, we sat outside," Erich told her. His eyes gleamed. "We drank fizzy ginger beer and watched the fight. That Mr. Blue, he sure can punch. He knocked the policeman to the floor," he said demonstrating the technique, his small fists clenched, face contorted. "And Mr. Fred tried to stop him and, bang, got hit with a chair."

Well that accounted for Blue's arrest and Fred's injury anyway.

"Hmm." Emma didn't want to comment on the fight. "And did you like the ginger beer?"

"Yes. May I have some more?"

Henry said something to Erich in German, sending a sideways look at Emma.

"But it's hot, Henry," Erich said. "And I'm still thirsty."

"I wouldn't mind a glass myself," Emma said. "Perhaps we could get a whole bottle of ginger beer. I'm sure Gertie would like some too, wouldn't you?" she asked jiggling the little girl on her hips. Gertie burped and Emma immediately stopped jiggling. Gertie looked as if she might already have had enough to eat and drink at the post office.

"Ooh, yes," Erich said.

Daniel had disappeared into the hotel with Mr. Penton. Emma and Erich went along to the verandah with Henry trailing reluctantly behind with Jack on his lead. Likely he didn't trust leaving Erich alone with her. They waited outside the open door of the hotel. Emma could hear voices and the sound of tables and chairs being moved about, but not what was being said. Then the voices grew louder and Emma moved a few steps to the side.

"I'll see the money gets paid, Penton," Daniel was saying as he stepped out onto the verandah, Mr. Penton behind him.

"Mr. Penton, may I get a bottle of ginger beer for the boys?" Emma asked.

"A bottle of ginger beer? Surely, ma'am."

The big man turned and called out to his barman and in due course the bottle was produced, cold and wet from being chilled in the pool beneath the building. Emma produced a coin from her pocket and handed it over. She gave the bottle to Erich to carry and he hugged it to himself proudly.

"He should have given you half a dozen bottles for what he's charging for damages to his rotten furniture," Daniel said as he accompanied them back to the *Mary B.*

"What happened exactly?" Emma asked.

"The constable was in the snug with a mate and he tried to arrest Blue and the other fellow, Jess Sharp, when a few punches were thrown. Fred tried to stop Blue and you know how that was always going to end."

Emma nodded. Once Blue was in a fighting mood he just lashed out. "Who's the police magistrate here?"

"Penton."

"Oh dear. Well, if he's got his compensation, surely he won't hold them?"

"He's going to let them cool their heels for a few hours, he said."

"Is he just being difficult because he can?"

"Sure seems that way. I've a good mind to leave Blue where he is and let him find his own way home."

"Shorty said they were fighting about the honour of the *Mary B*?" Surely that allowed for some consideration.

"Your honour, my girl. The whole crew thinks the sun rises and sets on you. As if you didn't already know. They think having you on the *Mary B* sets them apart from everyone else."

Emma stopped and stared at him. "Oh no, surely not. Daniel, you're not serious?"

"You never seem to be short of admirers, do you?" he said, sourly.

"If my presence on the *Mary B* is causing trouble Daniel, I'll leave."

"Not until we've bought Knowles out," he said, bringing up the boat builder and his seven-and-a-half percent share for the first time in months. "In the meantime, you take the place of another crew member as we arranged."

They stood staring at one another. Adversaries again. Emma became aware of the boys looking from her to Daniel and back, soaking up every word. "Come along," she said briskly, shepherding them onto the boat. "We'll go and open that bottle before it gets warm."

Jack went up the stairs with them, Erich holding his lead. They were halfway up when Fred called to Henry.

"That nanny goat could do with milking about now, lad. You can't expect Mrs. Berry to do everything for you."

"I'll do it soon," Henry replied.

"You'll do it now." Fred's tone and expression brooked no opposition, but Henry hesitated.

"I'll keep some ginger beer for you, Henry," Emma said knowing full well that wasn't what the boy was concerned about. Henry said something in German to Erich, the word '*vater*' prominent, before stomping back down the stairs. It was early to milk the nanny. Fred must have seen it as a chance for her to speak to Erich alone. That, or he needed to work off some irritation after the hotel fight.

"Is the Captain mad at you?" Erich asked, over his glass of ginger beer. Emma had Gertie on her lap. She gave her a sip of ginger beer from her own glass and the child coughed and spluttered at the taste.

"Oh, he's just upset because we can't leave until Mr. Blue gets out of the lockup," Emma said vaguely.

"Will we be here for a long time, then?" His little face looked concerned.

"No, no. We should be able to leave later today." Emma sipped at her ginger beer. It was cool and sharp, a rare treat after a diet of tea and water. Gertie reached with chubby hands for Emma's glass and another mouthful. It was time to start asking questions.

"You must have come out to this country on a ship, Erich. Do you remember that?" Emma asked, looking for a way in.

"I remember the sea. I don't like the sea. There is just water everywhere. You could be lost. I cried a bit," he admitted.

"Even grown up people cry sometimes. Sometimes everyone feels a bit like they are lost at sea."

"My mother cried sometimes."

"Did she? What did she cry about, do you know?"

"There was shouting, and she cried."

"Just words, was it, Erich?" she asked tentatively.

"Mr. Blue punched that man," Erich said. "People can hurt someone when they do that, can't they?"

"Yes, Erich, they can."

What was Erich trying to say? Had Zac been physically violent towards Hilda? And perhaps the boys as well? It was seeming more likely, though they had hidden it well from visitors if that were the case. Emma could imagine a woman afraid putting on a front so as not to annoy her aggressor. She shuddered at the idea. It was just that Hilda didn't seem afraid of Zac, however she looked at it. Was she reading too much into Erich's words? He was only seven. She put Gertie down on the floor and poured Erich and herself a little more ginger beer.

"Where did you go when you got off the ship?" she asked.

"We were in, um, Mel-bourne? Yeah. Then we go a long, long way on a train and a cart to Uncle Axel and Aunt Rosie's farm."

So, there was an Aunt Rosie as well. This was looking even better. So, from Melbourne, train to Bendigo and by cart to Kerang. A journey of almost two hundred miles heading northward. She felt she was gradually putting a picture together, but it raised more questions.

"So how old were you when you went to the farm? Was it long ago?"

Erich thought for a moment. "I think I must have been about, um, three? Yeah."

That meant they had been in the colonies for a good four years, at least half of it spent in Kerang possibly.

"And you remember everything? About the ship, and Melbourne and everything?" Emma asked, a little surprised.

"I remember the sea. Henry talks about it sometimes. He didn't want to come. He had friends at school."

"Hmm. I can understand Henry not wanting to leave his friends. Did he make new friends at Kerang? Did you?" Erich nodded into his glass. "Did your father work on Uncle Axel's farm?"

Erich froze. Wrong question. She shouldn't have mentioned his father.

Henry came into the saloon. He glanced sharply at Erich who was sipping his ginger beer and didn't look at his brother. Emma poured Henry a glass.

"Thank you for milking the goat," she said. "It's difficult to remember what needs to be done when your usual routines have been upset, isn't it?"

"*Danke*," Henry said, whether for the ginger beer or the understanding Emma wasn't sure.

Chapter Fourteen

"I'VE HUNG AROUND here longer than I intended," Captain Mallory was saying to Daniel. They were each standing on their respective boats, speaking across the short expanse of water that separated the two vessels. The *Lisette* was making ready to set off, smoke billowing from her funnel. "And I have to put the Company's interests ahead of any crew member."

"And who's going to pay this crew member's fare if I give him passage?" Daniel, hands on hips, wanted to know.

"He'll pay his own way of course if you carry him. Personally, you'd do yourself a favour to leave them both behind."

"You're probably right but that's my decision to make."

"It is. Well, we may see you further up. Good luck." Captain Mallory went off to his wheelhouse.

"If I had any sense. I would take his advice and leave Blue in the lockup," Daniel grumbled seeing Emma.

She knew he wouldn't but commiserating with him would help him feel better about the situation.

"It is annoying," she said not just meaning Blue's behaviour.

It was part of her job to act as a buffer between the crew and the captain. Which begged the question: had she been acting as too much of a buffer making life too easy for them? She had thought something was going on among the crew back at Kulkyne when Lieutenant

Forrester was questioning them all. She hadn't given it any thought since.

"That's one way to describe it," Daniel said. "He'll be doing without his tot of whisky for the rest of this trip, I can promise you that."

They watched as the *Lisette* pulled out from the wharf and turned upriver with a loud toot, toot from its horn. The sound of its engine soon receded into the distance.

Supper that evening was a subdued affair. Blue had still not been released from the lockup and Daniel was no longer expecting to leave Euston that evening. He decided that none of the crew were without blame for the delay.

"You should never have gone to the hotel, especially with the *Lisette*'s crew," he admonished them. "There was always going to be trouble. Now Penton's getting as much out of us as he can, including charging for the meals for the prisoners. We probably can't leave now until after breakfast, whatever time that will be."

The crew had little to say in their defence and Emma felt guilty about being the reason for the fight. As she was putting the boys to bed, she caught a smirk quickly wiped off Henry's face. Was he seeing this as another useful delay for his father to catch them up? As the crow flies, they were barely forty miles from the woodpile. Sometimes on the river it felt as if they were going round in circles.

=====

EMMA WOKE SEVERAL hours later to the sound of horses and voices. Checking her timepiece, she found it was just going on one o'clock. She pulled on a wrapper and slipped out onto the upper deck. The street and the river were lit with a soft blue light, the full moon Daniel had mentioned. He would hate missing such a good night for travelling. There was almost no need for the lamps that were alight outside the hotel and the brighter lamps of the mail coach that stood in front of it.

As she watched, two men unharnessed the coach horses in quick time, leading them off to the stables next door before bringing out a fresh set for the next stage. They worked quickly and efficiently. Cobb & Co had a strict timetable to meet. There were riders in the shadows of the lamps and several people in the street, passengers stretching their legs. The riders detached themselves and went past the wharf to the police station. Emma thought she recognised Lieutenant Forrester among them but wasn't sure. She didn't know how many troopers had gone out with him so couldn't tell if they had brought a prisoner back.

Light flared in the station yard and lit the open shed that served as a stable. She could see several troopers moving in and out of the light as they unsaddled the horses and rubbed them down. Hay was forked into the feed bins. A light came on in the station building. She wondered if the Lieutenant knew he had lodgers in the lockup. Constable Fogarty would no doubt give him that information, eventually.

She yawned. There wasn't much point in staying out here, pleasant as the evening was. The mail coach, a fresh set of horses harnessed and ready, its passengers refreshed, clattered past. Without the coach lamps the buildings along the street threw long shadows and everything was quiet again. The flares in the police station yard were extinguished as the troopers, having settled the horses, went off to their own beds somewhere.

Emma was about to return to hers when light spilled out at the back of the police station and three men made their way across the station yard to the lockup. Emma recognised Lieutenant Forrester in the light of the flare he was carrying. A trooper was escorting the third man.

There were voices, but Emma was too far off to hear what was said. The number of men at the lockup increased, decreased, moved. Two men broke away from the group and made their way toward the wharf. Blue she recognised by his size and shape and his loose-limbed walk. Only two men returned to the police station. The third man must have been locked up. Had they found Zac Zeller?

"Where's my bloody boat?" It was Jess Sharp, just discovering the *Lisette* had steamed off without him. More cursing followed.

"You can bunk aboard with us, mate," said Blue. Typical of him to have forgotten and forgiven their original disagreement.

Jess Sharp had some harsh words to say about Captain Mallory and the Company.

"Here," said Shorty's voice from below, "get aboard and stop your caterwauling. Some of us wants to sleep. You've caused us enough trouble for one day."

Blue and his companion came aboard quietly. Emma felt the relief of a mother hen when all her chicks were safe. She should make sure Daniel knew that Blue was back just in case he hadn't heard them. It would affect what time they left in the morning. His cabin was on the opposite side. To reach it she took a shortcut through the saloon. There was light showing around the edges of his curtain as she knocked on the door.

"Daniel," she called softly. "Did you hear? Blue is back."

His door opened immediately. He was already dressed apart from his boots, or still dressed, she wasn't sure which.

"Hardly likely to sleep through that racket," Daniel grumbled, clearly still annoyed at his crewmen. "We'll get away within the hour. Fred will take a turn at the wheel later and Blue can work as fireman for Summers." That would make life easier for the engineer anyway.

"I'll have Ah Lo put the kettle on."

"Captain Berry."

It was Lieutenant Forrester calling from the wharf. And there were the two of them in the moonlight, framed in the doorway of Daniel's cabin. Emma instinctively pulled her wrapper more tightly around her.

"What is it?" asked Daniel.

"I'm right glad to catch you still here. We need your presence at the inquest tomorrow."

"Not possible, Lieutenant. We need to be getting on. And you have our statements. There's nothing else we can add."

"I'm afraid the magistrate doesn't agree. We have arrested a person of interest. Your input at the inquest is vital if we are to commit him for trial."

"Damn Penton," Daniel muttered. "You've no right to hold us up, Forrester," he said more loudly. "We're running out of water to get us back to Echuca as it is without any more delays. I was planning on steaming off right now, in fact."

"Don't do anything stupid, Captain. There's room in the lockup for you if need be."

"Have you arrested Zac Zeller?" Emma asked.

"We've arrested a man on suspicion, ma'am. He's not calling himself Zeller. The inquest starts ten o'clock sharp in the hotel lounge."

"Thank you. We will be there."

"Thank you, ma'am. I will hold you to your word. Good night to you."

"There's nothing we can do about it, Daniel," Emma said as the Lieutenant disappeared into the police station. "There'll be trouble further along if we leave now. We'll still be able to get away late morning perhaps."

Daniel cursed softly and sighed. "I know but I don't have to like it. Next time we find a body we will be walking away. Let someone else deal with it."

She didn't blame him. She went back to her cabin and tried to sleep. She hadn't been to an inquest before.

Perhaps tomorrow they would find out the why and who of Hilda's death.

=====

HEAT SHIMMERED ALONG the street and a dust devil swirled in a current of hot air as Emma and Daniel, accompanied by Shorty, Blue, Willy, and Jess Sharp, made their way to the hotel. Fred and Ah Lo had remained behind on the *Mary B* to keep company with the boys and Gertie, while Jake Summers was keeping an eye on the boiler, which was stoked ready for departure as soon as they could leave.

A crowd had gathered outside the hotel and curious faces surveyed them as they entered. It looked as if every adult in the town had come along to see the entertainment. It wasn't every day an inquest was held on a murder. The lounge itself was crowded with standing room only but there was an empty bench at the front facing a table. Constable Fogarty was in attendance and directed them to take their seats there. Apparently, they were to be the star attraction. The iron roof creaked and pinged. The room was already hot and oppressive.

They had only been seated a few minutes when Mr. Penton took his place at the table facing his audience, Lieutenant Forrester standing nearby.

"At least we're starting on time," Daniel muttered.

Mr. Penton announced the intention of the inquest to consider the deaths of Hilda Zeller and James Franklin. Statements made would be read and questions asked as pertinent, he explained.

They began with James Franklin and dealt with it quickly. Mr. Penton called Daniel to the witness stand – a chair set beside the table – and read out the statement he had made the day before. Daniel was asked to confirm it, which he did.

"There was no evidence to indicate that anyone else was involved in this death?" Mr. Penton asked.

Daniel replied in the negative. Penton eyed the *Mary B*'s crewmen for a moment but didn't ask for confirmation from them. Emma thought he probably considered they would back their captain regardless, and James Franklin's death was declared to be a result of natural causes due to old age. Daniel was asked to remain seated where he was.

"We now turn to the matter of the death of Hilda Zeller," Mr. Penton intoned. Emma felt the atmosphere in the room tense in anticipation. Once again, Mr. Penton read out Daniel's statement on finding the body.

"You confirm this is your statement of the events that took place at the woodpile known as Zellers on Thursday January 13th of this year?" intoned Mr. Penton.

"Yes, that is correct."

"How long have you known the Zellers, Captain."

"Well, as long as they've had the woodpile. A year or two. But know them, not really at all. I only met Zac Zeller once, and his wife I saw a few times more, but just to exchange the time of day."

"When was it you saw Zac Zeller?"

"A year or so back. We spent a couple of hours with them on a Sunday."

"Who is we, Captain?"

"Myself, my late brother Sam and his wife."

"Thank you. And what was your impression of the family? Were there any signs of dissent?"

"No, quite the opposite in fact. I would have said they were comfortable together."

"So, you can shed no light on why Zac Zeller may have killed his wife?"

Daniel hesitated.

"Captain?"

"No, nothing at all. If indeed he did."

"Well, that is what we intend trying to establish here today. Have you any reason to suppose a third party may have been involved?"

"Only the evidence of his son. He insists his father went into the bush after someone."

"Ah, yes. We will get to his evidence later. Is the boy here, Lieutenant?" Mr. Penton asked.

The Lieutenants gaze swept the room.

"I'm not sure, sir."

"He's on the *Mary B*," Daniel said.

"Very well. We may need to call him later, but he doesn't need to hear everyone else's evidence. May in fact be better for his veracity if he does not, children being what they are. You have no reason yourself, Captain, to suppose anyone else was involved in this crime?"

"I have no opinion on the matter, either way."

"Now the location of the body, hidden in the woodpile. Did that not strike you as odd?"

"It did. It would be the last place to put a body if you were trying to conceal it. It was always going to be found quickly."

"Just so. Zac Zeller would have been aware of that, of all people, wouldn't you say?"

"I suppose."

"Thank you. That will be all for the moment, Captain. Please hold yourself available for further questions if needed."

"We need to be getting on with our journey, Mr. Penton," Daniel said. "You must be aware of the water levels. Every hour we delay we run the risk of being stranded."

"We appreciate your problem, Captain. We do require your presence, however, but we have every intention of completing this inquest quickly. We all have businesses to run."

Emma sniffed. Penton's business would be doing fine regardless. The bar would be as full as the lounge with updates on the inquest going back and forth. Daniel, looking disgruntled, took his seat again.

"I call Mrs. Emma Berry to the witness stand."

Emma identified herself as part owner of the *Mary B.* Mr. Penton read out the statement she had made the day before and asked her to confirm the contents. She did so.

"Very well. Now, you state here that you spoke to the dead woman on several occasions since that Sunday a year ago. Did you get any indication at these times of the state of her mind or the state of her marriage?"

"She seemed content enough with her lot, but I felt she was used to a more social life."

"But you also state that she was supposed to be leaving for Melbourne the very day you found her. She had in fact, arranged to travel on your boat. Is that correct."

"It is."

"Do you think her decision to leave could have precipitated the event that led to her death?"

"I have absolutely no idea. She was going on a holiday."

"That's what she told you." It was a statement rather than a question.

"I had no reason to doubt it."

"Mmm. Why do you think the body was hidden in the woodpile?"

Emma paused for a moment. To speak or not. "It made me think of a funeral pyre," she said simply.

There were murmurings from the assembled crowd.

"A funeral pyre? That is not something one would expect in a British country. And it wasn't set alight, was it? There was no evidence of burning?"

"No."

"So, there is nothing to show that was the idea?"

"No. But perhaps the person who did it was disturbed before he could finish what he set out to do."

"Disturbed by whom?"

"Well, it can't have been a riverboat, or they would have found the body before we did." Unless it was the arrival of the *Mary B* that disturbed the killer. Was that what Henry was hiding? That his father had been nearby all the time? "Perhaps Zac Zeller disturbed someone when he returned from his work," she said instead.

"That's a possibility if some unknown person was the culprit. But don't you think only a fool would consider lighting a large fire in these hot dry conditions? It would start a conflagration that could consume miles of bush, including the Zeller's shack and possibly anyone in it. Wouldn't you agree, Mrs. Berry?"

Emma had to admit they would indeed have to be a fool. "But whoever killed Hilda had already shown they didn't have much concern for human life. They may have wanted all trace of their crime obliterated, regardless of the cost to anyone else."

"Yes, well, I think we can put aside the idea of a funeral pyre," Mr. Penton announced to his audience, not impressed it seemed with Emma's comment. "Unless of course we find some Hindi, or such like person involved, but I haven't seen or heard of anyone of that type in the district." Emma felt he was enjoying himself at her expense and regretted mentioning the idea at all. "Now getting back to something more concrete, you say you searched the shack and found no gun though it was known that Zeller had one."

"That's correct." She would keep her answers short and to the point from now on.

"And you found nothing, according to your statement, that would shed any light on what might have happened? No signs of a struggle, for example?"

"No."

Penton was silent for a moment. Emma felt his eyes on her, but she continued to gaze out over the heads of the audience. He must realise he had a hostile witness now.

"Thank you, Mrs. Berry. That will be all for the moment. Again, I ask that you keep yourself available for any further questions."

"A funeral pyre?" Daniel murmured as she sat down.

"Stupid man," Emma muttered.

"I hope you're not referring to me."

Emma refrained from answering as Mr. Penton glanced at them and cleared his throat before beginning a summary of the evidence to date.

"We have established the conditions surrounding the death of Hilda Zeller: her discovery in the woodpile set up for the use of the riverboat traffic; her burial; the search of the family home; the removal of the children; the fact the Zeller family had spent several months at Pattin Downs station before taking up the timber lease; and that they arrived some several years before from Germany and may have spent time with relatives at Kerang.

"As far as we know, the only people the family seem to have had any contact with at their timber lease are the riverboat crews and the occasional contact with Kulkyne station. Before we proceed further, at this point I would ask if anyone else has any knowledge of the Zeller family that they can add?"

No one moved. Then a lone hand was raised from among those sitting on the bench with the *Mary B* crew.

Chapter Fifteen

MR. PENTON acknowledged the raised hand. "And you are?"

"Jess Sharp, PS *Lisette*."

"Ah yes. One of the combatants from yesterday. Come forward and take a seat."

Jess Sharp was an average looking fellow with a sour twist to his mouth and a hard look in his eye. Someone who thought the world had done him wrong and wasn't about to forgive it.

"In what capacity did you know the Zellers?" Mr. Penton asked when he had taken the chair.

"I knew 'em from the woodpile," Jess Sharp said.

"Yes?"

"Well, I knew of Mrs. Zeller. She were well known among rivermen for being free with her favours. She were partic'lar though. She only fancied officers and them with clean hands."

A babble of voices greeted this news. There were "oohs" and "aahs" and a few wise nodding heads and even an "I told you so."

"Quiet, quiet," demanded Mr. Penton.

Emma realised with some surprise that she didn't feel as shocked at the idea as she may have done. A little memory slipped into place. One visit, another boat had just left the woodpile and Hilda had come out of her bedroom, flushed, her hair dishevelled as if she had been sleeping. At least that was what Emma had thought at the time. The memory suddenly took on a different hue.

"What do you mean by them with clean hands?" Penton asked.

"Engineers need not apply," said Jess Sharp. "They 'ave oil under their fingernails. And deckhands were below 'er notice. Captains and officers and the better class passenger, providing they could pay."

"And this was common knowledge among rivermen?"

"I reckon so."

"Captain Berry? What have you to say on that?"

Daniel shifted uncomfortably in his seat. "I have heard rumours to that effect," he said quietly.

Emma looked at him. Why hadn't he told her? That put a completely different complexion on the situation. No wonder the Lieutenant had been suspicious when he interviewed them at Kulkyne.

What if Zac discovered what Hilda was doing and killed her? Or was her penchant for other men the reason he had taken her out into the bush in the first place, to get her away from opportunity? If so, that had failed dismally. One thing was clear – her annoyance at Daniel for not telling her.

"You have no personal knowledge of this, Captain?" Mr. Penton was asking.

A few sniggers greeted this remark.

"That is correct," Daniel replied curtly.

There would be those who suspected he lied, of course, and those who thought he didn't require the services of a Hilda Zeller when he had his widowed sister-in-law on board. She caught the eye of Lieutenant Forrester and gritted her teeth. He was of the latter opinion she was sure. Well, she had put herself in this position. Her mother had warned her.

"Do you have anything further to add, Mr. Sharp?" Mr. Penton asked the deckhand.

"No, nothing, 'cept what I'm saying is the truth of the matter."

"Very well, that will be all. I recall Mrs. Emma Berry to the chair."

Emma took her seat amidst murmurings from the assembled crowd. This inquest was turning into far more entertainment than anyone, including herself, had expected.

"Now, Mrs. Berry, what credence do you give these rumours about Hilda Zeller. I say rumours because no one here appears to have any personal knowledge – or none they are prepared to admit anyway."

This remark was greeted by a few sniggers among the audience.

"I have no knowledge either way," Emma said. "I hadn't heard any rumours."

"No knowledge at all? You saw nothing to suggest that Hilda Zeller was – ah – bestowing her favours on men from the riverboats?"

"No, I did not."

Hilda may really have just been woken from a nap on that day. To suggest anything else was pure conjecture and she refused to add to the stories. The funeral pyre was beginning to make more sense though if it was going to be some sort of purification. Was Zac of a religious bent? She had no idea. Mr. Penton looked at her speculatively for a moment but had no further questions.

Emma sat down again beside Daniel her hands clenched tightly in her lap, feeling as if a thousand eyes were on her from behind. Mr. Penton conferred quietly with Lieutenant Forrester. There was a palpable change of mood in the audience. Before, there had been curiosity and some indignation at what had been done to the 'poor woman.' That mood had changed with Jess Sharp's evidence. Now it seemed, if the mutterings were anything to judge by, the manner of Hilda's living had taken precedence over her death. The bad woman becoming the cause of her own downfall. The man's crime diminished in the light of her far greater one.

Emma's hands tightened as her anger rose. Whatever Hilda had done she had been an intelligent woman who carried herself well, was house proud and a good mother. She wasn't a slattern. Whatever it was that had driven her to behave as she had, supposing the stories were true, there had to have been some reason. Who were people to judge? Hilda was before a far greater judge now and Emma didn't believe He would condemn her so lightly.

The lounge had become unbearably hot and stuffy and people were getting restless, but no one left. Emma wanted to talk to Daniel but didn't want to do so where she may be overhead or draw more attention to herself. None of the *Mary B* crew would meet her eye. She felt alone and conspicuous. And very angry.

Mr. Penton called for quiet. "I have decided, under the circumstances not to call the Zeller lad to give evidence at this inquest. The police have already interviewed him and having read the result of that interview, and heard Lieutenant Forrester's opinion of it, I find that lad's evidence is clearly skewed toward protecting his father and is unreliable. Whether he knows of his mother's supposed activities is a moot point, but not one I wish to press on the lad. I now call Lieutenant Forrester of the New South Wales police force to give evidence."

As the Lieutenant moved to sit in the witness chair, stiffly upright, his cap held on his lap, Emma found herself reluctantly impressed with Mr. Penton's restraint and consideration for Henry. She may have felt more inclined to answer his questions, however, if he had shown any for her.

"Lieutenant, can you please describe your activities since hearing of the death of Hilda Zeller."

"We received a report of the suspicious death of Hilda Zeller through a telegraph from Kulkyne station on the evening of Thursday January 13th. I immediately proceeded there with a posse of three troopers, arriving late in the evening. Notice of the death had been brought by the PS *Mary B* and I proceeded to interview the Captain and crew, including the Zeller lad, and got an understanding of what had occurred. Early next morning we proceeded along the coach road and from there, made our way in toward the river and scouted about until we located the woodpile and the shack."

"Mrs. Berry of the PS *Mary B* had informed me of the note she had left on the kitchen table for Zeller should he return, letting him know that the children were safe. That note was not located but we could find no other evidence that anyone had been there. We then set out to search the bush up and down the river and back toward the coach road. At one point, we found a fresh camp site but no sign of our quarry.

"On the next day, we kept watch along sections of the coach road but still did not sight anyone. Late that evening, we stopped the mail coach and there found a passenger who had been picked up on the road several miles further west. This man denies he is Zac Zeller, but the circumstances strongly indicates that he is someone of interest. We have brought him in for questioning but have not had the opportunity of doing so, only arriving back here shortly after midnight."

"And you say this man was picked up by the mail coach in the vicinity of Zeller's timber lease?"

"That is correct, sir."

"Have him brought in and we will hear what he has to say for himself."

All eyes followed Lieutenant Forrester as he went out, returning almost immediately with two troopers escorting between them a tall well-built man, blue-eyed, with short raggedly cut blond hair in need of a wash. His reddish complexion told that he was a man from a cooler clime unused to the hot sun of the colonies. Emma estimated his age at somewhere in his forties. One thing about him she knew. He was not Zac Zeller.

The man was seated in the witness chair facing the audience, the troopers standing behind him though he was handcuffed. He looked around confidently at the people seated as if he hadn't a care in the world. Emma wasn't sure if it was an act, or not. The room was deathly quiet.

"State your name," ordered Mr. Penton.

"Jack Macklin," replied the man. His accent was English though from which part of the country Emma would have been hard pressed to tell except that it was not an educated voice. "You know me, your honour. I worked here for several weeks as yardman."

Mr. Penton looked at him more closely. He coloured slightly. "Ah, yes." He glared at Lieutenant Forrester. "Captain Berry, do you recognise this man?" he asked abruptly.

"I have never seen him before," said Daniel.

"He is not Zac Zeller?"

"No, he is not. The general description fits but this man is some ten years older and he does not have a German accent."

"I see. For the benefit of this inquest, what is your business in this district, Mr. Macklin?"

"I was travelling to see the country and pick up work," he said. "It is not a good time to travel, I've found. And work," he shrugged, "just a few days here and a few days there mostly."

"You have been travelling on foot?"

"Some, but I came down river by boat."

"Where were you before?"

"Melbourne."

"You were working there?"

"Yes."

"What was your occupation in Melbourne, Mr. Macklin?"

Macklin seemed to find the question amusing. "Labouring," he said.

"How long have you been in the colonies?"

"Four year about."

"And you've spent all that time in Melbourne?"

"Yes."

"What places have you worked in this district? Apart from this hotel."

"Thandam station was the last place. I tried to catch a boat to go back home but there were none, so I crossed the river and walked to the coach road. I expected someone would come along at some time and give me a lift."

"And you were picked up by the mail coach?"

"Yes."

"What do you know about the Zellers?"

"I know nothing about these people. I told the police that already. Some woman has been murdered apparently. What has that to do with me? Why pick on me?" A whining note had entered his voice. "This is supposed to be a free country, a British country. What have I done to be treated like this?" He raised his handcuffed hands toward Mr. Penton.

The hotelier looked annoyed. Emma could see his problem. The man had been in the vicinity of the Zeller's woodpile at his own admission but there was nothing to connect him to Hilda's death.

"Lieutenant, you searched this man's belongings?"

"I did."

"Was he carrying a gun of any sort?"

"No, he was not."

Emma thought he could have thrown it away in the bush or the river. It didn't prove anything either way. Not carrying a firearm in the bush could be considered suspicious but if he were a city man, unfamiliar with the Australian bush, it might not be unexpected.

"Take the prisoner out, Lieutenant," Mr. Penton ordered.

Lieutenant Forrester nodded to the troopers who moved to Macklin's side as the man stood.

"No, no. Wait a moment." Mr. Penton held up his hand and considered for a moment. "Yes. Go and fetch the Zeller boy, Lieutenant. Macklin, you will remain here for a little longer."

Emma looked at the man's face. If he was concerned about Henry recognising him, he didn't show it.

"I will find the lad on the boat, Captain?" the Lieutenant asked Daniel.

"He was there when we left," Daniel replied. Emma didn't blame him for not giving a more definite answer. Henry could have taken it into his head to run again.

The Lieutenant went out. A low buzz like so many bees filled the stuffy room as the crowd, released from its enforced silence, found their voices again. Jack Macklin sat quietly looking down at his hands. The voices grew louder as time ticked by on the large clock on the wall behind where Mr. Penton sat but it was only five minutes after closing that the lounge door opened again. Voices stilled and heads swivelled to see as Lieutenant Forrester came in with Henry. Macklin stared at the boy blandly.

"Come and stand here in front of me," Mr. Penton directed Henry. The lad stood in front of the table, his gaze on Mr. Penton. "For this inquest, tell me your name lad."

"Heinrich Zeller," he answered clearly.

"Good. Now, I need to ask you a question Heinrich, and I want you to answer me honestly. Take a good look at this man sitting here and tell me if you have ever seen him before."

Henry turned to look at Macklin who stared over his head with a bored expression.

'N-no," Henry stammered.

"Are you absolutely sure?"

Henry look back at Mr. Penton. "Yes, sir. Absolutely," he said, more firmly.

"Very well. Go and sit with Captain Berry." There was jostling on the bench as room was made for him. "If you have nothing with which to charge this man, I suggest he be released, Lieutenant. This inquest thanks you for your time," he said to Macklin.

"Hah, like I had a choice," Macklin grumbled as he was escorted from the room. Mr. Penton sat back and mopped his face with a large handkerchief. He looked around the room.

"That appears to be all the evidence available at the moment," he said. He considered his notes for a few minutes and then announced his conclusions.

"This inquest finds that Hilda Zeller died by misadventure possibly at the hands of her husband, Zac Zeller. A bulletin will be issued for Zeller's arrest. This inquest is closed."

Chapter Sixteen

"AT LAST. LET'S GET out of here," Daniel said getting to his feet. Emma was aware of curious eyes as they made their way out of the hotel lounge, most of the crowd making way for them. As they reached the door, Henry stumbled against her and she put her arm around his shoulder. He seemed to be struggling to keep his emotions in check, but he quickly pulled away from her refusing comfort.

Unpleasant as he was at times, Emma's heart went out to him. He must have been relieved on the one hand, at seeing a stranger under arrest on suspicion of his mother's murder but disappointed his father hadn't appeared. He must be doubting he would catch them up.

Jack barked an excited greeting as they boarded the *Mary B* and Fred, suitably notified of their arrival, appeared from the fore deck with Gertie and Erich. With the boiler well stoked Jake Summers soon had the engine turning over. Willy took the helm of the barge and Shorty and Blue wasted no time in letting off the mooring ropes for barge and boat.

Emma saw Henry take Erich aside in urgent conversation no doubt relaying his experience at the inquest, in German of course. She relieved Fred of Gertie and turned to the stairs to the upper deck. A shout came from across the street.

"Ahoy, Captain, wait up." Jack Macklin was waving to them as he ran across from the police station. He carried a travel bag and had a bed roll slung across his shoulder.

"What is it now?" Daniel asked, coming out from the wheelhouse onto the upper deck.

"Can I get passage with you?"

Daniel nodded. "Come along then. Mrs. Berry will deal with the details."

Shorty put back the boarding plank that he had been in the process of taking up and Macklin came aboard profuse with his thanks.

"I was afraid I was going to be stranded in this godforsaken place," he said. "You're a lifeline for a poor man who's been hard treated."

"You're welcome, Mr. Macklin," Emma said in the businesslike manner she kept for passengers. "We have an empty cabin. Come on up and we can deal with your fare." She turned again to the stairs as the *Mary B* pulled away from the wharf. Henry, Erich, and Jack stood watching a little way along the deck. Gertie began to grizzle, and Emma stopped and called Henry over.

"Can you look after Gertie, please. I'll be back down in a few minutes. You can ask Mr. Charley for a biscuit if you like."

"All right," the boy said almost cheerfully as he took his sister in his arms. Emma marvelled at the ability of children to recover their equanimity.

"Neat boat you've got here," Macklin said loudly over the sound of the engine as he followed Emma up the stairs. "Those young'uns are yours I take it. Nice family business, eh?"

"None of them are my children, Mr. Macklin," Emma replied. "They are all the children of that murdered woman you were arrested over."

"Really? All three of them? You don't say."

Emma showed him the available cabin which was on the opposite side of the boat to the cabin occupied by the children.

"This will do nicely," Macklin said dropping his bag onto the bed and throwing the bed roll into the corner. "Be good to have a soft bunk for a change."

"Are you planning on traveling all the way to Echuca?" Emma asked.

"I am, ma'am. Then down to Melbourne."

"The fare is five pounds ten shillings for the cabin, three meals a day and as much tea as you can drink." Emma told him and waited. Macklin rubbed his hand across his head.

"Well, there's the problem, see. I paid all my ready cash for the coach ticket. But I can work my passage. Never been one to shy away from work."

A freeloading passenger and they had already left the wharf.

"Well, there's a problem with that, Mr. Macklin. We don't need any work done. We have a full crew already."

He looked at her appealingly. Emma wasn't charmed.

"There must be something I can do," he said putting on the charm. Emma wasn't impressed.

"Nothing of any value to us," she said. "Tell me, you would have been paid by cheque at the places you worked, am I right?"

"Of course. I have a cheque from Thandam station. I was paid in ready money when I worked at the hotel, but I've spent all that as I told you, food and tobacco and the coach ticket." And the odd drink or two, no doubt.

"Why didn't you cash your cheque at the hotel?"

"When? In between leaving the police station and hailing you?"

She had to admit he had a point there. "I'll tell you what we'll do, Mr. Macklin. We will hold that cheque in lieu of your fare and cash it when we get to Swan Hill. We're already carrying the three Zeller children and they aren't paying passengers." And then there was Jess Sharp. There was no point in asking the *Lisette*'s deckhand for his fare until he received his back pay at journey's end. If they could catch up with him. "We can't afford to feed everyone for nothing. We are a business, after all?"

Macklin considered her for a moment. "You drive a hard bargain, ma'am. What choice do I have?"

Emma shrugged. "We can always put you off at the next property if you prefer. You could try the coach road again."

"No thanks. I've had enough of this country. I just want to get back to a civilized town life."

Emma waited. "The cheque?" she said, when he just stood there looking at her. Was she going to need some help with this man?

"Sure, sure." He bent and opened his bag. Rummaging around inside he gave an exclamation of surprise. "Well, I'll be. Look here." He held out a small handful of coins, most of them of small denomination but among them two gold one-sovereigns and several half-sovereigns. "Seems I overlooked this bit of coin. Must have just dropped it in the bag and forgot I had it."

Emma didn't comment, but seriously doubted Mr. Macklin had been unaware of what money he had. He handed over the sovereigns and a handful of silver coins of smaller denomination to make up the required fare.

"Thank you. Lunch will be in the saloon shortly. Let me know if you need anything." She left him to settle in wondering if he was going to be someone who needed an eye kept on.

=====

MACKLIN HESITATED IN the saloon doorway, taking in Emma and the children seated at lunch.

"Please come in, Mr. Macklin," Emma said. She indicated a place at the table. "Lunch is ready."

"The men will be along?" he asked although there were no other places set.

"No. When we are travelling, they take lunch wherever they happen to be."

Macklin looked uncomfortable. "Ah. I would prefer to do the same if you wouldn't mind. I'll take my plate along of my cabin." He picked up his tin plate, piled with potato, cabbage and mutton chops, which he eyed appreciatively.

"If you prefer," Emma said.

Perhaps he didn't feel comfortable sitting down at table in the 'polite' society of women and children only. She had met men like that as if afraid their table manners weren't up to standard and they might slurp their food or spill it down their shirt front and embarrass themselves. And then there were the men who felt such company was beneath their consideration. She wasn't sure into which category Jack Macklin fell.

"There's bread and butter pudding too," she told him. "If you take your plate down to the galley when you're done, Ah Lo will make sure you get some."

"Thank you," he said as he left.

Emma couldn't say she was sorry he had gone.

"I like bread and butter pudding," Erich announced.

"Me too," agreed Henry. Emma noted again how much more cheerful he seemed to be. Whatever the reason she was glad of it. Perhaps he wouldn't harass Erich so much. After lunch Emma put Gertie down for her nap and went up to the wheelhouse. It was the first chance she'd had to speak to Daniel about the inquest.

"Has our passenger settled in okay?" he asked her as she stepped in the doorway.

"I suppose so," she replied. "He's had his lunch anyway in his cabin. He didn't care for the company of myself and the children in the saloon. He tried to get out of paying his fare as well. Claimed he had no ready money on him and would work his passage."

"And did he? Have money I mean."

"Yes." Emma told him what had transpired.

"Hmm. A bit of a chancer then," Daniel said. "You get all sorts."

"Indeed. Why didn't you tell me there were rumours about Hilda?"

He looked at her before turning back to the river. "They were just that. Rumours. Does it matter?"

"What do you mean? Does it matter what she was doing, or does it matter I didn't know?"

"Why would you need to know? It was just talk."

"Well, I could have warned her people were talking, I guess."

"I doubt that would have changed anything, Emma."

Possibly not. But what else didn't he tell her? Had Daniel heard rumours he was keeping to himself about opium smuggling? She wouldn't be surprised, although he said he hadn't known about the packets marked China Tea. China Tea, of course. She could ask Ah Lo about the opium. She should have thought of that before.

"We'll be traveling til late tonight," Daniel said, breaking into her thoughts. "I want to reach Swan Hill by the end of tomorrow. I'll feel better once we're safely past the Bitch and Pups."

"Have you told the crew?"

"I'll leave that up to you."

They were traversing the seven-mile long Bumbang Island loop. The channel cutting off the loop was impassable at low water, but they were making good time, the river in the loop being wide and deep and the current slow. Emma saw the 662-mile marker tree slip by. That meant a hundred and fifty miles still to Swan Hill.

Emma found Fred sitting against the galley wall smoking his pipe and watching the boys play with Jack who seemed never to tire of fetching the ball they rolled for him. Shorty, his hat over his face, was taking a nap and Ah Lo was peeling potatoes for supper dropping them into a bowl of water so they wouldn't brown. After a glance at Shorty and Fred, neither of whom looked like moving, Blue went up to the wheelhouse to sit with Daniel. Willy was on the barge, and Emma had seen Jack Macklin on the upper deck, supposedly enjoying the view. "Where's Jess Sharp?" Emma wanted to know. "He did come back on board, didn't he?"

"Aye. He's about somewheres," Fred told her.

"Asleep in his cabin, probably," Shorty muttered.

She didn't say any more. She wasn't about to get into a discussion of Jess Sharp's evidence at the inquest supposing any one of her crew would talk to her about it. It wasn't a subject a man would discuss with a lady. Which was why she hadn't been told of it in the first place.

Was it why Hilda had wanted her company on this trip? As a buffer between herself and the men? Emma was certain it must have been. Her presence meant Hilda wouldn't have to interact with the crew in any way. And now here she was taking care of Hilda's children. It was as well she had agreed to come. It went without saying she would have preferred the journey to have turned out as planned.

Emma found a patch of shade on the foredeck, near where Shorty was gently snoring. Finding shade was a joke really. One moment the boat was heading south, the next west or east or north as it followed the twists and turns of the river. Shade and sun came and went as if on a whim of the river gods. She turned her mind to the opium smuggling. She was beginning to have some disquieting thoughts on the subject as she remembered a newspaper article some months back which described the squalor and degradation of addicts in an opium den in Maryborough.

Some of the claims had been refuted in later articles, but the idea of innocent young women caught up in the trade had stuck with Emma. It reminded her of Hilda's situation. Had she simply been caught up in a slightly different trade? Had Zac required Hilda to earn her keep?

152 · IRENE SAUMAN

If she had indeed been leaving with no intention to return, he may have objected to the loss of income.

She wondered if Ted Bell had been one of Hilda's clients. It would explain his discomfort at speaking to her about the Zellers. It was more likely than his being involved in her death. It was all speculation, anyway. She turned her thoughts back to the opium smuggling. It wouldn't hurt to ask.

"Fred," Emma said, her tone casual. "Have you heard anything about opium smuggling on the river?"

"Someone's always trying to smuggle something, lass," Fred said around his pipe.

"Hmm. You know that's why my brother was sent to Wentworth? To investigate opium smuggling?"

"Aye."

"Well, after we left, he found a commercial traveller on the coach carrying opium made up in packets marked China Tea."

"How do you know that?"

"I got a telegraph from him at Euston. I suspect Joe was afraid we may get a consignment of China Tea."

"You want to ask Charley about China tea and opium," Shorty mumbled through his hat. "You'd know about that, wouldn't you, Charley?"

"Someone having big joke?" Ah Lo asked, throwing a half-peeled potato into the bowl causing the water to splash.

"What do you mean?" Emma asked surprised at the Chinese cook's sudden display of irritation.

"You not hear of opium war?" he asked his voice rising.

"Well, yes, I've heard of it. But I don't remember much about it except it was something to do with trade between Britain and China, wasn't it?" She had a vague recollection of a history lesson, from the British viewpoint of course.

"Great and mighty Britain bring opium to China in exchange for tea. Now they blame Chinee for use opium. Say Chinee bad, ignorant. China tea. Hah." He got up and stalked off to his galley his face grim.

Emma was stunned. She hadn't just opened a wound she'd made it bleed profusely.

"I think you'd best not ask any more questions about opium smuggling, lass," advised Fred. "We don't want our cook going on strike now, do we?"

"No, Fred. I'll go talk to him. See if I can calm him down."

"Would be a good idea. And no remarks from you, lad," Fred warned Shorty. "Remember your stomach."

Shorty just grunted. Emma went to the galley door. Ah Lo had resumed peeling his potatoes at the small bench beside the stove. But the potato in his hand was being whittled down to the size of a small plum and was still shrinking.

"Ah Lo, I'm sorry I brought up the subject and upset you. You know we all hold you in the highest regard. It doesn't seem to matter who you are or where you come from, human beings are the same all over, good and bad alike."

Ah Lo didn't answer or look at her, but his hands stilled, and the whittling of the potato ceased. Emma left him to calm down. She would leave the opium issue to Joe from now on. It wasn't worth upsetting the equilibrium of her own boat.

Chapter Seventeen

DANIEL PUSHED THE *MARY B* along at full speed throughout the afternoon, trying to put as many miles as possible behind them before nightfall. Not long after leaving the Bumbang loop, they passed Belsar Island and pulled in at Meilman Station. Fred accompanied Emma on a quick visit to deliver some of her grandmother's herbal mixtures. Meilman was also on the New South Wales side of the river and Emma, after her conversations with Joe, was acutely aware they were trading illegally by not charging customs duties.

She felt a pang of guilt to think it might have a bad effect on Joe's career if that was discovered. But then she rationalised if she suddenly started to charge and remit the duties to the Customs Office as required, they might wonder at this sudden new trade and ask awkward questions. She wasn't prepared to take that risk. She'd go about business quietly, leaving things as they were and hope for the best. It wasn't her preferred mode of operation.

They steamed on into the evening, around Youngera Island with its derelict farm buildings and past Tala Station. It was one of those fresh air evenings that can come occasionally in the interior after a hot day. Supper was over and the children fast asleep lulled by the boat's movement. Fred was standing just inside the wheelhouse doorway keeping an extra eye on the river for Daniel at the wheel. Willy was piloting the barge and Emma, Shorty and Blue had gathered on the upper deck in front of the wheelhouse, the slight breeze of movement keeping the mosquitoes at bay. The steamers lamps lit up the water ahead of them while beneath their glow they sat in a companionable semi darkness. Macklin and Jess Sharp were both in their cabins or elsewhere on the boat.

"I'm going to go stay with my sister in Castlemaine," Blue said in answer to Shorty's question of what he was going to do during the off-season. It was as if everyone felt they had left all the trouble behind and they could now look forward, it being just a matter of days before they reached home port.

"Is she still having trouble with that man of hers?" asked Emma.

"He'd left, last letter I had," said Blue. "I just hope he stays that way." Emma did too, otherwise Blue could find himself in real trouble if he got involved in that domestic situation.

"I'm going to be digging my garden," Fred said. "The missus wants to grow more vegetables and I'm planning on putting in another crop of the sweet peas."

"The one thing I miss on the *Mary B* is a garden," Emma said. "Do you plant the sweet peas near a door or window where you can smell them indoors?"

"Well, they're on a trellis by the wash house so I suppose the missus gets to smell them when she does the wash."

Emma laughed. "That may be some small consolation."

"What are you going to be doing, Charley?" Shorty asked.

"Work in market garden," Ah Lo replied. He lived with several other Chinese men when he was in port and had a part share in a market garden supplying some of Echuca's fruit and vegetable shops.

"You going home, Boss?" Blue asked.

"Yes. I'll probably be helping my grandmother in her herb garden for some of the time. Seems as if everyone off the river wants to get their hands in some soil."

"What about you, Captain? You going to be doing some gardening?" Blue asked, leaning back in his chair and looking up toward the wheelhouse doorway.

Daniel didn't answer for a moment and Emma wondered if he had heard. What would he do? His girl had broken off their engagement back in May in favour of some local lad who was around all the time. She didn't know how he would spend his time off the river.

"I don't have any soil to get my hands in right now," Daniel said. "But it's an idea." He sent the signal for slow down to the stokehold and they drifted toward the bank. "We'll stop here," he said. "There are too many rocks in this section coming up and too many shadows on the water."

Emma estimated they were about five miles short of the Murrumbidgee junction. Not a bad day's run considering they had started late. They would do better tomorrow.

Before taking herself to her own cabin, Emma looked in on the children. The three of them were snuggled up together in the middle of the bed, Henry's arm thrown across his sister, her head against Erich' shoulder. The cotton blanket had been pushed down around their legs but the air flowing in through the open window was cooler than it had been when they went to bed. She pulled the blanket up, careful not to disturb them.

The next day dawned hot and hazy, the heavy air seeming to press down, the high banks and the trees closing them in as if they were travelling through a tunnel. They passed the Murrumbidgee junction and the 596-mile tree, the smoke from their funnel hanging lazily in the air behind.

Erich and Henry argued over a piece of toast at breakfast and Gertie was grizzly and wouldn't settle, even pushing Jack away when he came near. Emma wondered if she was teething and eventually resorted once again to a spoonful of cough mixture which seemed to help for a time.

About mid-morning Fred got the boys fishing again, one each side of the boat to stop arguments, and Emma left Gertie nearby in her harness while she went up to speak to Daniel. She had barely reached the wheelhouse when an angry shout came from below.

"Get out of it, you mongrel."

"That's Mr. Summers," Emma said stepping back onto the deck. Was Jack getting into mischief?

"What matter you," Ah Lo screeched back his voice high pitched.

He was sprawled on the lower deck, Jake Summers standing over him fists clenched. Even as she took in the scene Shorty and Fred intervened, but Summer's shook off their restraining hands. She could hear Jack barking but couldn't see the dog. Willy appeared beside her, having been leaning on the doorway on the opposite side of the wheelhouse.

"I'll deal with it, Daniel," Emma said and went quickly down the stairs. By the time she had reached the lower deck Ah Lo was on his feet – with a meat cleaver in his hand.

"No one call me mongrel," he screeched waving the cleaver menacingly and advancing on Summers.

"Ah Lo, put the cleaver down," Emma ordered.

Ah Lo stopped at the sound of her voice but continued to glare at Jake Summers who had retreated a step but continued to glare back at the cook. Fred and Shorty, either side of Jake, looked warily at Ah Lo. Gertie began to scream, startling everyone. Everything seemed to go into slow motion as Emma stepped in front of Jake. The signal to slow sounded in the stokehold but Jake Summers didn't move.

"Give me the cleaver, Ah Lo." She held out her hand.

"He knock me down, Missus, call me mongrel dog."

"Mr. Summers attend to your engine, please," Emma ordered as the signal sounded again. She only hoped Daniel was calling for slow speed because of what was going on down below and not because of some danger on the river. She was relieved when the movement of the boat eased but didn't take her eyes off the cook. "I heard, Ah Lo. I'll deal with it. Give me the cleaver, please." As she spoke Fred stepped up beside her.

"Come on now, Charley. You don't want to hurt anyone."

"I mind own business, he knock me down, call me mongrel dog," Ah Lo repeated, less strident now but the cleaver still held high.

"Minding your own business, my foot," Jake Summers bellowed from behind them. "You were messing about in my stokehold. I knew I shouldn't have let you in to cook them taties the other night. Give you an inch you'll take over, you and your blasted Chinee mates."

"I no touch your stinking engine," Ah Lo screeched. "I get coals. Fire in stove go out. You want eat, I need fire."

"Please be quiet Mr. Summers. You are not helping. You'll get your coals, Ah Lo," Emma said soothingly to the cook. "Just give me the cleaver."

Ah Lo wavered for a moment then lowered the meat cleaver. Fred took a quick step forward, grabbed the cook's arm and wrested the cleaver from him. Shrill words in Chinese filled the air.

"You'll go for a swim in a minute, you don't cool down," Fred told Ah Lo.

"And him," Ah Lo shouted pointing in Jake Summer's direction. "He start this."

"That's enough, Ah Lo. Get on with your work, now."

"No coals, no fire, no work," Ah Lo shouted triumphantly.

"Mr. Summers," she called into the stokehold, "Shorty will get some coals to restart the fire in the galley. I will speak with you in a moment."

Shorty picked up the tin bucket Ah Lo had dropped and stepped into the stokehold. Gertie's screams had subsided somewhat.

"Henry, are you there?" Emma called.

The boy appeared from around the corner of the engine room his face white, Gertie in his arms. Erich emerged slowly behind them eyes wide and frightened.

"Take Gertie up to your cabin and see if you can settle her down," Emma told Henry quietly. "I'll be up shortly." Erich scuttled after him. "In the galley, Ah Lo," Emma said, indicating for him to move. She stood in the doorway. "It isn't like you to let the fire in the stove go out during the day."

"Bad weather. Watch boy fish, fall asleep. Fire burn down."

"It burns down overnight as well. How do you start it then?"

"Mr. Summers, he get coal. Not let anyone in."

"Why didn't you just ask him for the coals this time?"

"He talk to little dog. I just slip in for moment. Not do any harm."

Shorty appeared beside her with the bucket in which a small shovelful of coals glowed. Emma stood aside and he handed the bucket to Ah Lo who promptly set about getting his stove alight.

"He don't let anyone in there," Shorty said. "He guards the place like it's a gold mine or something."

"Really? How long has that been going on?"

"Ever since he came on as engineer."

"Why wasn't I told about it?"

"Engineers are a funny lot, Boss. Best to humour them."

"I don't know about that. It seems a bit extreme. Does this have anything to do with Mr. Summers' pistol?" She should be grateful Summers hadn't had a chance to pull it on Ah Lo. There had been some reaction from the crew during Lieutenant Forrester's questioning when they learnt the pistol wasn't loaded. She should have followed up with Fred as she'd intended but other things had intruded. Her lack may have precipitated this trouble. It wasn't a pleasant thought. "Has he been threatening anyone with it?" she asked.

"Probably afraid some un's goin' to steal his new mattress," Shorty muttered.

"A new mattress?"

"He picked it up in Wentworth. He went shopping and came back with a lad hauling it on a hand cart. Right pleased with himself he was."

All this over a mattress? Perhaps Shorty was right, and engineers were an odd lot. Mr. Shankton was another of that group. "Well, it's his money. If he wants to pay for his own bedding, I guess that's his business. Are you all right now, Ah Lo? No more fighting?"

"He call me mongrel," Ah Lo grumbled, but it was clear he had calmed down somewhat.

"He's going to apologise for that," Emma promised hoping she could make good on it. She didn't want the matter to escalate with Ah Lo seeking retribution by putting something nasty in the engineer's meals.

She knew little about Jake Summers. He had been hired on at the recommendation of boat builder Knowles after the *Mary B*'s repairs back in September. Whatever his past he did know engines and had clearly worked on boats before.

The real problem was she had no authority over him as purser and loadmaster. The engineer's position was equal to her own. They both answered to Daniel. But as part owner of the *Mary B* she was also his employer and that was the only role she could take. Emma stood at the opening to the stokehold, causing a shadow to fall. Jake Summers studiously ignored her as he checked the oil level, a greasy cloth in his hand.

"This behaviour is not good enough, Mr. Summers," she began. "I understand your concern for your engine but..."

She felt a hand on her shoulder and turned in surprise to find Daniel glowering down at her. The *Mary B* was still moving. Fred must have gone up to the wheelhouse.

"Upstairs," Daniel said.

What was the matter with him now? "I haven't finished speaking to Mr. Summers and I need to check on the children."

"Later." He ushered her up the stairs ahead of him and along to the saloon. "What the devil did you think you were doing?" he said, his voice deathly quiet before the door was barely closed behind them. "You could have been hurt, putting yourself in the middle of men with knives and guns."

"One man with one knife," she responded. Was everything she did always going to annoy him? "And yes, someone could have gotten hurt or worse, but Ah Lo wasn't going to hurt me. Fred or someone else might have had to use force against him, but I didn't need to."

"You couldn't be sure of that. You don't know what goes on in his head."

"I know that much, Daniel." She couldn't resist a jab. "And it was my job to deal with it. The job you insisted I take on. And another thing," she went on, warming to her subject, "what do you imagine hauling me away like that has done for my status on this boat? You're supposed to back me up not pull me away for a ticking off."

He glared at her for moment then shook his head before wrenching open the saloon door and leaving her standing there. Emma sank onto a chair her legs a little shaky. What had that been about? She supposed it must have been frightening when Willy reported that Ah Lo had pulled out a meat cleaver and then when Mr. Summers didn't respond immediately to the signal. But she had dealt with it and she didn't deserve to be chastised. He should have trusted her.

She stirred herself and went along to check on the children. She found the boys very subdued. Gertie, still grizzling intermittently, was lying on her stomach while Henry rubbed her back, but she was almost asleep.

"Everything is all right," she assured them, sitting down on the edge of the bed. They didn't look convinced. Even Henry looked shaken still and he always did his best to appear in control. "Sometimes," she went on, "when people spend a lot of time together in a small space, they get a bit fed up with one another and little things become big problems. But it's all sorted out now."

"I thought Mr. Charley was going to chop someone up," Erich said, his eyes large.

"But he didn't Erich and he's calmed down." She wanted to say that nothing bad would happen, but it already had as far as their lives were concerned.

"Weren't you afraid?" Henry asked, surprising her.

Had she been? She didn't think it had occurred to her at the time. Perhaps she should have been. Was Daniel right when he said she couldn't have known how Ah Lo would react? But wasn't part of a boss's job to know his or her men? Ah Lo's reaction was at least partly her fault anyway. He was already upset at the conversation about China tea and opium and having to babysit Gertie making him late to get lunch the other day. It wouldn't have taken much more to set him off.

"I didn't really think about it, Henry," she replied. "It was just something that had to be done. Now," she said brightly, "as soon as Gertie is asleep, we'll go along to the saloon and have some biscuits and something cool to drink. It will make us all feel better."

At her name Gertie sat up, suddenly wide awake, and it was all four of them who went to the saloon. Too bad if it spoiled their appetite for lunch. They needed something comforting after what they had witnessed. Gertie's reaction particularly bothered her. If only the little girl could speak her mother's death might be known in a moment.

Chapter Eighteen

THEY WERE APPROACHING another bend when the *Mary B*'s warning whistle was answered. The engine speed slowed, keeping just enough headway to get around the bend without drifting. Ahead of them, laid up in the mouth of Wee Wee Creek on the New South Wales bank was the *Lisette*. There was activity around the paddle box on her portside and one crew member was up to his waist in the river. The *Mary B* eased to the bank behind her.

"Glad to see you," Captain Mallory called up as Daniel left the wheelhouse and looked down from the upper deck. "Thought you would have caught up with us before now. Was beginning to think you'd crept past us in the night. Had more trouble?"

"Not us," Daniel replied his voice non-committal. "Looks as if you have."

Mallory pushed his cap back and scratched his head. "Got a snag through the portside paddle box first thing this morning. Having a job fixing it sufficient to be going on with. Several paddles are broken."

"Anything we can do to help?"

"It should be done in an hour or two. The problem is, I don't think the repair will allow us to make any headway with the barge in tow. Too much pressure and it won't hold." The question hadn't been put in actual words, but it was clear what Mallory was hoping for.

"You want me to take on your barge? That's going to slow us down. Mine's fully loaded."

"You've got a good enough engine."

"That's as may be. Towing two barges in this water level gives us twice the problems. Not to mention a second barge will add extra drag and add to our fuel costs. If I take it on, I'll want the Company to cover charges for our wood from here to Swan Hill. You can get the paddle repaired properly there."

Mallory glared for a moment. He knew he was being repaid for dumping his errant deckhand on them and abandoning them at the first problem after suggesting they travel together. Finally, he nodded.

"I'd appreciate if you could travel behind us til we get there," he said. "There's no guarantee this repair will hold in these waters. One bump and it could all be over."

"That's fine." Daniel went down to the lower deck where Emma had been listening.

"You would have taken his barge, in any case," she said to him.

Daniel grinned. "He knows that too, but he couldn't refuse the arrangement once I put it to him. The Company's pockets are deeper than ours."

Emma smiled back and saw Jess Sharp slip off the *Mary B* and onto the *Lisette*. Well, that was one passenger dealt with, not that he had been any trouble. As far as she knew anyway. She wasn't sure her crew would tell her what was going on anymore.

"Can we take Jack for a run?" Henry asked coming up with the dog on his leash, Erich following.

Emma looked out at the thick bush. "Oh, I don't know Henry. We won't be here for long and I don't want to have to send someone out looking for you."

"We won't go far. Please?"

"How about I go with them, Mrs. Berry?" Emma turned to see Jack Macklin behind her. She hesitated. "I'll keep an eye on them. I could do with stretching my legs. Just sound the horn if we're not back when you're ready to leave."

"That's kind of you, Mr. Macklin. You two make sure you do as you're told now."

"We will," Henry assured her eagerly.

Emma watched as Macklin casually followed the boys and the dog off the boat. She wondered idly at his offer, but her attention was taken by Gertie crying as she saw her brothers and Jack disappearing. She went to attend to the child. Food was always a good way of quietening her and it was almost lunch time. Ah Lo was about somewhere so she put together a glass of goat's milk and heated some leftover vegetables in a pan, with grated cheese on top.

"You take over my job, Missus?" Ah Lo was at the galley door sounding a little put out.

"Absolutely not, Ah Lo. But you have enough to do feeding a hungry crew without adding a small child at all hours." He was becoming almost as protective of his area as Jake Summers. "How are they doing with the repairs to the *Lisette*?"

Ah Lo shrugged. "Not my business."

So much for changing the subject. Emma quickly slid Gertie's food onto a plate.

"I'll just give this pan a quick wipe."

"I do it," Ah Lo said as he stood aside for her to leave. He didn't look at her. Emma wasn't sure if he was embarrassed about his behaviour earlier or annoyed because she had intervened. She heard him bang the pan on the stove top. Just as well the season was ending. Clearly everyone was in need of a break.

When the *Lisette*'s barge, *Georgia*, had been put in place behind the *Owen*, the *Mary B*'s crew returned for lunch. Work was still ongoing on the *Lisette*'s paddle wheel. Jack Macklin and the boys hadn't returned and with lunch ready, Emma had Daniel sound the whistle for them. A few minutes later they emerged from the bush. The boys walked in front, Macklin ambling along behind.

They could have been a family group. Macklin and Henry had the same sturdy build, while Erich was finer, not having grown as much yet. All three were blond, blue eyed, with clear complexions but there was no closer resemblance. Macklin could be mistaken for a German, but he had an English accent. Many Englishmen were blond and blue-eyed, descended as they were from Viking stock. She could understand why Lieutenant Forrester had thought him a worthy subject for suspicion. She was uneasy about him also. Was that simply because she didn't like the man? But there was his proximity to the scene of Hilda's death as well. She wished she knew more about him.

=====

DANIEL GAVE THE *LISETTE* a ten-minute start, before following. He didn't want any danger of running into her turning in circles somewhere ahead. Mallory had said he would be making about four miles an hour against the current at three quarter speed, so Daniel set the *Mary B* to match it.

A little further on from Wee Wee creek they passed the junction of the Wakool River. The Murray changed its character here. From a wide ambling river, it became a narrower stream that wriggled its way through the landscape with sharp bends and swift currents, although the currents weren't such an issue at this time of year. Instead, it was the rocks and hard clay bars that called for careful navigation in the low water levels. This section of the Murray River all the way past Echuca to the Barmah Forrest was a newer channel. Sometime in the distant past a geological upheaval had created this three-hundred-mile southern loop.

Emma, standing on the upper deck gazing out at the countryside, was not thinking about the history of the river or its navigation issues. She needed to talk to someone to make sense of her jumbled thoughts about the

Zellers and Jack Macklin. It was at times like these she missed the female members of her family. In an all-male enclave, conversations were usually short, many subjects simply never raised, and her own opinions not always well received.

Gertie was having her afternoon nap and the boys were somewhere down below, keeping out of mischief she hoped. The crew, whoever was there, could deal with them. She went to the galley and got mugs of tea to take up to the wheelhouse where Fred was keeping Daniel company. They welcomed the tea but when it came down to it, she found she couldn't broach her thoughts about Macklin. They were too nebulous. She left the two men to battle with the charts and the river and took herself to her cabin to dig out her notebook. If she couldn't talk about it, she would write it.

Twenty minutes later Emma looked at the notes she had made. There was little to substantiate a relationship between Macklin and the Zellers. The boys didn't appear to know him. He hadn't been carrying a gun of any sort, much less a pistol or rifle, when picked up by the police. There was nothing to suggest Macklin was of a violent nature and Henry's reluctance to talk about his father weighed heavily on the side of Zac Zeller being the culprit.

Against Jack Macklin was the fact that he was within a few miles of the Zeller's shack when found two days after Hilda's death and was known to have been in the area for some time. There was the matter of money possibly missing from the shack and Macklin having cash money he didn't want to draw attention too. But Zac could have taken any money they had if he were on the run, and Macklin might have tried to hide what he had just to get a free ride.

Emma knew nothing about the man except for what he had said when questioned at the inquest: an Englishman travelling around the colony taking work here and there. Nothing suspicious in that unless he had chanced his hand with Hilda and the situation had turned ugly. He could have thrown away the pistol that killed her, whether it was his or Hilda's. She could have had a weapon of her own, given her occupation.

Emma sighed. You could make up scenarios all day long, but it didn't mean anything without evidence. She put her notebook away and turned her mind to her work. They would reach the Bitch and Pups soon. If they made it safely through, they had another twelve miles of clay bank hazards and rocks before they reached Tooleybuc. They would spend the night there. Towing two barges in the dark was not smart. Daniels' hope of reaching Swan Hill tonight would not be realised.

Gertie woke and she took the child with her up to the wheelhouse for a better view ahead. As the *Mary B* rounded a curving bend, a shepherd's camp was visible, the hurdles still empty but probably not for long. The sheep would already be on their way back at this time of day. The next bend would bring them almost onto the rock shelf that formed the major hazard at the Bitch and Pups.

Daniel sounded the *Mary B*'s whistle. Emma, from her position at the wheelhouse doorway, waited to hear a warning whistle in return, but none came. The *Lisette* had made it safely over. Then they saw her on the far side waiting for them.

"And so she should be," Daniel muttered.

He rang for slow ahead and the *Mary B* floated to the bank where it was quickly made fast. The job now was to manhandle the barges across the rock shelf, the Bitch as it was called, avoiding the smaller rocks around that represented the Pups. Emma marvelled at the imagination of whoever had named the feature. Once the barges were on the other side, the *Mary B* would be taken over and the barges picked up again. There was about two feet of water running over the rocks. Barely enough.

The *Lisette*'s crew trudged up the bank to join them. Ropes were tied to the barges and with all hands to the task, the barges were hauled and coaxed one at a time through the narrow slip. It was heavy work, but an hour later both barges were against the bank on the far side.

"How easily did you get your boat across?" Daniel asked Mallory.

"It was touch and go," Captain Mallory admitted. "But she's bigger and heavier than your tub. Take it steady you shouldn't have a problem."

Daniel nodded. "Well, if I get stuck, we've enough hands to get her off I should think. Either that or I should go full steam and take her over on the wash."

Captain Mallory laughed and Emma got the impression he would like to see that. Emma was sure Sam would have taken it full steam just for the fun of it, necessary or not. Daniel chose the middle option. Not full speed, but faster than he had been travelling with the barges behind. He reversed the *Mary B* to get a run up and then, hands firm on the wheel, legs apart, set her straight at the slip. The boat went over cleanly on a bow wave to a cheer from everyone. The barges were hooked up again and they set off for Tooleybuc following the *Lisette* and breathing a sigh of relief that the worst, they believed, was past.

Chapter Nineteen

THEY REACHED TOOLEYBUC just as the sun was setting, mooring side-on against the bank. Apart from the boats' navigation lights the only other light came from the ferryman's house, an oil lamp glowing at his front door. The crew floated the two barges alongside the *Mary B* and made them fast for the night.

Captain Mallory came over and invited the senior crew to join them for dinner on the *Lisette*. That meant Daniel, herself, and Jake Summers. Emma was tempted to politely refuse the offer. She didn't want to meet up again with Mr. Shankton the *Lisette*'s engineer but decided she wouldn't be churlish. She would just try to ensure she sat further down the table, preferably on the same side.

She gave the children their supper and put Gertie down to sleep, leaving the boys under Fred's supervision. She wasn't intending to be late back tonight in any case. It had been a particularly trying and stressful week. Tomorrow they would reach Swan Hill and her time on the river would be at an end until the water levels rose again.

Present at dinner, apart from their party of three from the *Mary B*, were Captain Mallory, Mr. Shankton, loadmaster Albert Fryling, and three male passengers. Fortunately, the *Lisette*'s engineer was seated several places down near his captain, though Emma did have to suffer a snub as he turned his back on her when she arrived. It must be hurting him to have to be civil to Daniel who was seated opposite on the other side of Captain Mallory.

Emma was a little surprised that she had been included in the invitation as the only woman, but then if he was nothing else the good captain was a gentleman even if his attitude was one of humouring the little ladies. She had decided some time ago that if she were to survive on the river, she couldn't afford to be thin skinned about the attitude of some of the men. Her actions would have to speak for themselves.

It came as something of a surprise, however, when her attitude was put to further test that night. It was while she was enjoying a nice slice of roast beef that Albert Fryling, sitting on her right, asked her how they had come to lose part of the *Owen*'s cargo in the river. She hadn't spoken to him at the time of the event.

"The bargeman was at fault, was he?" Fryling said.

Was he giving her the opportunity to pass the blame?

"Not at all," she replied pleasantly. "Blue Higgins is very experienced, and the load was balanced correctly."

"Really? How did it come to slip in that case?"

"Two of the ties came loose."

"Hmm," he said, swallowing a mouthful. "Careless. If you'll take my advice it is best to check these things every day. Easy to overlook something, let things get a little slack, be too friendly."

For a moment Emma thought she would choke on her food. There wasn't much of a response she could give to such patronising talk. This was a moment when she could have done with her support crew to stand by her, but Daniel was further up the table in conversation with Captain Mallory and there was no one else present who would put in a word for her.

"I'll consider what you say," she said trying to keep the coolness from her voice.

"The crew have a theory about that episode," Jake Summers, who was sitting opposite Fryling, spoke up somewhat grudgingly. Emma looked at him in surprise.

"Really?" said Fryling. "And what, pray, is that?"

"It's reckoned to be a bit of mischief by the young Zeller lad. He may have loosened a couple of the ties."

"Hilda Zeller's boy? And why would he do that?"

"Who knows. Just a boy's mischief. Some think that's the only way them bales could've ended up in the river."

"But it just goes to prove what I was saying about checking the load every day," said Fryling, sounding a bit put out.

"You're quite right," Emma agreed, her spirits somewhat restored. Had she won some grudging respect from Jake Summers with her handling of the confrontation with Ah Lo? "And certainly, when we carry passengers who like to play pranks."

"Is there a problem with them?" Fryling said.

"Henry, the older boy, didn't want to leave the shack but we didn't feel we could leave them there on their own despite his insisting their father would be returning."

"And you didn't think he would be?"

"We didn't know. Still don't, really. He may have returned since."

He sighed and said as if to himself, "She was an attractive woman."

"You knew Hilda, Mr. Fryling?"

He looked startled, as if surprised that he had spoken out loud.

"Ah, well, that is to say..."

He took a gulp of his wine. Emma waited intrigued. Had he made use of her services? As a loadmaster he would have qualified if Jess Sharp's claims were true. She would have liked to ask Mr. Fryling if he thought the rumours had any substance. His reaction if not his answer might settle her mind on the matter. Rumours, she knew, should not be taken at face value. Just look at the one that seemed to be circulating about her relationship with

Daniel. But Mr. Fryling immediately turned to Jake Summers.

"Was the *Mary B*'s towing power increased during the boat's recent refurbishment?" he asked.

"I've no idea on that," Jake told him looking amused. "You would have to ask Mrs. Berry."

"Mr. Summers has only been our engineer since the repairs were completed," Emma explained. She went on to tell them the towing power had increased by twenty percent due to the installation of a more powerful engine. Mr. Fryling thanked her for the information and afterwards concentrated solely on the person seated on his right.

"This woman that was reported murdered, she was killed by her husband?" asked Mr. George, an elderly passenger sitting directly across from Emma and who seemed to have a perpetual worried expression if the wrinkles on his forehead were anything to judge by.

"We don't know," Emma replied. "Certainly, the husband is missing. According to his son he went off after someone in the bush."

"You mean a random killer could be at large?" He looked thoroughly alarmed.

"I don't think people really kill at random, do they?" she asked, intending to calm his mind.

"Oh, I don't know about that," said Colonel Anstey who was sitting on the other side of her. "I've been out in Africa when there was a rogue elephant wrecking villages and killing people, what. Just gone to the bad. Same thing occurs occasionally with men, don't you know."

"Perhaps the elephant felt he had a reason, Colonel," Emma said. "Perhaps he objected to being hunted for his ivory tusks."

"You're supposing they have intelligence, ma'am."

"Well, they must have some level of thought. They take care of their young, protect the weaker members of their group."

"Instinct, that's all that is," said the Colonel.

Emma thought the Colonel's argument went against his own theory of a rogue human being: instinct on the one hand, intelligence on the other. Mr. George was still looking worried.

"The police are on the case, Mr. George," Emma assured him. "And we are many miles from where it happened."

"Killing of any sort is hardly a conversation for a civilised table and with a lady present," he said, with a reproachful glance at her.

That was rich considering he had raised the matter. She wondered what topics of conversation the ladies of his circle engaged in. Knitting patterns and cake recipes, perhaps.

"Murder is so outside the bounds of civilised behaviour it can bring out the worst in us all I'm afraid, Mr. George," she said.

"Very true," agreed the Colonel. "We are on the frontier, here. Life can sometimes come down to the bare bones, you know."

"You would understand that of course as a military man, Colonel," Emma said, attempting to turn the subject.

"I do. Ex India, ma'am, retired. Enjoying a little travel. Do you have any tales about smuggling on the river?" he asked. "Captain Mallory was regaling us with some last night. He told us the one about the little girl who crossed on the punt from Moama to Echuca every day for her violin lessons. After weeks of this some customs officer decided to check the violin case on the way back one day and found it full of food items, butter, and the like. She never was taking violin lessons, don't you know, but gathering her family's dinner, duty free. Hah."

"Wrong will always be found out in the end," Mr. George intoned dismally from across the table. The Colonel harrumphed.

"Well, the customs officers are on the lookout for opium smuggling at the moment," Emma said. "The high customs duty on opium is making it an attractive proposition."

"We must protect ourselves from the Chinese," said Mr. George portentously. "They corrupt all with their heathen ways."

"Doesn't the *Lisette* have a Chinese cook?" Emma asked with feigned innocence.

"Hah. Got you there, Mr. George," said the Colonel. Emma got the impression from Mr. George's sour look that there was no love lost between the two. She was tempted to mention the opium war shamelessly echoing Ah Lo, but the Colonel went on. "Never had any trouble with the Chinese m'self," he said. "Had more to do with the Indian wallahs during my years there. Excitable fellows. Difficult to understand at times, what."

"Are they?" Emma said thinking of Ah Lo's ability to get excited. "I've never met anyone from India. Neighbours down river from my family's pastoral station raise horses for the Indian remount trade. That's about the limit of my knowledge of the country, I'm afraid."

"Do they indeed," said the Colonel. "May have had my leg over one or two of their horses then, ma'am, during my years of service, begging your pardon."

"Quite possible I suppose, Colonel."

"What's the story on this opium smuggling lark, then?" he asked.

"Oh. Well strange to say, the customs officer at Wentworth has caught a commercial traveller with opium made up as small packets of China tea." No need to mention the customs officer was her brother. The Colonel harrumphed again.

"Doesn't seem a very sensible way of moving the stuff," he said. "Having to package and label it, you know. One would have thought some large-scale method would make more sense. Simple matter of efficiency, what."

"I suppose it is," Emma said not having thought on it herself.

Perhaps the commercial traveller Joe had discovered was just a small-time smuggler working for himself for a few extra shillings, smuggling across the South Australian border to Wentworth and disposing of his wares locally.

"Certainly, in my experience," the Colonel was saying. "I know about managing a large group of men who need to be fed three times a day, ma'am. Logistics of scale, that's what it's about. And I've seen opium grown in India. Fields of it. Mark my words, if anyone is smuggling the stuff it won't be in small packets. Simply not economic, what."

"That's very interesting," Emma said and spent the rest of the meal hearing more about his service in India.

When it came time to leave, and despite her best efforts, Mr. Fryling managed to avoid speaking to her by making sure he was in earnest conversation with someone else. It was frustrating but also interesting. He was confirming her suspicion that he might have known Hilda quite well.

As they picked their way along the darkened bank to the *Mary B*, Gertie's distressed cries could be heard. Jake Summers muttered something under his breath and Emma sighed. She wouldn't be getting to bed just yet. Mr. Summers went to his stokehold and she and Daniel went upstairs. Fred was sitting on the top step, an empty glass in his hand. She imagined the crew had helped themselves to more than their single tot tonight.

"How long has she been awake?" Emma asked as Daniel went on to the saloon. She could hear the rest of the crew there playing a noisy game of cards. They were likely the reason Gertie had woken.

"About twenty minutes. Seems a lot longer. I haven't been able to settle her," he said. "She screams worse when I go in there."

"She's missing her mother and doesn't understand what's happening, poor little thing. You should have come and got me." Fred just grunted. "Go off to bed now, Fred. I'll deal with it."

She went to her cabin first for the bottle of cough syrup. In the children's cabin, Gertie had worked herself into a fine state and the boys were awake and bleary eyed. Henry's wary look was back but Erich at least seemed relieved to see her and snuggled back down, turning his back on his sister.

Emma managed to get a spoonful of the syrup into the little girl and then decided to take the child to her own bed. Once there, she quickly undressed and climbed in with Gertie who was already quietening down, the syrup taking effect. She held the little girl to her and the next thing she was conscious of was Jack barking and voices in the early dawn.

Chapter Twenty

"YOU COULD AT LEAST HAVE waited for us to get out of bed before calling in," Emma heard Daniel complain, his voice bleary with sleep.

"And give you time to hide your contraband?" came a voice Emma didn't recognise. "I'm sure given the river conditions you would want an early start in any case. You should be thanking me."

That didn't sound good. The only person who would make a comment such as that was a customs officer. And not a friendly one. Emma's guilty mind flew immediately to the trunk under her bed where she stored the packages of herbal remedies. But no, it was empty. She'd delivered the last order at Meilman Station. They didn't have anything to worry about on that account. She did a quick mental inventory of their cargo; the wool collected from Thandam and Pattin Downs stations and the pile of hides tucked away at the stern with the nanny goat. The cargo list was up to date because it was her job to see to it, but it was always possible to miss some small item.

Emma reached across Gertie's warm body and picked up the little timepiece on the side table. Just on five o'clock. She sighed and untangled herself carefully from Gertie before quickly getting dressed. Outside, the sun was just making an appearance through the trees and a slight mist hung low over the water. It would burn off quickly. The air was already hot. The smell of bacon wafted from the *Lisette*. Someone else was also up early.

Daniel appeared on the deck below with another man. She recognized him immediately. Aubrey Sinclair nicknamed the Weasel by the rivermen. The least popular customs officer in New South Wales. Rumour had it he was transferred regularly from place to place as even many of his fellow officers disliked him and his methods. She would have liked to leave him to Daniel to deal with, but as purser and loadmaster it was her job that would come under scrutiny. May as well get it over with. She went to the saloon and collected the cargo book and bills of lading from the credenza.

"Ah, Mrs. Berry," Albury Sinclair greeted her when she went down. "Has your brother caught those opium smugglers yet?" He was barely her height and had red hair, a long nose, and a supercilious look. She didn't like his tone as if he thought Joe wasn't capable of the job. He no doubt thought it should have been him who got the post. Emma doubted Mr. Sinclair would ever find himself in charge of a customs office.

"You would have to ask him about that, Mr. Sinclair," Emma replied in her best offhand manner. He looked at her for a moment and then turned to Daniel, effectively dismissing her.

"Let's have a look at what's on the barge, Captain."

Daniel held out his hand to Emma for the paperwork and she gladly handed it over. If Mr. Sinclair didn't want to deal with her, she had no objection to leaving Daniel to handle it. She collected a bucket and went to the stern to milk the nanny goat. Jack followed, sitting beside her his head cocked to one side as she worked, the warm jets of milk sounding a rhythmic splurt as they hit the bucket.

"We'll just keep out of his way, eh, Jack," she said. Jack gave a small bark in response and the nanny shifted her leg, hitting the bucket and sending it over as Emma made a futile grab. Milk spilled, soaking into the hay spread over the floor of the pen.

"Drat."

She took the bucket back to the galley to wash out and found Ah Lo blowing on the coals to get his cooking fire going.

"Why everyone early?" he complained. The cook didn't drink so Emma couldn't blame a sore head for his truculence, though he'd probably only missed out on half an hour's extra sleep.

"We've a customs officer on board, Ah Lo. You can blame him for waking us. And there's Gertie awake now and no fresh milk," Emma said as she heard the first wail from her cabin.

"Any chance of a cuppa, Charley?" Shorty, roused by the noise and looking a little the worse for wear, joined her at the galley doorway.

"Too early. Fire just start," Ah Lo replied.

Emma left them waiting for the kettle to boil and went to attend to Gertie. When she came out of her cabin with the little girl, Aubrey Sinclair was making a big thing out of counting the wool bales on the *Owen*. Good luck with that. Daniel stood on the *Mary B* arms folded, waiting not all that patiently she imagined. Blue and Willy had surfaced, and the three crewmen were hanging about waiting for a restorative cup of tea.

"I'd kill for a bit o' bacon and bread," Shorty muttered, as the smell of bacon cooking continued to waft temptingly from the *Lisette*.

Willy just grunted. He was standing but his eyes were closed. Emma shook her head at the folly of men and went to fetch the jug of powdered milk from behind the paddle box. She dipped the sack over the side to wet it again before taking up the jug and covering the rest of the food items.

She didn't know how long it would be before they were on their way. She had a feeling Mr. Sinclair was going to be very thorough. Gertie gulped down her milk and Emma wiped the white moustache from the child's upper lip. The action seemed to trigger something as the little girl began to cry. Emma crooned and smoothed her head, but it was the biscuit Ah Lo gave her that eventually soothed her cries.

Daniel strode past them to the front of the boat at that moment and shouted across to the *Lisette* for Captain Mallory. Emma wandered after him.

The *Lisette*'s cook stuck his head out of the galley.

"He eat breakfast. No disturb."

"That's fine with me. I'll just leave his barge behind here in charge of the customs officer."

Mr. Fryling appeared at the saloon doorway. "What's the problem, Captain?"

"Customs Officer Sinclair would like the paperwork for your barge cargo, Mr. Fryling."

"Ah." Mr. Fryling glanced at Emma standing off to the side. She could almost see his mind working. As loadmaster for the *Lisette*, he would have to board the *Mary B* now and run the risk of encountering her. She didn't hear it, but she was sure he sighed. "Very well, I'll handle it."

"The paperwork for the wool was in order, wasn't it?" Emma asked.

"You know it was," Daniel replied.

"Well, you never can tell with someone like Sinclair," she said. "I might not have dotted an 'i' somewhere."

"He's going to search the whole boat, you know. You haven't any more of those herbals around have you?"

"Nothing except what we use ourselves."

"We should be all right then. The sooner it's done the sooner we can get on. At least Sinclair is dealing with us first. We can leave Mallory to his own devices today."

"Aren't we taking his barge on, then?"

"Oh yes, I'll do that, but I'm not waiting for him. If his repair held to get him here it should hold til Swan Hill."

Emma thought Daniel must be really fed up if he was planning to abandon the *Lisette*. It wasn't like him.

"Tea's up," Ah Lo sang out.

Daniel grabbed a cup as Mr. Fryling came on board. The *Lisette*'s loadmaster nodded to Emma and immediately turned his attention to Daniel. That was the second time this morning she had been dismissed.

"Tea?" offered Daniel.

Mr. Fryling shook his head. "Just finished breakfast, thanks," he replied.

"You were up early," Emma heard Daniel comment as the two of them made their way along the *Mary B*'s deck.

Emma didn't hear what Mr. Fryling had to say but she imagined Captain Mallory was eager for the *Mary B* to travel behind him as backup in case his repair didn't hold. She put Gertie on the foredeck in her harness with a slice of bread and butter and Jack for company. The dog would probably get a share of the bread but it hardly mattered if the child were happy.

She wanted to catch Mr. Fryling before he left. If, as she half suspected, he would try and leave the *Mary B* by coming down the starboard side to avoid the galley area she would need to lay in wait for him there. It would also be a more private spot for the conversation she wanted to have.

At least she had hoped it would be. Erich came scurrying down the stairs on his way to the bathroom. She wondered if all little boys found that such an urgent errand first thing in the morning. When he came out, she sent him to ask Ah Lo for some bread and butter for himself promising a more filling breakfast shortly. Then it was Henry's turn though at a more leisurely pace. Neither boy returned from the galley. Soon the smell of mutton chops and fried potatoes told her that Ah Lo was well on the way with breakfast. A riverboat crew didn't travel on toast and jam.

And there was Mr. Fryling coming down the starboard deck as expected. She stepped out preventing him getting to the boarding plank.

"Mr. Fryling. A quiet word if you please."

He stopped dismay evident. "I'm rather busy, Mrs. Berry. If you wouldn't mind." He took a step as if to go on, but she didn't move. "Ma'am."

"I'm sorry Mr. Fryling but it is important, or I wouldn't be bothering you. You've no doubt heard by now what Jess Sharp said about Hilda Zeller at the inquest? The rumours?"

He stiffened and turned his head to stare out at the landscape. From the side view of his face Emma could see his jaw tighten, the strain of some emotion he was trying to contain. Was it simply distaste for the subject matter, something that was hardly a topic of conversation between a man and a woman who barely knew each other, or an indication of something stronger?

"Mr. Fryling," she said gently. "I considered Hilda a friend and I'm concerned about the manner of her death, that is all. Please. I need to know. Was it true…what Jess Sharp said about her?"

He struggled with his feelings for a moment longer. "She wasn't free with her favours," he finally spat out, anger seeming predominant. "Sharp had no right to vilify her."

"I don't understand. Did he lie then?"

Mr. Fryling turned his head and glared at her. "No, he didn't lie." The words came out through gritted teeth. "But he had no right, no right…"

"I'm sorry." He seemed to have felt strongly about Hilda. "Is there anything you can tell me that might help discover who killed her?"

"It had to have been her husband, hadn't it? She did say she would be leaving the place soon. He must have objected."

"She was going on holiday."

"A holiday? No, she was leaving for good. Returning to her family in Germany, I understood. A woman like that should never have been living in those conditions."

"Mr. Fryling." Captain Mallory's voice pierced the air. "When you are quite ready."

Emma looked round to see the *Lisette*'s captain looking down on them from his upper deck. She sighed as Mr. Fryling brushed past her and off the *Mary B*. Hilda's transactions may have been of a monetary nature but at least one of her clients had parted with more than coin. If what he said was correct, it confirmed the suspicions of several people that Hilda had no intention of returning to the timber lease. It gave Zac a strong motive.

"There you are," Daniel said, coming around from the front of the boat. "Sinclair is ready to look through the cabins. You might want to be there for your own at least."

Emma followed the two men to the upper deck and along to the wheelhouse. She and Daniel watched as Sinclair tapped the timber panelling of the walls and searched the shelves where the charts were stored. When he pulled a small screwdriver from his jacket pocket and began to remove the shelf, Emma found herself reliving the last moment she had seen Sam alive.

She turned away, her throat tightening and caught a look of understanding from Daniel. She stared out across the river and drew in a deep breath to calm herself. She would not shed tears in front of Sinclair. He would probably take it as fear of what he might find and tear the *Mary B* apart from bow to stern to discover the cause. That thought lightened her mood in a grim way and chased away the threat of tears.

Finding nothing in the shelf cavity, Sinclair moved on to the saloon.

"Are you looking for anything in particular, Sinclair?" Daniel asked boredom evident.

"We've had a report of opium being disguised in packets of China tea," the customs officer said absently, his head in the credenza.

"Really? Where did the report come from?" Emma asked in all innocence.

"That's confidential information."

"Probably just a one-man affair," Emma said sotto voce to Daniel. "Colonel Anstey said last night it wouldn't be economic to move opium in such small amounts. He was in India where most of the opium is grown and he has experience in large scale economies."

"Indeed?" Daniel said catching her mood. "You'd think the customs men would realise that then, wouldn't you?"

"I would have thought so."

Mr. Sinclair's ears were turning red. "Your brother thought fit to pass the information down the line," he said.

"Well, he would have to make the report, wouldn't he? I don't suppose he expected anyone to take it up along the river. Riverboats buy their tea in bulk. I mean, a titchy packet wouldn't last more than five minutes among a crew."

"But it isn't tea that's in the packets." Sinclair was getting upset.

"So why would we buy it?" Daniel asked. Emma stifled a snort of laughter.

"I'll take your cabins, next," Sinclair said his face now matching the colour of his ears. He started with Emma's room. After a quick search through her drawers she thought his face was even redder if that was possible. Then he turned his attention to her bunk.

"Well, what do we have here?" he asked, a note of triumph in his voice as he pulled the trunk from beneath it, a triumph quickly quelled when he saw it was empty.

"What was in this?" he demanded glaring at Emma.

"Food," Emma replied, crossing her fingers behind her back. "Of course, we've eaten it all now.'

Mr. Sinclair sniffed inside the trunk. "There's a..." sniff, "...flowery smell."

"I used to keep clothes in it with some lavender sachets. Keeps the moths away, you know."

"You said you kept food in it lately. It doesn't smell of food."

"Of course not. It wasn't fresh food. Preserves mostly. In jars."

He gave her a look that clearly said he didn't believe her but there was nothing he could do about it without evidence. He repeated the process in the children's cabin, poking about under the bed and pawing through their poor bag of clothes. He picked out the book of Hilda's that Emma had given Henry to take when they left the shack.

"Please don't do that, you'll break the spine," Emma told him sharply as he bent back the covers and shook the little book to make its leaves flutter. "It's all the children have of their mother's."

"Hmph." He dropped the book back in the bag.

Daniel and Emma followed him around the upper deck to the cabins on the starboard side. Mr. Macklin was still in bed when Mr. Sinclair opened his door. Emma stepped away, modesty prevailing.

"Wha – what's going on?" she heard Macklin ask blearily. "Who are you?"

"Customs inspection," Sinclair informed him stepping in. "I need to look in your bag."

"You'll do nothing of the damned sort." There was the sound of a scuffle and Mr. Sinclair was projected out of the cabin his jacket askew. He was about to dash back in when Daniel grabbed his arm.

"He's still on the river, Sinclair. He hasn't landed anything yet and he'll be checked when he does. I've been accommodating up to now, but another show of force and you'll be off my boat and I'll be lodging a complaint. There's no need for this behaviour."

Sinclair pulled his arm from Daniel's grasp and shrugged his jacket straight, glaring between Daniel and Macklin, who had come to his cabin doorway. Emma could just make out that the man was wearing very little and turned her back.

"I'll look over the lower deck," she heard Sinclair say followed by the sound of Macklin's cabin door slamming shut. She wished she could have seen Sinclair go through Macklin's bag. She might have learnt something about him.

The three of them trooped down the stairs, Sinclair in the lead. Below, the crew were standing and sitting about the galley drinking tea, eating breakfast and yarning.

"What's this?" Jake Summers demanded when the little party stopped at his stokehold.

"Custom's inspection," Sinclair informed him. "I'll be checking everything down here. Nothing to worry about unless you're carrying contraband." He stepped inside.

"Here, hold up," Jake demanded stepping past him and blocking his progress. "Capt'n?" he appealed to Daniel.

Daniel shrugged. "He has the right. Sooner done the sooner we can be rid of him."

There was no longer any pretence at cordiality. Jake Summers did not look happy at his captain's response. He stood, breakfast plate in one hand fork clutched like a weapon in the other, eyes glaring in his ruddy face. Emma heard the rest of the crew assembling behind her interested no doubt in some entertainment.

"Don't go touching this here engine," Jake Summers said. "No one touches this engine bar me."

Sinclair bristled and stared at the machinery, at the fan wheel, the rudder chains, the boiler with its fire box, the fire just getting worked up. He peered around and behind, up and down, looking in every corner and crevice. The engine and its immediate surroundings were spotless. There was nowhere to hide anything.

He looked back at Jake Summers as if assessing the man, and then around the stokehold, his eyes roving over the bedding leaning against the back wall, a shelf above holding a photograph and a shaving mug and several books. He moved closer, peering at the bedding.

"Why do you have two mattresses?" he asked.

"I likes a soft mattress. The one they give me here was hard," Jake Summers told him moving to stand in front of the offending items.

Sinclair reached past him and poked at the mattresses. "Where did you get this one?" his hand on the one at the back the fatter of the two.

"Had it for years," Jake Summers blustered. "Brought it on board when I joined this boat."

Emma, standing just outside the stokehold with Daniel remembered what Shorty had said about Mr. Summers getting a new mattress in Wentworth. Surely not. He wouldn't be that stupid. Would he?

"What's going on?" Blue asked from the back of the group.

"Mr. Summers is gettin' his new mattress inspected," Shorty said.

"Uh oh."

"What do you know about this?" Emma asked sharply turning to Blue who flushed almost as red as his hair under her scrutiny.

"Just speculation," Fred answered for him. They could be like a music hall chorus sometimes.

Emma turned back in time to see Sinclair pull the older mattress away and peer between the two. "Looks mighty new to me. Fresh clean cloth. No hollows. Doesn't look as if it's ever been slept on." He prodded at it then pulled a pen knife from his pocket and flicked it open. Jake

Summers dropped the fork he had been holding and grabbed Sinclair's wrist forcing him to drop the knife.

"Don't you pull a knife on me, you mongrel."

"That what he call me, mongrel dog," Ah Lo growled from behind. Some things died hard.

"Sinclair, what do you think you're doing?" Daniel stepped into the stokehold. "I warned you. No violence."

"I want to see what's inside this mattress. I need to cut it open. And there'll be a charge for assault in any case. You need to have better control of your men, Berry."

"You'll ruin a perfectly good mattress, man," Jake complained still holding Sinclair's arm. "You going to compensate me for that?"

"Only if I'm wrong."

Jake Summers glared between Sinclair and Daniel for a moment as if assessing his options, then pushed Sinclair from him and stormed out of the stokehold his breakfast going flying in the process.

"Hiee," cried Ah Lo as Summers pushed by. "That man nothing but trouble."

"Don't let him get away. I want to talk to him," Sinclair shouted but no one moved. Emma felt the *Mary B* rock slightly as Mr. Summers hit the boarding plank. If he wasn't guilty of any wrongdoing he was certainly acting as if he was.

Inside the stokehold Sinclair retrieved his penknife. He cut along the top edge of the mattress, slicing through the outside fabric and then a layer of muslin-covered flock padding. He put his hand in through the cut and withdrew it holding something. When he opened his hand tiny grey/blue and brown seeds fell in a fine shower to the stokehold floor.

"Opium. Dried opium," he announced triumphantly. "What do you say now, Captain?"

Chapter Twenty-One

"WELL, WELL, WHO WOULD have thought. The *Mary B* smuggling opium." Sinclair was gloating as he finished his paperwork in the saloon with Daniel and Emma present as the *Mary B*'s owners.

"Unbeknown to us," Daniel replied roughly clearly annoyed at the embarrassment Jake Summers had caused them.

"So you say, so you say. And out of Wentworth, too. I wonder how your brother will feel about that, Mrs. Berry, when he hears it. Loaded under his very nose so to speak. Makes those – what did you call them – titchy packets? Makes them look like small fry now, don't it?"

There was nothing Emma could say to that. The worm had turned, and it rankled.

"Well, now," he went on, "what are we going to do with the contraband?" He sat back and looked thoughtful. "I could have it taken on to Swan Hill, but that would be awkward. I can't transport it on horseback. If I leave it on board without being present, there's no guarantee it will reach its destination."

"I beg your pardon?" Daniel glared at the man. "What do you think we would do with it?"

"It's anyone's guess, isn't it? You've had a smuggler in your crew without knowing. So you say."

Daniel smacked his fist on the table and Sinclair almost tipped himself backwards out of his chair.

"You accuse me of anything again and you and that damn mattress will find yourselves in the river. Do you hear?"

"I'm not accusing you of anything," Sinclair spluttered, looking decidedly paler than usual.

"You had better not be."

"In any case," Sinclair went on gathering himself, "the contraband will be destroyed when it gets to Swan Hill. We may as well do that here. Save the trouble and have ourselves a nice little bonfire."

"There is no 'we' in any of this, Sinclair," Daniel told him in no uncertain manner.

"You're going to burn the mattress?" Emma asked. All that opium going up in, well, smoke.

"Simplest way to handle it," Sinclair said. "In the meantime, I still have to pay a visit to the *Lisette*. Put the mattress out on the bank, Captain. I will set it alight and let it burn while I get on with that. Save myself some time."

"You intend to burn it while we are moored here?" Emma asked in amazement before Daniel could respond. Was the man mad? "You'll have us all asleep within the hour with the smoke. Yourself included, most likely." Sinclair stared at her. "You do realise how much smoke that much opium is going to produce? It could smoulder for hours."

"Well..."

"You'll wait until we've left before doing anything," Daniel told him. "The mattress will stay where it is until we are ready to go."

"You can't tell me..."

"I can and I will. This is still my boat. Take it or leave it."

"I could impound your boat, Berry, charge you with smuggling that opium."

Daniel got to his feet and loomed over Sinclair. "I'd like to see you try."

Sinclair grabbed up his paperwork and his hat. "That mattress had better be out on the bank before you leave or you'll find the police waiting for you at Swan Hill," he shot back as he scuttled out of the saloon.

"I thought for one dreadful moment we were going to have his company all the way to Swan Hill," Emma said with a weak laugh. Daniel smacked his fist on the table again. "Calm down," she said quietly. "I know he's irritating but we'll just be inviting trouble if we do anything to the man. He's not one to let something like that go."

"I'd like to see if he could swim," Daniel growled.

"The river's not deep enough for him to need to at the moment."

"Oh, I'd find a deep enough hole, don't you worry about that."

She was sure he could just as she was sure he wouldn't. That might have been something Sam would have done, but not Daniel. She giggled.

"What?"

"I'm just picturing Sinclair overcome by the smoke from his bonfire. It would almost be worth waiting across the river to see it."

"You'll have to imagine it, I'm afraid," Daniel said. "The sooner we leave him behind the better."

"I guess, but I can dream. Do you suppose Knowles knew anything about this smuggling? Perhaps he's getting a cut of the profit. They could be in it together."

"Capt'n?" came a whispered voice. Emma spun round as Jake Summers crept into the saloon. "Can you pay me off, Capt'n? I'll make me own way."

Daniel took a step toward him. "Damn you, Summers. Have you any idea the damage you've caused us? I've a good mind to hand you over to Sinclair and let you sweat for it."

"I'm already out of pocket for the opium, I can't afford to pay a fine as well," Summers argued sullenly. "A hundred pounds it is. I'd be working the rest of my life to pay it off."

Daniel snorted with disgust. "And you're leaving us without an engineer."

"Croaker can do it," Summers said, referring to Fred. "Just tell him to take care with the regulator. It's a bit stiff. You'll need to get that looked at before next season."

"That's as may be. He can't fix the engine if it breaks down. What on earth made you think you could get away with this?"

Jake Summers shrugged. "It's hard getting enough work during the off season. Just got unlucky this time."

"This time?" Emma said, the words coming of their own volition, her voice sounding higher pitched even to her ears.

"It worked okay the last two trips."

Emma stared at him open-mouthed. "Are you saying the *Mary B* has been smuggling opium for the past two months?" How could she not have suspected something?

"You'd better not let that get around, Summers," Daniel told him. "And don't bother trying to get any work on the river again. I'll be warning off any skipper you apply to. Not that it will be safe for you on the river in any case. You don't imagine Sinclair is going to let this lie, do you? He'll have the police put out a warrant for you. He'll want to get that fine paid or have you do time for it."

Jake Summers bridled at that. "What am I supposed to do for work?"

"I don't care. You're a liability on the river and a liability to yourself from what I can see." Daniel went to the credenza and pulled out a notebook. He consulted it for moment. "Here," he said, writing out a cheque. "Here's your wages to date. Now get off my boat."

Jake looked at the cheque. "Hey, this is a few pounds short."

"You might have signed on for the season, Summers, but you can't expect to be paid for the time you aren't here, I hope?" Summers stuffed the cheque into his vest pocket, the sullen look back. "I wouldn't complain too much about the way we're treating you," Daniel said a warning note in his voice. "I've good cause not to pay you anything."

"Nah, can't say I can," he admitted. "Seen worse." Emma remembered his reluctant defence of her to Mr. Fryling last night at dinner. He seemed to have his own version of honesty. Anyone who had a soft spot for a Jack Russell couldn't be all bad, she supposed.

"I'll just slip down and get my bag," Summers said opening the saloon door on the starboard side and peering out. Next moment he was gone the door left swinging, his rapid footsteps disappearing along the deck and down the stairs.

A few minutes later a shout went up. Aubrey Sinclair had spotted him from the *Lisette*. Emma and Daniel watched from the saloon window as Jake Summers headed for the safety of the bush. No one went in pursuit. The only one who cared about catching him was the customs officer.

Emma followed Daniel down to the lower deck. She'd been neglecting the children this morning. Not that she need have worried. The crew were watching the play with Jack and Gertie who were rolling together on the deck.

"Ack," Gertie cried laughing as Jack licked her face. That dog had a sixth sense of where he was needed.

"How are we doing Capt'n?" Fred broached the question, cup of tea poised for a sip.

"Well, we're down an engineer, Fred," Daniel replied. "I'm going to have to rely on you to do the honours. Summers said to tell you the regulator is a bit stiff."

"I know it," Fred said.

"The customs bloke didn't get him then," observed Shorty. "You gotta hand it to him. Opium in a mattress. Not a bad dodge." There were heads nodding all round.

"Just as long as no one else gets the idea to try something similar," Daniel said a warning note in his voice. "Otherwise you'll end up like Summers, on the run, out of home and out of work. Though I would be sorely tempted to put the next person who pulls a trick like that in the hands of the customs. You've been warned."

"Aye, Capt'n," came the sober chorus.

"Don't expect any leniency from me, either," Emma said in answer to a look from Shorty. "I am in perfect agreement with the Captain."

She hadn't forgotten that they had been suspicious of Jake Summers' new mattress – apparently the third in several months – and not a word said. They were like a bunch of men playing at boys. Or was that boys playing at men? She wasn't sure.

Underneath her annoyance was the niggling thought that she should have seen the engineer bringing in those new mattresses. He must have been careful enough to do it when she was engaged elsewhere but that didn't help her feeling that she was missing things she shouldn't. She had handled the Summers-Ah Lo confrontation neatly, though. She would have to remind herself of that success even if Daniel had issues with her about it.

"I hope that mattress is still in the stokehold?" Daniel wanted to know.

"Aye, it is," Fred replied. "You want I should move it?"

"Not yet. We're off loading it before we leave. Sinclair is going to burn it here."

"Oh ho," Shorty chortled. "I'd like to see that. He'll have the birds falling out of the sky."

She saw Aubrey Sinclair leave the *Lisette* and make his way to the ferryman's cottage. As soon as he was out of earshot, Captain Mallory appeared at the *Mary B*'s boarding plank. With him were his two bargemen.

"How did your inspection go?" Daniel asked.

"Better than yours I hear, Berry," Captain Mallory as his bargemen came aboard and went immediately to clamber across to the *Georgia* lashed alongside the *Owen*. "Dashed bad luck if you ask me. I do appreciate your help with the barge, Berry. We'll see you later today at Swan Hill, all going well."

He left and minutes later the *Lisette* pulled out from the bank with a blast of its whistle. So much for the *Mary B* leaving first. It would take a little time for the barges to get into position.

"He's very affable this morning," Emma commented.

"Feeling relieved to be given a clean bill of health by our customs officer I should imagine. Where is the man anyway?"

"I saw him go to the ferryman's cottage. Perhaps he needs to borrow some matches."

"More likely cadging a cup of tea and some breakfast. He knew better than to ask for it here."

"Ready when you are, Capt'n," Fred called to Daniel from the stokehold doorway. "Steam's up."

"Right. Shorty get that mattress out onto the bank now," Daniel said and headed up to the wheelhouse taking the stairs two at a time.

"You'd better give him a hand, Willy," Emma said, "and then cast of at once."

"Aye, Boss."

"Henry, Erich," Emma said, addressing the boys, "take Gertie up to the saloon. We'll be leaving in a few minutes."

She didn't allow them to stay on deck during the cast off in case they got in the way. Henry picked up his sister and followed by Erich, went up the stairs. Emma checked the barges as they floated back on the current behind the

Mary B, the *Lisette*'s barge tapping the bank behind the *Owen*. The river was too low and the channel too narrow for towing in tandem.

A long loud note sounded on the horn sending the magpies into the air from the trees. Mr. Sinclair appeared hurriedly from the ferryman's cottage, a can of something in his hand. Kerosene perhaps? He waved. He'd seen the mattress left on the bank. Emma still considered it the height of stupidity to be burning the mattress here.

"All clear, Captain," Emma called up to the wheelhouse. A signal sounded down to the stokehold and the *Mary B* moved smoothly out into the river. Emma watched to see the barges safely follow at the end of the towing ropes. The thrum of the engine vibrated through her feet.

Back on the bank she saw Sinclair begin to splash kerosene over the mattress. She hoped the combination of kerosene and opium wouldn't prove lethal to anything. Now he was bending over poking at the mattress. Now he was shaking his fist at the *Mary B* and jumping around as if his tail was on fire.

She heard a noise behind her and turned to see Shorty bent double and shaking. Was everyone going mad? She looked back to the bank and caught a last glimpse of Sinclair waving his arms wildly before the trees blocked her view.

"Oh, my goodness. You didn't. Tell me you didn't," Emma said as realisation dawned. She hadn't watched Shorty and Willy unload the mattress being concerned with keeping an eye on the barges.

Shorty nodded. "Wrong mattress," he spluttered.

Emma put her hand to her mouth. There would be repercussions she knew, but it was funny.

"Shorty Mason, you'll be the death of us," she said eventually. "What on earth are we going to do with a mattress full of opium?"

"No idea, Boss," he said, swiping his hand across his eyes.

"I'm going to have to tell the Captain, you realise that?"

"It was his idea, Boss."

Emma stared and then shook her head in wonder. Daniel really was stretching his wings. She went up to the saloon to the children.

"We'll be at Swan Hill later today," she told them. "And tomorrow we'll get someone to take us to Kerang to your Uncle and Aunt's farm."

"Tomorrow?" Henry said, as if he found it sooner than expected.

"Do you know how to get there?" Erich asked eagerly.

"Not yet, but I'm sure someone will be able to tell us. The police perhaps."

"Why do you want to talk to the police?" asked Henry. "I know where the farm is."

"You remember the way? Well, that's good." She would check anyway. She hoped someone from the livery stable or a carter would be able to take them tomorrow, otherwise they might have to spend an extra night in the town.

"Going to Uncle's farm. Going to Uncle's farm," Erich chanted, jigging up and down on the bed.

Henry opened his mouth as if to tell his brother to be quiet but shut it again when Emma looked at him. He didn't seem as excited about seeing his Aunt and Uncle as Erich obviously was. Instead he looked worried. Did he think they wouldn't be welcome?

The boys went down to the lower deck and Emma went along to the wheelhouse Gertie on her hip. Shorty was sitting in the corner. He grinned at her.

"That was amusing, Daniel," Emma said, "but you've made an enemy there, and I'm not sure what you expect to gain from it."

Daniel chuckled. "Made me feel better," he said giving the wheel a turn as he negotiated past a sandbank. "I didn't like the idea of all that opium being burnt there on the river. Seemed a pretty stupid thing to be doing all told."

"My thoughts exactly. It will cost us a new mattress though," Emma pointed out. She stood Gertie on the chart shelf and held her so she could see out the window. "Ook," the child pointed to the birds rising in front of the boat and clapped her hands. A bark at the doorway announced Jack agreeing with her.

"It was worth it," Daniel said. "I'll hand the opium in at Swan Hill and I'll make a report about Sinclair at Echuca. Not my fault a crewman unloaded the wrong mattress. He wasn't to know which one it was."

"I'm just a dumb ole deckhand," Shorty agreed mournfully.

"Uhuh."

Chapter Twenty-Two

EMMA LEFT DANIEL AND SHORTY in the wheelhouse. Shorty was telling stories in between helping on the sharp bends. She could understand why Daniel preferred Fred or Willy's quiet presence. They had passed the wreck of the barge Eileen stranded on a wide bend, its planks rotting, and eased around Murphy's Island, when a warning whistle sounded up ahead. They had caught up to the *Lisette* limping along, her damaged paddle obviously giving trouble.

Daniel rang down for reduced speed and they followed the *Lisette* at a distance. The time seemed to drag with their destination so close. It would have been faster to walk. The boys became bored with fishing, neither of them having caught anything, and had become argumentative. Even Jack had deserted them, sitting by the stokehold instead.

Emma sent Henry up to their cabin to get the book she had given him at the shack and had him read aloud to Erich for an hour. The book was in German, so she didn't understand a word of it but was happy to listen to the sounds. Gertie seemed to find the sounds comforting too and at least it kept the boys from fighting for a while.

"I'm hungry," Erich said in the middle of a story. Emma wondered if there had been something in there about food.

"I suppose it's time for morning tea. You did have breakfast rather early."

"Good," Henry said relieved, closing the book.

The change from German to English was noticeable. Neither boy had a pronounced accent, unlike their parents.

"You both speak English very well. Had you learnt English before coming to the colonies?"

"Everyone in England speaks English," Henry said as if Emma was being especially obtuse. "I'll just go put the book away." He pounded off up the stairs.

It took a moment for Emma to register what he had said. She was reminded of Claude Devereaux who she had met more than two years ago in connection with another murder. A Frenchman who had grown up in England and spoke both languages fluently. Why had Hilda never spoken of England? Could England be the connection with Jack Macklin?

======

EMMA WANDERED RESTLESSLY. She had tried reading in the saloon with Gertie playing around, but her concentration kept wandering. Now, standing on the upper deck Gertie in her arms, she was aware that they had almost reached Merrim Station. They weren't stopping there which was just as well. Mr. Fraser, never the friendliest, didn't welcome the *Mary B* after Emma had found alternative employment for his housekeeper and stable hand. They might have visited Sam's grave, but she doubted Daniel wanted to stop even for that today.

She hadn't seen Macklin since he had ejected the customs officer from his cabin. She went further along the deck. There he was below, leaning on the railing near the bow surveying the view, cigarette smoke drifting up around him. Ah Lo was poking his head out the galley doorway every now and then saying something to Fred. She couldn't see the entry to the stokehold from where she stood, but she could picture Fred leaning in the opening, one eye on the engine gauges. If she were going to do anything about checking up on Macklin now could be the only chance she would get, but she had to take care of Gertie first.

She hurried down to the lower deck, not giving herself time to think. She found the boys at the stern, fishing lines in the water again with Willy sitting nearby. She put Gertie in her harness and tasked Henry with looking after her for a time. Jack immediately went to the child licking her face. Emma stopped at the galley and collected a cup of tea from Ah Lo.

"I need to sort out the paperwork. Mr. Sinclair left it in a mess," Emma said to Fred as she passed.

He looked at her oddly, or perhaps it was just her guilty conscience. She needn't have said anything. Macklin still stood at the bow seemingly lost in his own thoughts. Back upstairs, Emma quickly spread some papers out on the table beside her cup of tea. Anyone who came looking for her would think she had just stepped out for a moment. She took one last look at Macklin through the saloon window. He hadn't moved. She slipped out the door on the far side. There was no one to see her but the ever-present eucalypts lining the riverbank and several ibis wading in the shallows.

Quickly along the deck to Macklin's cabin, a quick look either way and in she went heart thumping. If he came back while she was here, she had no excuse. She'd thought of bringing a broom and pan and pretending to be sweeping but had decided it was just as easy not to be encumbered with anything. She doubted he would believe her in any case.

She couldn't see the bag. Surely, he didn't have it with him. It wasn't under the bed. She tried the cupboard. There it was tucked in the corner under the shelf. Grabbing it out she dropped it onto the bed and undid the buckle fastening the strap, her fingers fumbling. There were two shirts, one clean, one not so, a pair of trousers, two neckerchiefs, and a change of long johns which she didn't touch. She put the clothes aside quickly on the bed. No need to dwell on them. She pulled out a nice leather pouch and found inside a shaving kit and a gold pocket watch. Expensive. Had that been honestly come by? She put the pouch on top of the clothes and dived back into the bag. A dog-eared copy of Henry Kendall's Poems and Songs came next to hand. Beneath was a scatter of coins and a pocketknife.

She jumped at the sound of the *Mary B*'s horn, sending her heart into her throat. She shouldn't be here. What did she think she was doing snooping in a passenger's belongings? Daniel would be furious if he knew. He would ban her from the *Mary B* forever. And for nothing. She grabbed at the leather pouch about to pack everything away again. And stopped. There was a wedge of folded paper in the corner amongst the coins. It looked as if it had been crushed. She couldn't pass up seeing what it was.

Her fingers were all thumbs in her haste to unfold it, her ears attuned for any sound outside though she was afraid she mightn't hear someone creeping up quietly over the noise of the engine. That thought didn't help her nerves either. She struggled to open the sheet of paper without tearing. How had it gotten into this state? She could see a government crest and coaxed the paper further apart.

It was a notice of discharge from Melbourne Gaol. One Joseph Heinrich Paulsmire discharged after serving four years for manslaughter. Manslaughter. They had an ex-convict on board travelling under an assumed name. Why would he do that unless he had something to hide? And he was German despite his English accent. The coincidence was too much. But what was the connection?

Emma's hands shook as she tried to fold the paper the way it had been but was only partly successful. If he looked at it at all, Macklin...Paulsmire...would be able to tell it had been opened. She could only hope he would have no reason to do so. Lieutenant Forrester can't have seen this. Had the man hidden it in his boot? It would account for its condition. She tossed the book and the leather pouch back into the bag and packed the clothes in on top, hoping they were as close as possible to the way they had been.

With the bag safely back in the closet she stood for a moment with her hand on the cabin door. Heart thumping, she took a deep breath and opened it slowly. All clear. She slipped out closing the door quietly behind her. She managed to restrain herself from running along the deck to the saloon. She wasn't cut out to be a burglar. She opened the saloon door and started, her hand flying to her chest. Erich was standing in the saloon.

"What is it?" she asked more sharply than intended.

"Jack bit Gertie," he said taking a step back. Thoughts of blood and infection immediately filled Emma's mind.

"Is it bad?" she asked as she followed him out. She could hear Gertie's cries now.

"I don't know. Henry smacked him."

"Before or after he bit Gertie?"

"After." They had reached the bottom of the stairs.

"Nice biskit," Ah Lo was saying trying to temp the child but Gertie wasn't having anything to do with it. "It not bad, Missus. No blood," he said when he saw Emma. "I not know what happen. I busy in galley."

"It's not your responsibility, Ah Lo. Thanks for trying to help." She knelt beside Gertie who was sitting on the deck. "Here, now. Let me have a look." She took the hand that the child was holding out. There was a red mark on one finger, but no skin broken. "Let me just kiss it better," she soothed. "There, it's better now." Gertie's cries quietened as she examined the spot. "Jack, come here." The dog was sitting a little way off out of reach. "Come on." He came slowly. Emma let him come right up before she reached out and patted his head.

"There, Jack didn't mean to hurt you. Did you grab Jack too hard? Did you frighten him?" she asked.

"He shouldn't have bit her," Henry put in.

"No, but it was just a nip, Henry. No harm done. I think Gertie might have been a bit rough with him, that's all."

"I'll whack him harder next time," Henry promised with relish.

Emma hadn't thought about whether Jack would go with the children when they left but she decided now. If she had a choice in the matter, he would stay on the *Mary B*. Whether Jack agreed was something still to be discovered.

Thinking it might be best if they had some time apart, she picked up Gertie to take her to the saloon. This time the child was happy to accept the biscuit from Ah Lo. As Emma reached the stairs, she came face to face with Macklin. She hadn't realised how cold his blue eyes were. She turned quickly, feeling her face flush, and all but stumbled at the bottom step. His hand, warm, gripped her arm and she flinched.

"Steady. You don't want to trip now ma'am, not with the child."

Emma steadied herself not looking at him. "Thank you, Mr. M-Macklin." Oh, lordy. She couldn't even say his name properly. "Clearly I wasn't paying attention to what I was doing."

He let go of her arm. "I startled you."

"No, no. It was my own fault. Thank you," she said again. She forced herself to ascend the stairs slowly, one hand holding Gertie on her hip while at the same time gripping her skirt to keep from tripping and not expose too much ankle, her other hand steadying herself on the stair rail. It wasn't the most elegant way to traverse the steep stairs. The hairs on her neck prickled as she imagined him watching her, but at the top she saw from the corner of her eye he was gone.

He must be heading back to his cabin. He would be checking his bag and finding some telltale sign that someone had opened it. He would realise that she was the only one who could have been there. He would put two and two together and know the reason for her confusion. She expected any moment he would confront her.

Emma was glad she would be leaving the *Mary B* at Swan Hill. Macklin was to go on to Echuca and catch the train to Melbourne. She wouldn't see him again after today. She wasn't sure if it was what she had done or what she knew about him that disturbed her more, but she resolved to tell the police at Swan Hill what she knew. There was reason now, she felt, for the police to investigate him further. Perhaps the people at Kerang would know of him.

Which brought another thought. A not so pleasant one. What if they were Paulsmire's family? Dare she ask Henry and see if she got a reaction to the name?

At midday, she went down and offered to help Ah Lo with lunch. They had to feed the two *Lisette* bargemen as well, though they were one mouth short themselves without Jake Summers. It would be an awkward transfer of food with the two barges on the narrow channel. As it turned out it didn't matter. They had to stop for wood at Harolds and Ah Lo had the bargemen's lunches ready and delivered by the time the *Mary B* started off again.

Emma took the children up to the saloon for their lunch. Erich was still talking about Uncle Axel's farm, excited at the prospect of seeing it again.

"I used to help Aunt Rosie feed the chickens," he said. "And the poddy calves." He laughed. "Poddy calves. That's funny, isn't it? One knocked me over when I was trying to give its bottle of milk."

"You were too little to remember all that," Henry told him. "You've just heard stories."

"I have not, Henry. I was five. Mama baked me a birthday cake."

At the mention of their mother both boys fell silent.

"I used to feed the orphan lambs," Emma told them. "They'd pull and tug on the bottle and their tails wagged all the time."

"The poddy calves wagged their tails too," Erich said. Emma smiled back at him.

"Sheep don't have long tails," said Henry.

"The farmer docks the tails while they are still young," Emma explained hoping they wouldn't ask for details. "I'm looking forward to meeting your Aunt Rosie and Uncle Axel tomorrow," she said as she spooned another mouthful of mashed potato into Gertie's waiting mouth. She could have let the child feed herself, but she wasn't keen on having to get mashed potato out of the little girl's hair. "Are there any other children at the farm?"

Erich frowned. "There was a baby," he said. "Um, I don't remember its name. We didn't have Gertie then."

Henry glared at his brother. He didn't seem to like the talk about Uncle Axel and Aunt Rosie and the farm. Didn't he have the same enjoyable memories of the place as his brother? Emma decided at the last moment not to mention the Paulsmire name. She was nervous about knowing it at all with the man so near.

"Eat your lunch before it gets cold, Erich," she said.

======

SEVERAL COTTAGES AND a handful of vegetable gardens and small orchards marked the approach to Swan Hill on the Victorian side of the river. On the New South Wales side, grey canvas and bark huts marked a blacks' camp. Emma could hear the shouts of the children as they sported in the water. Some of them swam toward the *Mary B*. Fred warned them off and pointed out the barges following. They called out cheekily, laughing and splashing. It was a refreshing change from the uninhabited spaces and almost constant view of Mallee scrub they had been passing through for the past week.

Emma was watching from the upper deck having just got Gertie up from a rather long afternoon nap and the boys were hanging around the galley drawn by the smell of Ah Lo's fresh baked oat biscuits, as the two riverboats approached the wharf. Emma called the boys upstairs to the saloon to stay with Gertie while she supervised the mooring. Not that she ever had much to do. The crew knew their business, but they were a man short right now and it was ostensibly her responsibility.

"Bring a biscuit for Gertie," she called as the boys started up, each juggling a hot biscuit. Henry dashed back to the galley to get it.

The *Mary B* nestled up to the wharf behind the *Lisette*. The low water level meant that even the top deck of the boats was below the level with the wharf. Shorty leaned out and got a rope around one of the wharf pylons. He tied it off with enough slack for the *Mary B* to float free without rubbing against the timbers. Steam hissed from the funnel as Fred released the boiler pressure and Blue and Willy floated the *Owen* up behind, the *Lisette*'s barge tapping in behind it.

"I can smell Charley's oat biscuits," Emma heard Blue say as he stepped onto the walkway and tied off the barge. "Just what I need." He eyed the *Mary B* as it gently floated toward the wharf and away and timed a jump, his long legs carrying him safely to the deck.

He headed for the galley. Ah Lo cackled as Blue grabbed a handful of biscuits. "You leave some for others, mister."

Daniel came down to the lower deck. "That job is finished with anyway," he said to Fred nodding toward the *Lisette*'s barge. "We'll make better time for the rest of the trip. Hello, what's up?"

Chapter Twenty-Three

A POLICE OFFICER AND two troopers were leaving the *Lisette* and coming their way. Emma's heart constricted. The opium. Could Sinclair have gotten to Swan Hill ahead of them? No, he would be here himself if he had, ready to gloat and charge them with smuggling. A telegraph perhaps? But there wasn't a telegraph station between Tooleybuc and Swan Hill. Unless one of the pastoral stations had installed it for their own use. Some had, though she hadn't heard of any in that section of the river. And why would they be checking the *Lisette* if they were here for the opium?

Daniel moved to the bow to meet the police and Emma followed as the men picked their way along the narrow walkway. There was a yard of greasy brown water separating the *Mary B* from the wharf timbers.

"Captain Whitaker, Victoria Police," the officer introduced himself. "We're looking for a man who may have taken passage on your boat. A Joseph Paulsmire."

Had she been right to be concerned about the man?

"We only have one passenger," Daniel said. "An Englishman, Jack Macklin."

"I believe he is Joseph Paulsmire," Emma spoke up, knowing as she did her knowledge of his identity was going to cause her problems with Daniel.

He stared at her now, open mouthed. "What?"

Emma nodded. "If it's the Joseph Paulsmire who has recently served four years at Melbourne Gaol for manslaughter, he is your man, I think," she told Captain Whitaker.

"You seem to be very well informed, ma'am," he said not hiding his suspicion.

"Indeed." Daniel stared hands on hips with the annoyed expression she had come to expect of late.

Emma ignored him. "Well unless he's carrying another man's discharge papers. Is this to do with the death of Hilda Zeller? Have you been informed of that?"

"He's wanted for questioning," the police officer said clearly not about to elaborate.

"Shorty get the boarding plank down," Daniel ordered. Captain Whitaker and one trooper made ready to board, while the second trooper was ordered to stay on the walkway.

Emma looked back along the deck. She hadn't seen Paulsmire for some time. At least now she could safely think of him by his proper name. Had he seen the policemen on the walkway? She was about to tell the Captain he wasn't armed when Willy, still on the walkway, hissed.

"Capt'n. Capt'n, that Macklin bloke has just snaffled our shotgun."

"What?" Daniel started toward the stern but was immediately stopped by Captain Whitaker who had just stepped onto the *Mary B.*

"Wait up. If he's armed, we need to proceed with caution. Where did you see him?" he asked Willy.

"At the stern. He lifted the shotgun off the wall where we keep it and nipped around starboard."

"Blimey," said Blue, spraying biscuits crumbs.

"Get everyone off the deck. If we must shoot, we don't want someone in the way."

"Give us another biscuit, Charley," Blue said. "It might be me last."

"Get in the stokehold and stop mucking about," Daniel told him.

Blue grumbled but he joined Shorty and Fred in the stokehold. Ah Lo hunkered down in his galley.

"There are children upstairs, Captain," Emma informed him, standing her ground. "I'll just get them."

"You'll stay down here out of the way. I'll send the children down if it's safe."

"But..."

"And I don't want any heroics, understood?"

"Understood," Daniel assured him, as he pushed Emma into the stokehold ahead of him. "I'll look forward to hearing how you knew his name when this is over," he told her. Emma decided later was time enough to concern herself about that. It was standing room only in the stokehold. The heat from the boiler fire made the space uncomfortably warm, despite it having been burning down for some time.

"I thought they were comin' for this 'ere mattress," Shorty said his voice muted. "That Sinclair was fit to be tied after the trick we played on 'im back there."

"Ssh. I want to be able to hear the children," Emma said.

She strained her ears to hear what was happening. She could hear voices and movement up on the wharf and the slop of water against the timbers, but there was no sound from the saloon that she could tell. What if the boys tired of waiting for her to tell them they could come down? They could step out into a gunfight. Paulsmire must have seen the police on the walkway, otherwise why arm himself. He'd not been under any threat until now.

If she were Paulsmire, what would she do to get away? Slip down the deck and over the bow into the water, drift downstream close to the wharf and get out further along where the bank was low. Simple. You would soon dry off in the heat and be long gone before anyone figured where you were.

But what if he couldn't swim? The walkway wasn't available with the trooper waiting there. If he were really desperate, he could go overboard and cling to the side of the boat in the hope he could remain unseen until the searchers gave up or it got too dark to see.

It was stuffy in the cramped stokehold. She wrinkled her nose at the odour of sweaty bodies that was taking over. There were mutterings behind her as the silence outside continued. Then Gertie wailed. Emma's nerves prickled. She leaned forward quickly and managed to get a look toward the stern before Daniel jerked her back his hand on her shoulder.

"Don't do that," he scolded.

"There's no one there. I think he's jumped ship. He saw the police and went into the river."

"You don't know that."

"Well, they don't appear to have caught him. They've had time to go round the boat twice already."

"Hardly. It just seems that long. We'd have seen them go past. They'll be checking the cabins upstairs."

Emma brushed her hands down her skirt. Gertie's cries seemed to be escalating. The child needed comforting. It called to her nurturing instincts and reminded her of the way Gertie had cried when the boys had disappeared at Pattin Downs. It was the cry of a child abandoned. Emma could just imagine her crying like that after her mother disappeared, before the boys and their father came back to the shack that day. What had happened to the boys? Everything was quiet. No footsteps.

The police weren't likely to mistake her for Paulsmire if they saw her on the deck. She relaxed, trying to give Daniel the idea she wasn't about to bolt. Then she was out before he could react. She felt a brief tug on her skirt then she was free. She heard Daniel curse behind her. It took but a moment to slip along the stokehold wall and round and up the stairs. She didn't look about, just ran to the saloon and in. Gertie was sitting under the table, but the boys were gone. The child's cries turned to sobs as Emma grabbed her into her arms and held her tight.

"There, there. You're safe now."

She would have a piece of Henry for abandoning his sister. But had he a choice? Had Paulsmire taken the boys hostage? Emma looked out the saloon windows to the starboard side. Not that it told her much. She couldn't see down to the lower deck, but she couldn't hear anything.

Opening the saloon door, she peeked left then right. No one on the upper deck. She made her way up to the wheelhouse. It was empty. That left the two cabins, Daniel's own and Paulsmire's. She stopped at Daniel's cabin door.

What would she do if she found the boys with the wanted man? She would just have to brazen it out. Henry would help. He was solid enough. All that work gathering timber had told.

"Henry are you there?" she called quietly and opened Daniel's door. The cabin was empty. She breathed deeply and moved down to the next cabin, thankful that Gertie cries were down to the odd sniffle.

"Henry?" Her hand was on the door handle when it was flung open and she found herself staring into the barrel of a shotgun. Then Gertie's scream in her ear made her jump and she was pulled into the cabin the door slamming behind her.

"Shut the child up," Paulsmire ordered roughly.

"You'll need to put the gun down," Emma told him. "It frightens her." She was more annoyed than frightened. That might come later.

"Step back," Paulsmire told her. She did so, now standing nearer the boys who were sitting on the bunk.

Paulsmire lowered the gun as asked and Gertie magically quietened as if a tap had been turned off.

"Are you all right?" she asked turning to the boys. She could see Erich's eyes were as large as saucers although Henry wouldn't look at her. It made her angry to think Paulsmire was frightening them.

"Of course, they are. What do you take me for?"

"Someone who takes children as hostages."

"Yes, that's just what I'm doing. They're my ticket off this boat, these two."

"You can't have thought it through. What are you going to do with them after you get away? You can't just abandon them somewhere. They can't look after themselves."

"I want to go to Uncle Axel's farm," Erich spoke up, shakily.

"You know what has happened to their mother," Emma said. "They need to be with family right now. They don't need this."

"What do you care? They aren't your boys."

"I was a friend of their mother," Emma explained hitching Gertie into a more comfortable position on her hip. "I don't know why she died the way she did but the least I can do is make sure the children are settled somewhere safe. They have family at Kerang, Uncle Axel's farm as Erich says. Look, why don't you leave them and take me instead. I'd be a much better hostage and you could leave me anywhere without it having to bother your conscience." Supposing he had one.

She saw Henry look quickly at Paulsmire. There was something in that look. It wasn't the look you gave a stranger who was threatening you. It was – what – looking to someone for direction? Someone you knew and trusted?

Emma caught her breath. All those times Henry had scolded Erich in German with warnings about 'vater.' The truth of what he said when he told what his father had done, choosing his words carefully. Everyone thought he was referring to Zac, and sometimes he was when it suited his story, but sometimes he was referring to Paulsmire. Paulsmire who had been away for four years. Long enough for his wife to take up with someone else. Long enough for young Erich to forget. Or not like what he remembered. And long enough for Hilda to try and hide herself away in the bush.

The words tumbled from her lips. "Hilda was your wife. The boys are yours." Paulsmire stared at her as if trying to make up his mind whether to deny it or not. "The police won't believe you when you try to use them as hostages. They'll know you wouldn't hurt your own children."

"Lucky you came along then, isn't it?"

Well, she had offered. At least he wasn't going to shoot her. Not right away anyway.

"What happened to Hilda? Why did she have to die?"

Paulsmire glanced at Henry and shifted his feet. "It was an accident. The gun went off when I tried to take it from her."

"But she wasn't shot with a shotgun."

"She had a pistol."

He was quick with the answers, but Emma saw Henry's head go up. Poor lad. He must know his mother didn't have a pistol.

"Then tell the police that," Emma challenged.

"They're going to believe me?" His tone was bitter. More self-pity. A man who thought he was hard done by, that nothing was his fault.

"Why not?" Emma asked though she knew the answer. Apart from the fact he was an ex-convict, that story was for the benefit of Henry. But why were the police here looking for him? What did they know? "What happened to Zac Zeller?" Emma asked.

"No idea," he said glancing out the window. He was lying. Zac must be dead as well.

"Joseph Paulsmire. Come out with your hands in the air." Captain Whitaker had tracked them down. He may have been listening outside the door for some time.

"I'd be careful if I were you," Paulsmire called back grimly. "I have the boys and the lady. You wouldn't want any of them to get hurt, now would you?"

"The boys are his," Emma called out. "He wouldn't hurt them." Gertie, she realised, couldn't be.

Paulsmire glared at her. "I'll be glad to take you as a hostage," he said. "I can think of any number of places in this god-forsaken country to leave you, too."

"Dad."

"It's all right, son. Calm down. Of course, I don't mean it." Emma didn't believe that either.

"You can't stay in there forever, man," Captain Whitaker was saying. "Come on out now, slowly."

"Leave the girl," Paulsmire ordered.

Emma put Gertie on the bunk and Henry patted his sister's arm as she began to grizzle. For a moment she saw he was torn.

"Henry?"

He looked away. Whatever he felt about his father's behaviour there would be no help there. Not right now, anyway. She stepped back from the bunk. Paulsmire gestured for her to approach the door and then pulled her in front of him his arm across her throat, the gun at her back, the muzzle cold at the base of her neck. It was awkward. But he could still blow the back of her head off.

"We're coming out," he shouted. "You'd better step back. The woman is coming out first and I've a gun on her. Open the door," he ordered Emma. She did as she was told. This wasn't the moment for heroics. Captain Whitaker stood gun raised, facing the door as Emma eased it open. He did not look pleased to see her.

"Put the gun down," Paulsmire ordered. "I'm taking the woman with me. And the boys. Anyone tries to stop us her blood will be on your hands. Now," he barked spitting out the words as Captain Whitaker hesitated. "Put your guns down and move to the stairs."

The policeman gave one last glare at Emma and slowly lowered his weapon. He nodded to someone out of her line of sight.

"Out now," Paulsmire told the boys and they slipped out onto the deck. Emma noticed for the first time that Henry had both their own and his father's bags with him. They had been well organised. That little walk to stretch their legs while the *Mary B* waited at Wee Creek for the repair to *Lisette*'s paddle wheel had been a perfect opportunity to cement their plans.

Emma and Paulsmire followed the boys along the deck. Captain Whitaker and the trooper were both standing at the top of the stairs. A pistol and a rifle lay on the deck where they had placed them. Emma was afraid Paulsmire might swap his cumbersome shotgun for the Captain's pistol, but it either didn't occur to him or he felt he would be vulnerable during the changeover as he just motioned the policemen to proceed them down the stairs. The boys followed, then Emma, held by Paulsmire.

The descent wasn't easy. Emma couldn't look down at the steps with his arm around her throat. She took them carefully, both feet on each step before she stepped down to the next one, one hand gripping the railing.

It would have been tempting to trip and send him sprawling but she probably wouldn't survive it herself. She would have to pick her moment. If she got one. As they reached the bottom of the stairs, she saw Daniel, Blue and Shorty standing a little way along the deck. Daniel's face looked drained beneath his tan. She carefully raised a hand in a stop sign. She hoped they wouldn't try any heroics. She seemed to have done more than enough of that already.

They continued along the deck, the two policemen sidling along in front keeping an eye on what was happening behind them. Emma hoped they wouldn't get it into their heads to grab one of the boys. They came level with the stokehold. Fred was standing in the doorway a large shifting wrench gripped in his hand. Emma gave him the stop sign. He might be able to knock Paulsmire down, but even if she escaped getting shot there were too many other people around who could get hurt including the boys.

"Hiya." Ah Lo leapt out of the galley in front of them brandishing his meat cleaver.

Chapter Twenty-Four

EMMA FELT THE SHOTGUN move against her neck and Paulsmire's arm tighten. Her mind clouded over as everything went into slow motion. Voices came to life behind her. Some choice curses reached her ears, Blue threatening to use the cleaver on the cook himself and Shorty shouting about a mad Chinese. Among it all, she heard Daniel order Ah Lo to put the cleaver down.

Ah Lo in a half crouch, looked uncertain.

"Put it down, Ah Lo, please," Emma managed to whisper.

She could see Henry behind the cook looking to his father for direction. It wouldn't do for the boy to get involved either.

"You'd better do as the lady says, Charley." Paulsmire's voice was showing the strain. He shifted his feet. "I could blow her head off right here." Which would be his own death sentence, but it didn't help to hear the threat. No one seemed to be even breathing. The air crackled with tension.

"Please, Ah Lo."

"You sure, Missus? I chop into little pieces. Just say word."

"Another time, Ah Lo."

"If you say, Missus." His eyes not leaving Paulsmire, Ah Lo leaned into the galley and replaced the cleaver. Emma closed her eyes.

"Move ahead, Charley," Paulsmire ordered. They reached the bow and the boarding plank. The trooper stood at the walkway end his gun aimed at them. "Order him to lay down his weapon and move away," Paulsmire told Captain Whitaker.

"Do as he says, trooper."

When the trooper was several yards from the boarding plank Paulsmire sent the boys across.

"Up the stairs at the end and wait on the wharf," he directed.

"I don't want to go," Erich objected.

"You'll do as you're told, lad. Henry, help him along."

"Come on. It'll be all right," Henry told his brother.

"I don't like it," Erich complained but Henry herded him along in front and there was nowhere else for him to go but along the plank.

Paulsmire waited until they were well on their way. "Our turn."

Emma stepped onto the plank. It moved a little as the *Mary B* dipped slightly. Paulsmire's arm tightened around her throat.

"You're choking me, and I can't see where I'm putting my feet," Emma complained. "I'll have us both over." She swayed slightly to give credence to her words. The pressure on her throat was released and he gripped her left shoulder instead. She winced as his fingers bit and he held her close. The shotgun hadn't moved, still pressing at the base of her head. She hoped it didn't have a hair trigger.

She took two small steps into the centre of the plank. It was now or never. She ducked, twisting sharply to the left, bending and pushing back in one fluid movement. She felt her body connect his and felt his grip loosen as he lost his balance, an explosion by her right ear and a ringing noise as she fell. Water closed over her head as she went down.

Emma kicked upwards and to the side. She'd just escaped getting shot. She didn't want now to be crushed between the boat and the wharf. Had Paulsmire kept his feet or fallen on the other side of the plank? Her head broke the surface and the wharf loomed close. She reached up for a hold on the walkway. Someone grabbed her hand and pulled. It was the trooper. Other hands joined his and she was hauled from the water to find Mr. Fryling beside her. There was confusion in the water. The other trooper was trying to deal with a thrashing, drowning Paulsmire. Daniel suddenly appeared at her side.

She saw his mouth moving, concern and irritation warring on his face. Emma put a hand to her ear and shook her head.

"I can't hear you."

He nodded and took her hand, trying to lead her back to the boarding plank. She pulled back.

"No. We need to get the boys."

Daniel turned to the *Mary B* and a moment later Shorty and Fred hurried across and up to the wharf. Emma wondered if the boys had seen what had happened below. She saw Daniel's lips moving again as he tried to get her to move along the walkway.

"Wait, please," she said.

She was dimly aware that her clothes were clinging to her body and her hair hanging wetly around her face, but she needed to know the boys were safe first. It was a few minutes before she saw the crewmen coming back down with them. Henry's face was screwed tight. He was trying not to cry. Erich already was. She allowed Daniel to hand her back across the plank. Paulsmire was being pulled up onto the *Mary B* and handcuffed as she stepped aboard but she didn't stop. He wasn't her problem now.

"I have to see to Gertie," she said when Daniel tried to speak to her.

There was something almost pleasant about not being able to hear what people were saying. You could pretend they weren't there. She hurried around and up the stairs to Paulsmire's cabin. All was quiet. Inside she found Gertie asleep, exhausted after her upsets. Emma left her there. She would only get the child as wet as herself if she tried to move her right now and sleep was the best healing she could prescribe.

She went to her cabin to get into a change of dry clothes and found the tin bath already set up. Ah Lo appeared at the door with two kettles, one hot, one cold. Emma suddenly felt very tired and shaky. She sat down on the edge of her bunk, her arms wrapped around herself and managed to smile and nod as Ah Lo filled the tub and with some dramatic hand signals, left her to her ablutions. She could have done with Nella or her grandmother right now. And a cup of tea.

Emma didn't know how much later it was when she started awake. She shivered. The bathwater was cold, and she could smell something cooking. Chicken. She was sure it was chicken. Where had Ah Lo got that? She realised she was hungry. She dragged herself out of the tub, feeling only slightly refreshed, and got herself dried off and dressed in her wrapper. She was still towelling her hair when Daniel knocked on her cabin door.

"Emma?" She realised the ringing in her ears had lessened enough to hear him, although he sounded a long way off. She wrapped the towel around her head, turban style, and let him in. "How are you feeling?" He stood awkwardly in the small space left between the door and the tub.

She shrugged. "How are the boys? And Gertie? Has anyone seen to her? I fell asleep."

"They're being looked after. What did you think you were doing?" he asked, unable it seemed to hide the note of exasperation in his voice.

"I thought he'd taken the boys hostage. What else could I do? I didn't know they were his. Did you?" she challenged tiredly.

"What? No, of course not. How did you know who he was? You could have got yourself killed."

"But I didn't," she said, not answering his question. "Why did the police want to talk to him? Was it about Hilda?"

Daniel nodded. "They had a telegraph from Euston. Apparently, Zeller staggered into Kulkyne station exhausted and with a gunshot wound to his shoulder claiming Paulsmire tried to kill him. He thought Paulsmire had taken Hilda and the children and all he could do was get help for himself."

"Poor man."

Her hand went to the towel around her head. "Daniel, I need to get ready for dinner."

"You're not taking the children to Kerang tomorrow..."

"What? No. After all they've been through, they need to be with whatever is left of their family. Daniel, you can't..."

He put his hand up. "Will you hear me out? It's a ten-twelve-hour journey by cart from here. If we go on to Gonn Crossing, we can get transport there and be at Kerang in less than half the time. It's directly south."

"Oh."

It made sense. A ten-hour slow cart ride with three children in the heat of summer would be no picnic. And to arrive unannounced at a stranger's farm in the dark was not the best way to introduce herself and three motherless children. She hadn't thought further ahead than the need to get them there and her own need to return to Swan Hill to get the coach home.

When she entered the saloon a little later, she found Daniel about to carve the chicken and everyone helping themselves to the heaped platter of roast vegetables.

"Just in time," he said as Blue jumped up to pull out a chair for her.

"How's the hearing?" Fred asked.

"It's getting better, thanks Fred. Some ringing in my ears, still."

"I said life on the *Mary B* would be interestin', didn't I lads?" Shorty announced to the room in general. No one disagreed.

They tucked into their food. Emma found herself almost inhaling it she was so hungry. Erich did justice to his food too. He looked happy enough. Paulsmire must have been a stranger to him, absent from his young life for four years. Henry on the other hand looked miserable, pushing his food around his plate grieving she imagined for both parents.

"We've still got that mattress full of opium, Capt'n," Shorty said his fork halfway to his mouth.

"Struth," said Blue. "We'd better deliver it to the police station first thing afore we all get done for smuggling."

"Better do it tonight, I reckon," advised Fred. "That Sinclair fellow can't be far away by now. You can bet he won't be wasting any time to get here."

"You're right, Fred. It completely slipped my mind," Daniel said. "And I want to get away first thing tomorrow. We're going to be laid up for a day at Gonn Crossing as it is."

He explained to the crew their plan for delivering the children to Kerang and Emma realised for the first time that he was intending to accompany her. She found a little tension drain away. Not that she needed his help, but it would be nice not to have to do it on her own. She should have realised she wouldn't have been allowed to, but she hadn't thought that far ahead.

"We'll get a day's fishing and lazing around," said Fred. They were definitely ready for the off-season.

As soon as they had finished eating, Blue and Willy were co-opted to carry the opium filled mattress to the police station. It was only across from the wharf, so it wasn't as if it was an onerous task.

"Can I go with you?" Henry asked, tentatively.

"You're going as well aren't you, Daniel?" Emma asked.

"Yes, of course."

"Yeah. The police wouldn't take the word of these two reprobates," Shorty joked.

"Well at least with Willy and me carryin' it they won't think it's a mattress on legs," Blue responded.

"You'll make sure Henry gets to speak to his father, won't you?" Emma said to Daniel, ignoring the crew's banter.

The quick glance Henry gave her was one of surprise as if she had read his mind. Which in fact she had but it hadn't been difficult. It was obvious why he had made the request. Daniel just nodded.

Emma, Fred, Shorty and Ah Lo were playing 'Old Maid' with Erich when the men finally returned. Gertie was under the table feeding Jack with table scraps. Emma thought time in quiet company was a good idea for them right now. And it would be soon enough tomorrow not to have them around anymore.

"Where's Henry?" Emma asked, when the saloon door had closed and there was no sign of the boy.

"He's gone to his cabin. He's got some hard thinking to do, I imagine."

Emma nodded. She'd check on him when she tucked in the younger two.

"You wouldn't credit, Boss," Blue said, bursting with the news, "but that Sinclair bloke turned up at the station just as we were leaving. Struth, was he beside himself. Looked about to have a seizure or something."

"He was a bit upset, all right," Daniel agreed. "He'll go over the *Mary B* with a fine-tooth comb whenever he sees us from now on. Your grandmother's herbals are going to have to go on the cargo listing in future, Emma."

Emma wasn't about to comment on the future of the herbals. She didn't imagine her grandmother would increase their price. The custom duties would come off the top if they paid it. It was the principle of the thing.

"Did you learn anything about Hilda?" she asked.

Daniel nodded as he poured a tot of whiskey for himself and the crewmen. "Captain Whitaker took a statement from Henry too. They'd received a telegraph from Euston reporting Hilda's death and mentioning family at Kerang. They were already keeping a lookout for Zeller, checking the riverboats and the coaches, and they got Paulsmire's name and the situation with him from the people at Kerang."

"That's Axel and Rosie?"

"Yes. Becke is their name. She is Hilda's sister."

"Oh, I'm glad it's Hilda's family," Emma said relieved. "Have they been told we are bringing the children?"

"Ah, that I don't know. I didn't ask Whitaker if that information had been passed on from Euston."

Emma nodded. "They'll find out soon enough, I guess. Did Paulsmire have anything to say?"

"Quite a lot. When he learned Zac was alive and could tell his own story there wasn't much point in holding back, and I guess he wanted to get his own version across."

As Daniel told it, Henry and Erich had returned to the shack with Zac after working all day and found Paulsmire waiting for them. Paulsmire had shot at Zac and he'd run off into the bush. Paulsmire went after him, but not before telling the boys their mother had gone away and they were to wait for him and not tell anyone he was around.

"He came back while we were there at the shack," Daniel told her. "He saw us bury Hilda."

Emma shivered. "He was there watching us? Why?" she asked, and then answered her own question. "I suppose there were too many of us."

"Possibly, but we helped him out. When he saw what we were doing he decided to let us take the children and he'd get the coach and catch up with the boys later. He guessed they'd probably end up back at Kerang eventually if he missed them on the way, and it saved him having to bother with Gertie. He hadn't known about her."

"Thank heaven for that," Emma said, wondering where Gertie would have ended up if they hadn't got to the shack before Paulsmire. But then if they had been a day earlier Hilda would still be alive too. It didn't bear thinking on. "And putting Hilda in the woodpile? Did he say what that was about?"

"Apparently he wanted her found and Zac blamed for her death but didn't want the boys to see her. The woodpile was the only place he could think of. Nothing to do with a funeral pyre."

Emma shrugged. It had just been an idea. "He must have thought all the luck was on his side when he ended up on the *Mary B* with the boys. But how did he come to kill Hilda?"

"He wanted to take the boys and she resisted. She had a pistol and when he tried to take it from her, she was shot."

"One might have been able to understand that if she really did have a pistol and hadn't been shot clean through the heart," Emma said. "I could see Henry didn't believe him about the pistol when Paulsmire told me that was what had happened."

"The lad might convince himself of it in any case," Fred suggested. "Better than thinking his father killed his mother on purpose." There was silence in the saloon as they pondered the idea.

"Did he say what happened to the pistol?" Emma asked.

"Threw it away in disgust when he realised what he'd done. So he said."

"So he said," she echoed in disbelief. "Threw it away so he wouldn't be caught with it would be more to the truth. Probably did the same with Zac's shotgun. Perhaps we'll learn more about Hilda's story from the Beckes."

Chapter Twenty-Five

GONN CROSSING HAD GROWN from a simple river crossing to a gathering of adhoc buildings. There was a shed for the customs officer who collected the duties on stock that crossed from New South Wales to Victoria, and a depot where goods ordered could be picked up and produce left by the local farmers for delivery to market. Several fishermen had shacks and small boats there as well.

It was a pretty spot, with peppermint willows among the gum trees lining the bank. With the worst of the shallow water levels behind them, Daniel didn't seem to mind stopping there mid-afternoon the following day, after a leisurely fifty miles had been travelled from Swan Hill.

The *Mary B* moored above the crossing out of the way, and Daniel arranged at the depot to hire their delivery cart for the next day with a draught horse called Samson to pull it. When Daniel told him where they were going the owner of the depot, a Mark Stevens, asked Daniel to deliver a wheel Axel Becke had left for repair. Daniel agreed and in return Stevens provided a canvas canopy to shade the cart passengers.

They left at six o'clock the next morning. Jack barked farewell to them from the deck, making it clear he wasn't about to leave the *Mary B*. He was now officially a member of the crew and not just another passenger. Well, for as long as he wanted to be anyway. Emma was secretly glad though she would not have let on to the children.

They did, however, have the nanny goat with them, settled in the back corner with hay and water.

Samson plodded patiently along the dusty bush track that meandered over open spaces and wound around clumps of trees that provided some welcome but short-lived shade. It was hot under the canvas, but hotter without. Samson didn't walk fast enough to create a breeze.

Gertie was grizzly, unsettled by yet another change in her routine and Jack not around to distract her. Henry was quiet. At least he didn't scold Erich who couldn't stop talking and had trouble sitting still.

They didn't stop to heat the billy at lunch time, eating Ah Lo's packed lunch as they went along. He'd given them a goodly supply of oat biscuits and they had several jars of water, so they wanted for nothing. They saw evidence of pastoral stations along the way, several rough homesteads through the trees. Halfway through the morning they exchanged greetings with the driver of another cart and several people on horseback heading in the direction of the crossing. It was early afternoon when they reached the Becke's farm, Henry giving directions for the last few miles as memory of the area where they had spent almost two years returned with the familiar landscape.

The wagon pulled up in the front yard of a slab house of reasonable proportions. The yard was dusty with scratching hens, but there was a fenced vegetable garden flourishing beside the house. A woman, tall and rounded, her blonde hair done up in plaits the way Hilda's had been watched from the doorway as they climbed down from the wagon. Emma, Gertie in her arms and herding Henry and Erich in front of her walked up to the door. Erich was suddenly shy.

"Welcome home," the woman said hugging Erich and then Henry. She put her apron up to her eyes. "My poor sister." She touched Gertie's cheek. "Come in please, come in."

A man was sent to fetch Axel Becke in from his work. He was heavily built, dark haired and barely as tall as Emma, but he had a good humoured face. He shook both boys by the hand and seemed pleased to see them.

"Sit, sit," Rosie insisted.

Everyone sat at the kitchen table and plates of cake and biscuits were brought out with hot tea for the visitors and coffee for the Beckes. Rosie Becke kept looking at Gertie sitting on Emma's lap.

"She is just like our Hilda," she marvelled.

The boys ate and drank but were clearly restless after being on the wagon. Axel sent them outside to look around and get to know the place again.

"Now, you can tell us what happens," Rosie said. "How do you have the children?"

Emma told how she had first met Hilda at their woodpile shack a year or more ago and went on from there. She didn't mention Hilda's activities and she knew Daniel wouldn't. Let it die with her if it could. She decided to believe that Hilda had been earning money to escape to some place where Paulsmire couldn't find her. Rosie shuddered when she heard of their finding Hilda's body. She looked to her husband.

"In the woodpile? Would he cremate her?" she asked. Axel patted her hand but didn't reply.

Emma explained what Paulsmire had told the police about not wanting the boys to see her body and wanting Zac blamed for her death.

"He was a vindictive man, Joseph," Alex said, and Rosie nodded.

Emma and Daniel had a lot to tell filling in Hilda's journey west through Pattin Downs and Kulkyne stations, her life at the woodpile, and what had happened on the way back with the children. Finally, Daniel described how Paulsmire had been captured.

Rosie drew in a sharp breath. "But he could have killed you," she said to Emma.

Emma just shook her head.

"My sister-in-law acts first and thinks later in these matters," Daniel informed the Beckes with some asperity. It must really rankle with him.

"Ah. You are not husband and wife?" Rosie said surprised. "You mourn for a husband?"

Emma nodded. Rosie patted her hand and murmured "*Es tut mir leid.* I am sorry."

"Will Joseph hang for Hilda's death?" Axel asked. "I don't like to think he comes back for the boys."

"He may argue that Hilda's death was an accident," Daniel said, "but this is the second death he has been responsible for and he tried to kill Zeller as well. I can't see him being around for many years, if at all."

"He should not," Rosie said firmly. "I hadn't seen Hilda for years after they left Germany, just letters we wrote back and forth since he took her to England." Her voice broke. Axel took up the story as Rosie wiped her eyes on the corner of her apron.

"Joseph Paulsmire arrives in Weiden from England to visit old family, back when we were all much younger," he said. "He has been in England since himself a child. Henry had just been born but his father has already died and Hilda..."

"Paulsmire is not Henry's father?" Emma interrupted. "But he is German?"

Rosie answered. "German born, *ja*. But no, Erich's father only," Rosie explained. "Henry's father was..."

"Franz Krueger?"

"How did you know that?" Rosie looked at her, amazed. "Did Hilda tell you? Has she told Henry at last?"

"His name was in several books at the shack. But Henry said he didn't know the name Krueger."

Rosie looked at her husband. "So, she has not told him. Not even yet."

"Joseph wouldn't let her," Axel said to Daniel and Emma, "and she is afraid to go against him in anything."

Rosie took up the story again. "Joseph, he stays a while in Weiden. Hilda is grieving for Franz and wanting company, so," she gestured with her hands. "Then there is some trouble..."

"There is always trouble around Joseph Paulsmire," Axel growled.

"He takes her and Henry away to England. I know Hilda is not happy," Rosie went on warming to her tale. "I read her letters. Paulsmire is not a good husband. There is no money." She faltered and Emma got a prickly feeling in her skin. Had Paulsmire forced Hilda to work the streets? Had that been the start of it? Rosie gathered herself. "Then Erich is born. When we come here, I write her to come. Life would be better here. So, they come, but at Melbourne there is more trouble and Joseph goes to prison. When Hilda is here on the farm, she is happy. The boys are happy.

"Then she meets Zac. He work for Mr. Chappell down the road. And then she is expecting a child. Oh, I offer to take it, to raise it. Joseph doesn't need to know but Hilda say no. She is afraid to face him. Afraid she will betray herself with the child. They leave, and I don't hear from her anymore." Silent tears trickled down her round cheeks. "I wonder all this time where she is. Then Joseph comes to look for her. He is angry. We can't tell him where she goes but he ask around and then he goes. He goes to find her."

"He has been gone for months," Axel said. "He was determined to find them. We have been expecting this day. But Zac? He has been shot, you say? He will not live?"

"We haven't heard anything further on that," Daniel said. "But he can't be too badly hurt if he was able to get to Kulkyne on foot."

"Well, we will hear in time, I guess. He will want to see his daughter is taken care of. He would not abandon her, I'm thinking."

"A man on his own cannot raise a child," Rosie said. "He will want to leave Gertie with us." She looked longingly as the child. "So like our Hilda," she said softly. She got to her feet and rummaged in a dresser drawer. She handed Emma a small portrait in a gilt frame. It could have been Henry with a slightly older face.

"This is Henry's father?"

"It is Franz Krueger, *ja*. When he was eighteen his parents had that done. He and Hilda were childhood sweethearts. She was heartbroken when he dies in an accident. Hilda asks me to keep this for her. She always hides it from Joseph." Rosie teared up again.

"We will tell Henry the truth," Axel said.

Emma hoped it would be of benefit to the boy to know he had no blood relationship with Paulsmire. For Erich, being younger and more like his mother the relationship might not be such an issue. Unless he wasn't Paulsmire's child either, but that would never be known. Perhaps the boys would take the Becke name. They seemed to have already had several.

"Does Mr. Paulsmire speak German?" Emma asked, trying to tie up the loose ends in her mind.

"Oh, *ja*. His parents always spoke it, so he grew up with it. But he and the boys all speak with an accent."

Emma smiled. "I certainly wouldn't have picked up on that."

There was a wail from another room and Rosie Becke got to her feet to attend to the child whose voice it was.

Daniel gave Emma a speaking look and she nodded. They had to be leaving soon. It was clear the Beckes were prepared to accept the children and take care of them. Rosie returned with a girl in her arms, about a year older than Gertie.

"This is your cousin Agneth, Gertie," she said. "Agneth, Gertie will be living with us. Give her a kiss and be friends now." But Agneth did not appear to have woken in a good frame of mind and ignored her mother's request to kiss her cousin.

"That reminds me," Emma said. "I found a quilt in a trunk in Hilda's bedroom. It looked quite precious." She described it to Rosie.

"That is the one our *Oma* made for when Henry was born. It is still there? Hilda still has it?"

"It was there a week ago. Daniel, how can we get Hilda's belongings? The Bells' do you think?"

"We could telegraph from Echuca and ask Ted to collect it," Daniel suggested. "It might be some months before they can be sent on," he said to Rosie, "as the riverboats aren't running."

"If you could, *ja*. I would want to have that quilt."

"Zac might want some things if he lives," Axel told his wife.

"Tell him I will give the quilt to Gertie when she is older," Rosie promised. "That is as it should be."

"Do you still have family in Germany?" Emma asked.

"Lots of family," Axel replied. "We are hoping some will come out and join us here eventually."

"It's just that someone who knew Hilda told me she was planning to return to Germany."

Axel looked at his wife. "Perhaps she goes to the Kruegers."

"*Ja*," Rosie agreed. "She would be safer there from Joseph."

Emma couldn't help thinking how close Hilda came to being safe. At that moment Erich burst into the room followed more sedately by Henry.

"I collected some eggs, Aunt Rosie," he said eagerly, holding out his hands, three eggs in each. "But I couldn't carry them all."

"Put them in the basket, Erich," his Aunt said placidly, indicating a basket on the kitchen bench. "You will have an omelette for breakfast." Erich beamed and did as he was told, managing not to break any. "And this is your cousin Agneth." Agneth proved much more interested in the boys, smiling, and saying "hallo".

Emma laughed. "Little girls always like boys," she said to them. "You will have a shadow." Henry pulled a rueful face and his uncle laughed and clapped him on the back.

"We must be leaving," Daniel said.

"You are welcome to stay the night. It will be late when you get back to the river," Axel said.

"Thank you, but we must be getting on. We have an hour or two of light left and there should be sufficient moonlight. I was assured that Samson knew his way home, in any case."

"Well. And thank you for bringing the wheel, I must say."

"And the nanny goat. We have two, but another is needed now. And thank you for taking such good care of the children," Rosie said to Emma, giving her a huge hug. "You are a good friend to Hilda. God was watching over her for you to be there. I take some comfort in that."

"It was the least we could do," Emma replied. "I am just glad the children are in a good place now."

Axel Becke nodded. "They are family."

And a work force, Emma couldn't help thinking. But it could be far worse. While the men went out to the barn, where Samson had been fed and watered, Rosie Becke busied herself putting a food parcel together for their journey home. Emma protested that they still had enough but she insisted it would be spoiled in the heat by now.

"So much heat. I do miss our German winters."

By the time Rosie Becke had the food packaged Samson had been hitched back up to the cart. The farewells with the children were not without some tears on both sides. Daniel shook hands all around and Emma hugged Gertie and Erich as Henry stood stolidly by. She hesitated only a moment before taking a step and pulling the boy into her arms. She felt his arms about her waist as he briefly hugged her back.

"*Danke*," he whispered before turning away.

It was all she needed.

"How are you feeling?" Daniel asked quietly sometime later. They had been travelling in silence, the heat of the day beginning to ease as dusk settled.

Emma felt herself close to tears at his question. She swallowed. "Leaving Gertie behind was harder than I imagined," she said.

He didn't answer for a moment, perhaps thinking about the fact Sam hadn't been her only loss.

"You did a great job with the three of them. But you are going to have to stop putting yourself in danger. I don't think I could survive much more of it."

"Oh." Emma hesitated. He didn't sound angry, more as if her safety mattered. Could they possibly be getting back to something like friends again? "I don't do it on purpose, Daniel. We just seem to have had some incidents lately."

"We have, but I would prefer if you weren't so quick to step in. Think about it, would you? A good purser isn't that easy to find."

Emma laughed. It felt good. "Right. I'll keep it in mind, then."

"I'd appreciate it."

She was dozing, her head on Daniel's shoulder when Samson stopped some hours later.

"We're here," Daniel said waking her gently. A lamp hung from the side of a shed illuminating a section of the yard behind the depot. He helped Emma down, her body stiff from sitting for so long. Daniel had stood part of the way, reins in his hands, but since she had been sleeping he hadn't moved and was likely as stiff as she felt.

Mr. Stevens appeared from the shadows, pulling his braces onto his shoulders. "You made the trip okay, then," he said as he helped Daniel unhitch Samson. "I see you've come back without your little load."

"Yes, they're back with their family," Daniel said. "Nice people."

Mr. Stevens clearly would have liked to know more but no doubt he would get the story eventually.

"I'll feed and water this fellow," he said. "You better get on. The lady's about to fall asleep on her feet."

"Thanks. Much obliged to you."

The mooring lights of the *Mary B* were a welcome sight. Daniel whistled and was answered by a bark from Jack. Fred appeared and put the boarding plank down for them.

"All went well, then?" Fred said, seeing just the two of them.

"All went well, Fred," Emma replied. "But it will seem a little lonely for a while, I fear."

"Aye, lass. It will that."

Epilogue

SIX DAYS LATER Emma was handed down from the Cobb and Co coach, stiff and tired once again. It was early morning the sky just tinged with colour. The only thing marking the stopping place from all other similar places along the sandy bush lined track was the Wirramilla letter box, a round drum nailed to a post. The drum was only used for mail in the off-season now. For the rest of the year the riverboats carried the mail. Emma already had a bundle of letters and papers from the mailbag the coach was carrying.

"Are you being met?" The only other female passenger, on her way to Adelaide, put her head out the window and inquired anxiously.

"It's only two miles to the homestead," Emma replied more cheerfully than she felt. First the hundred-mile journey from Echuca to Bendigo by train, a forgotten comfort, then a days' wait for the coach to leave late at night. That had been followed by three days and nights rattling and bouncing over ruts and stumps or dragging through sand, with brief stops to change horses and occasionally eat at less than salubrious inns, a constant cloud of dust enveloping everything. The walk ahead was not enticing.

The lady passenger shuddered and drew her head in no doubt imagining Emma wandering lost in the featureless bush. The coach rattled off again at speed and she turned to the track that led north to the river and a bath and a comfortable bed. That was when she saw the glow through the trees, the embers of a campfire.

"G'day, Emma." Jacky Wirra appeared from the dimness of the trees his white teeth a beacon in his brown face as he grinned.

"You are a sight for sore eyes," Emma told him. He took her bag and she followed him to his campsite. Tethered nearby was his own horse and hers, Pepper. "Been here long?" He would have made trips back to the homestead between coaches.

"A few days. You're late."

"Hmm. Thanks for waiting."

"You know the Boss wouldn't let you walk home if he could help it."

The Boss. Her father this time, not herself. Emma silently thanked him for his thoughtfulness. Half an hour later, she left Pepper at the stable with Jacky and walked into the Wirramilla kitchen.

Janey was shoving wood into the fire under a singing kettle and Lucy was shaping a loaf of bread ready for the oven.

"I hope there's enough hot water for a good long bath," Emma said by way of greeting.

"You look like you could do with one, Missy," Lucy said, giving her a hug, while trying not to get doughy hands on her dress. "Welcome home."

Janey grinned at her and wrinkled her nose. Emma didn't need to be reminded she wasn't as sweet on the nose as usual. She pulled a face at Janey and left the girl to organise the bathwater, leaving the letters and newspapers on the table in the morning room on the way to her room. After a long soak and dressed in clean clothes, she felt almost human again. She went into the morning room looking forward to a cup of tea, and toast with slatherings of fresh butter and Lucy's best jam.

Her mother was the only one at the table, a pile of opened mail beside her.

"Emma, there you are," Rose Haythorne said as if her daughter had just come for her breakfast and not been away for several weeks. She waved a letter.

"Catherine has put a note for you in with mine," she said handing it over.

Emma took the letter eagerly. Perhaps her sister-in-law had some good news about the estrangement of Matty and Dotty Keogh. She'd had barely time to think of it while she was away. She slid her knife under the small dot of wax Catherine had used to seal the letter. Had Joe told Catherine to do that to keep Rose from prying? What did the letter contain to require that?

Dearest Emma.

I hope all is well and you are safely back at Wirra-milla. We heard the Mary B had found the body of the woodcutter's wife. Much to tell, I am sure.

At this end, Mrs. Keogh didn't believe the story you told Dotty of Matty abandoning her because he was upset by Sam's death and your unhappiness. I had to tell her the truth. It seemed the only answer.

Mrs. Keogh then spoke to Bea about it. I hadn't told her Bea didn't know about the promise. I'm not sure it would have stopped her if I had done, as Bea not know-ing has raised her suspicions again. Now she wants to hear direct from the source that you do not have Matty Macdonald on a string.

Your presence is required in Wentworth tuit de suite, lovey.

Yours ever, Catherine.

PS. You are going to have to be convincing. Mrs. Keogh is a tough mother hen protecting her chick. As to Bea, well, I will have to leave that to you as well.

C.

Poor Bea was Emma's first thought. Nothing good had come of that old promise. It had driven wedges into too many relationships. Mrs. Keogh was least on her mind but still, she would have to be dealt with.

Some sharp words in French rose to Emma's tongue to alleviate her frustration. Her mother would not understand them. But her grandmother appeared with Floss on her heels at that moment and she had to choke the words back and smile a greeting instead.

THE END

Next in Series

Book #4
Murder at the Mill

Emma is there to visit friends, but the Lockwood family have other plans for her.
Now two men are dead, and Deelie's husband is under suspicion. Was it an accident, honour defended, or did sibling rivalry go a step too far? Emma is drawn into the family's drama while needing to step lightly to protect her friend. Who is telling the truth? What is really going on between the Lockwood brothers? The handsome Lieutenant Forrester reaches a conclusion about the deaths, but Emma isn't sure it's the right one.

And while she tries to placate Mrs. Keogh and put an end to the fallout from that old promise, she finds herself the main attraction in another matchmaking effort. Then a friendly beagle gets involved and Emma wonders if Daniel will ever allow her back on the *Mary B*.

Set on the Murray River in the 1870s when the paddle steamers' whistles could be heard day and night between Echuca and Goolwa.

Available in paperback at all online retailers.

Don't miss a new release.
Sign up for Irene's newsletter and get updates, book recommendations and special offers. And a free ebook (pdf format available)
https://www.subscribepage.com/irene-sauman

Brief Note on the Riverboats

THE FIRST PADDLE STEAMERS on the Murray River were the result of a prize offered by the Governor of South Australia to see just how navigable the river was for trade. What followed changed the landscape, with large cattle stations giving way to sheep stations. Wool could be carried quickly and reliably and in large quantities on the riverboats, and wool brought a much greater financial return than cattle. Unlike the stern-wheel paddle steamers that plied some of the major rivers of the USA, the paddle steamers on the Murray were side-wheelers, allowing them to pull barges.

As well as transporting the wool to market, the riverboats provided the pastoral stations with all the supplies they needed. Echuca, the largest port on the river, was connected to the seaport of Melbourne by 134 miles (215 kilometres) of railway. Two other rivers formed part of what is known as the Murray-Darling System: the Darling River 914 miles (1,472 kilometres) and the Murrumbidgee 923 miles (1,485 kilometres). Both fed into the Murray. These rivers originate in New South Wales and were also involved in the riverboat trade.

Several government-owned snagging boats kept the Murray clear of fallen timbers from the eucalypts and other trees that lined the waterways. Hand drawn charts, and mileages marked on trees along the bank, helped with navigation on the winding rivers. As well as the working riverboats, there were also large pleasure boats, while regular passenger boats operated to a schedule just like a bus.

In colonial times, before Federation created the nation of Australia in 1901, each state was a separate political entity. Just as you might go through Customs at an airport, so there were Customs at state boundaries. The Murray River was a major trade boundary, and there was much smuggling between Victoria and New South Wales to avoid payment of the trade tariffs that were imposed. Customs offices were set up along the river at the major towns and ports to monitor the movement of stock and goods, but it was impossible to monitor every mile of river over such a long distance.

When Emma delivered her grandmother's herbal remedies on the PS *Mary B*, she didn't bother too much about collecting the tariffs, causing a conflict of conscience for her brother, Joe, a Customs officer.

Acknowledgements

National Library of Australia, newspaper archives online.
https://trove.nla.gov.au/newspaper/

Echuca Historical Society
https://echucahistoricalsociety.org.au/

Acknowledging also the vast amount of information available on the history of Australia and its people and the Murray River paddle steamers.

About the Author

IRENE IS A RETIRED HISTORIAN who grew up and went to school in New South Wales, by the mighty Murray River. Now living in Western Australia, she has three children and four grandchildren, and a sister who beta reads her books for plot holes and to see how quickly she can solve the mystery. (So far, she's not winning, which Irene finds rather pleasing but is carefully refraining from boasting, family relations being important, after all.)

When not writing, Irene reads, watches tennis, plays croquet (old age and treachery will defeat youth and enthusiasm every time) and has a reasonably green thumb, which means very little dies in her garden, unlike in her cozy mysteries.

I hope you enjoyed this read and will be kind enough to leave a rating, or even a few lines of review, on your favourite online retailer or on Goodreads. It helps the author and lets other readers know if a book is worth their time.

THANK YOU!

Books by Irene Sauman

Emma Berry Mysteries

Saddled with Death
A Gem of a Problem
A Body in the Woodpile
Murder at the Mill

Irene's cozy mysteries are available as ebooks and paperback at all major online retailers. You can also order your print copies through your local bookstore.

Irene is also on BookBub and Goodreads, and her Pinterest boards showcase photos relating to her Emma Berry Mystery series. She loves to hear from her readers and can be contacted at irene@jakadabooks.com

Bookbub:
https://www.bookbub.com/authors/irene-sauman
Goodreads:
http://www.goodreads.com/author/show/15332065
Pinterest:
https://au.pinterest.com/irenesauman
Facebook:
https://www.facebook.com/irenesaumanwriter

Lightning Source UK Ltd.
Milton Keynes UK
UKHW020636300920
370791UK00012B/756